FORTUNE'S ASHES

FIREBRAND
BOOK SEVEN

HELEN HARPER

ONE

My inarticulate cry of frustration echoed around the gloomy room. From the far corner, where a teenage gremlin was sitting hunched over a laptop, its dim glow giving her youthful face an eerie hue, there was a loud tut followed by a hissed mutter. 'Shhhh!'

I pulled a face, aware that she couldn't see my expression but still feeling slightly guilty, then slammed the heavy book shut and added it to my pile of rejects. I'd been coming to the Arcane Works section of the Carlyle Library for days. I'd pored over countless books, both modern and ancient, and not a single one of them had given any suggestion as to how a Cassandra could rid themselves of their powers.

I knew bitter rage was getting the better of me, but I couldn't help myself. This was my *life* I was worried about. My *future*. I didn't want to babble random prophecies or deal with visions of what was to come; I had enough on my plate already.

I raised my hand, preparing to sweep the towering stack of books to the floor in a fit of pique, then I thought better of it. I pushed back my chair and trudged towards the furthest shelves. I had to be missing something. There had to be a clue somewhere about what I could do, but I'd covered most of the shelves and I was running out of options.

I picked up a heavy tome that I'd already looked through. It was several inches thick and last time I'd only skimmed through the index. It was possible I'd not examined it closely enough.

Before I could heft it over to my little table, my pocket started to vibrate. I frowned; mobile reception down here was patchy at best, so it was a wonder that any calls made it through. I returned the book to its original position and slid out my phone to check the caller ID. Detective Chief Inspector Lucinda Barnes. That didn't bode well.

I pressed the little green button with the base of my thumb, genuinely intending to answer it in a professional tone of voice with a smooth greeting. Barnes was my boss after all, and I truly respected her.

'What is it?' I snapped. Then I winced at myself.

The line crackled. '...Bellamy? ... need ... get ... problem. Man....'

There was an annoyed tut from the studious gremlin. I ignored her and scowled at the phone, holding it up in the air to try and get a better signal.

'Come ... headquarters ... best...'

For fuck's sake. I rolled my eyes. 'This isn't a good line,' I said loudly. 'I can't hear you properly and I'm busy right now. You'd better contact DS Grace and ask him instead.'

The only answer I received was the spit of static. I looked at the phone again, realised I'd been cut off and sighed heavily. Damn it all to hell. I ought to go and see what Barnes wanted.

Supe Squad had been quiet for what seemed like endless days, with little more to deal with than a stolen bicycle last week, which turned out only to have been misplaced, and some misguided graffiti that had pissed off a few pixies. I needed something to focus on beyond my own woes and, despite my best efforts, the Carlyle Library clearly wasn't going to yield any helpful secrets.

I grunted to myself and tidied away the books, preparing to head out. When I reached for my bag and looked up, the young gremlin was glaring at me. 'I'm sorry about the noise,' I said.

Her nose twitched. 'I am trying to study!'

The youth of today. 'Sorry,' I repeated. I meant it; I knew I had to get a grip on myself and my emotions, I just wasn't quite sure how to do it. I nodded at her to emphasise my apology and silently vowed to do better, then I left. I had to accept that I wasn't going to find the answer to my problems in books. Not this time.

Once I was outside in the warm air of the early summer, I tried calling Barnes back but she didn't pick up. I'd worked out enough from the stuttering phone call to know that she wanted me to go to the Met headquarters. New Scotland Yard wasn't too far away so I grudgingly set off in that direction.

I ignored the three vamps who peeled away from the wall of the Carlyle Library and followed me. If they were all I had to worry about then I'd cope. Unfortunately, before I'd even crossed the busy road to retrieve Tallulah and make the short drive to see Barnes, I was joined by another vamp.

'Good afternoon, detective,' she said.

I didn't look at Scarlett and I didn't ask her why she was there. Instead I shoved my hands in my pockets and marched ahead. Despite her extraordinary stilettoes, she kept pace with me, Unless I decided to break into a sprint to escape her, I wasn't going to avoid this chat. I scowled and waited for the inevitable.

'We've been told,' she said, in a mellifluous drawl that set my teeth on edge, 'not to approach you.'

'And yet here you are,' I replied. I jerked my thumb at the trio of trailing vamps. 'And there they are.'

'They won't come near you,' Scarlett said cheerfully. 'They're only following to keep you safe.'

Lukas knew I could look after myself – I didn't need babysitters – but there was no point arguing with Scarlett. None of this was her fault. To be fair, none of it was Lukas's, either.

'Aren't you worried that they'll rat you out for chatting to me?' I asked.

'I am completely loyal to my lord,' she replied. 'But sometimes he doesn't know what's good for him. Apparently neither do you. He's been storming around for weeks now, yelling at anyone who puts a foot wrong and plenty who don't. It's time somebody put a stop to it.'

'My relationship with Lukas Horvath is none of your business.' My tone was icy. I skirted around a wide-eyed group of men in suits, all of whom were staring at Scarlett with their tongues hanging out. I looked her over properly for the first time and registered that she was wearing a skin-tight red-leather catsuit. Scarlett didn't do quiet and unobtrusive.

'I'm not asking you to tell me what the problem is,' she said. 'I'm asking you to tell *him*. He proposed to you and you ran away. He's confused and he's angry, and the very least he deserves is an explanation.'

A well of sadness rose up from the pit of my belly, threatening to overwhelm me. I swallowed it with an effort but the stabbing pain in my heart refused to go.

'He loves you,' Scarlett said. 'Heart and soul. Until recently, I believed that you felt the same. If you don't, if you were only playing with him, he deserves to hear it from you so he can move on.'

A sudden flash of fury zipped through me and I stopped walking and turned to her. I bared my teeth in an animal snarl. Scarlett's expression didn't alter. 'I was not "playing with him",' I bit out. 'And I love him as much as he loves me.'

I saw the faintest spark of answering anger in her eyes. She was here for Lukas and she wanted nothing more than to protect him. 'Then what the fuck is your problem?' she hissed.

The threat of violence simmered between us. I took a step back in a bid to give us some space – and to clear the air. 'He told me that he gave you five million pounds to buy a ring that allowed the wearer to see into the future. And that once you'd gotten the ring for him, he had it destroyed.'

The tiniest frown appeared between her eyes. 'Is this about money?' she asked disbelievingly.

'Don't be ridiculous,' I snapped. 'It's about power. Lukas despised the idea that such a ring could even exist, and he despises the existence of Cassandras who can also see into the future. He can't help himself. He knows it's blind prejudice and it's not their fault, but he still hates them.'

Scarlett shrugged. 'So?' I folded my arms and gave her a hard look. 'Wait,' she said slowly. 'Are you telling me that you're...'

I jerked my head angrily in assent.

Her mouth dropped open. 'You've been a Cassandra all this time and you kept it quiet?'

'No, It's a new development.' I muttered an expletive under my breath. I had no idea why I was telling Scarlett all this, because I hadn't told anyone else. Maybe it was because I thought she was the only person who might understand. After all, she knew Lukas; she probably knew him better than I did.

'Look,' I said, 'I know Lukas loves me. I have no doubts on that score. But I'm now a Cassandra and I know how much he hates *them*. If I tell him what's happened to me – if I tell him what I've become – he'll hug and kiss me and tell me everything will be alright. He'll tell himself the same thing. He'll believe he can still love me and that we'll be fine.'

Scarlett watched me with dull horror.

'And then,' I continued bitterly, 'I'll get to spend the next months or years, or however bloody long it takes, watching the love in his eyes turn to disgust. It'll be a slow death rather than a quick one. He deserves better than that.' I sniffed. 'So do I. So it has to be this way.'

Scarlett didn't say anything.

'I'd appreciate it if you didn't tell him any of this,' I said stiffly. She still didn't utter a word. 'Scarlett,' I warned.

She held up her hands. 'I won't tell him. It's not my place to do that. But you're kidding yourself if you think you can keep this from him. He's not going to slink away into the shadows, not where you're concerned. Sooner or later, you'll have to tell him the truth.'

I looked away. I might yet find a cure and, if I didn't, maybe the break would give me the strength I needed not only to tell Lukas the truth but also to make him realise that our relationship had to end. I couldn't bear to watch his love for me change to hatred. I wasn't strong enough to deal with that.

'Who else knows?' Scarlett asked, her voice much softer now.

A single tear rolled unbidden down my cheek. I dashed it away with my fist. 'Nobody. You're the only person I've told.'

She shifted her weight from foot to foot, her discomfort obvious. 'You can't keep it secret forever. True Cassandras can't control their visions, and they often can't control what they say.'

I lifted my hands in frustration. 'And that is a huge part of the problem.'

She licked her lips, displaying her single fang. 'Yeah,' she admitted. 'I can see that.'

Her sympathy was harder to deal with than her anger. I took another step backwards, suddenly desperate to get away.

'I won't tell him,' Scarlett repeated. 'But he's going to find out. If you need someone to talk to before then, I'm here for you, Emma. Any time.' She reached into the tiny bag hanging from her shoulder and drew out a small white envelope. 'Here. I was going to give this to you anyway, so you might as well take it. My phone number is inside. Call me,' she said. '*Whenever* you need.'

I swallowed hard. Scarlett and I weren't enemies but we'd never been friends, and her offer of help was almost too much. 'Thank you,' I whispered. I took the envelope. 'What is this anyway?' I asked.

A faint smile crossed her mouth and I registered sudden reluctance in her eyes. She didn't want to tell me, but I was obviously going to find out sooner or later. 'It's a wedding invitation,' she admitted.

My mouth dropped open. No wonder she hadn't wanted to tell me. 'Yours?'

She nodded. Despite the seriousness of our conversation, she couldn't keep the glow from her eyes.

'To...' I shook my head in vague disbelief. 'To *Devereau Webb*?'

'Crazy, right?' She raised her eyebrows meaningfully. 'If that idiotic werewolf and I can get it together, then you can do the same with Lord Horvath.'

I wasn't so sure about that. 'Congratulations. He's a lucky man.' A very lucky man.

'He certainly is.' She winked at me, but I could see that her delight at her own good fortune didn't erase her worry or discomfort.

'Lukas will be fine,' I said firmly. 'We both will.' I hesitated, then added for my own benefit as well as hers, 'Sometimes things simply aren't meant to be.'

TWO

It wasn't easy to put my conversation with Scarlett out of my mind. She'd understood as soon as I'd explained the situation to her, but I guessed part of me had been hoping she'd tell me I was being stupid and Lukas wouldn't give a flying fuck that I could glimpse the future. The fact that she hadn't argued suggested that she agreed with me – leaving him was the best course of action, no matter how much it hurt. Or made me physically sick.

I rubbed a hand across my eyes and passed through the main doors of New Scotland Yard, waiting for a second or two at the metal detectors while I tried to focus on my job and not my messy personal life. Coming here was good, I told myself. I needed the distraction.

Barnes wasn't in her office but a woman passing by told me she was conducting an interview on the third floor. Vaguely irritated, I headed up there and announced myself to a young man sitting at a desk by the lift. He looked more relieved than surprised when I told him my name. Huh. So Barnes really did want to speak to me in person, then.

I cooled my heels for several minutes. First I sat down on

one of the uncomfortable chairs along the wall, then I stood up and paced around. Nausea was continuing to plague my poor stomach in such a way that I wasn't convinced Scarlett's unexpected chat was the cause. I tried to remember when I'd last eaten. I was certain I'd had breakfast, if not today then yesterday.

Just as I was debating the practicalities of finding the nearest loo and heading in there to stick my finger down my throat to make myself throw up, I heard DSI Barnes' shoes squeaking along the shiny corridor. I turned around and raised a hand in greeting. She smiled at me but it didn't reach her eyes. Hmm. Something was definitely up.

'Emma,' she said. 'Thank you for coming.'

I bowed with more of a sarcastic flourish than I'd intended. 'Far be it from me to gainsay an order from you, ma'am,' I said.

Barnes raised an eyebrow. 'Did you get out of the wrong side of bed this morning?' she enquired. 'Or is your recent break-up with Lord Horvath causing you problems?'

I shouldn't have been surprised that she'd heard that Lukas and I were no longer living together. I knew she kept tabs on both Supe Squad and the supes themselves.

She peered at me more closely. 'While you have my sympathy,' she continued, 'it's important that you don't allow your personal problems to affect your professional life. It's fine between the two of us, and I'm always here if you need someone to talk to, but I am the exception. You need to leave your home life at the door.'

'I'm not on shift yet,' I said. Barnes looked at me. My shoulders slumped an inch. 'I'll do better,' I mumbled.

Her expression wasn't judgmental. 'I often find that immersing oneself in work can help. Are there any interesting developments at Supe Squad? Any cases to help focus your thoughts?'

I was certain she already knew the answer to that. 'Not really.'

'Hmm. Well, I'm sure something will come up soon enough,' she said. 'Not that I'm wishing for any crimes to be committed just to keep you busy, you understand.'

I nodded then I lifted my chin. 'I couldn't catch much on the phone – you kept breaking up. Why did you ask me to come in?'

She pursed her lips. 'We've received a complaint.'

Uh-oh. 'Against Supe Squad?'

Barnes met my eyes. 'Against you.'

My stomach lurched with even greater force. Bugger. Although I was well aware that my attitude in recent weeks hadn't been perfect, I didn't think I'd done anything to warrant a formal complaint. I'd certainly not done anything that justified a summons like this. 'Okay,' I said warily. 'What have I done?'

'It's not *what* you've done that's the problem, Emma,' Barnes told me. 'It's who you are.'

DSI BARNES led me into an empty room and gestured at a chair beside the table. Exhaling loudly, I sat down; the strong smell of disinfectant in the room wasn't doing me any favours. I spotted the water cooler in the corner and stood up, grabbed a cup of water and gulped it down.

Barnes was watching me. 'Are you alright? You look a bit ill – and rather tired.'

In other words, I looked like shit. I pasted on a smile. 'I'm fine,' I told her.

'You don't look fine. You look as if you're about to throw up.'

'It's the cleaning fluids in here, they're a bit too strong for me.' I sat down once more. 'It's not a problem. Tell me what's going on.'

Barnes looked as if she were going to say something else, then shrugged and leaned forward. 'Have you heard of the name Alan Cobain?'

I frowned; it didn't ring any bells. 'I don't think so. Is he the person who's complained about me? What's the basis for his complaint?'

'Mr Cobain is claiming identity theft.' Barnes paused. 'Of a sort.'

I shook my head. 'I don't understand.'

'He says that he's the phoenix.' She scrutinised me carefully.

'Uh...' I scratched my head. 'But all the literature states that there's only ever one phoenix.'

Barnes nodded. 'That's what he says.'

I warmed to my topic. 'I mean, there's nothing anywhere that suggests there can ever be more than one.'

She nodded again. 'Yep.'

'And I'm the phoenix.' I jabbed at my chest. 'I die. I *have* died. Several times, in fact. Then I'm reborn twelve hours later with some smelly fire and annoying scorch marks. It's happened more than once.'

'I'm well aware of that fact, Emma.'

'Other people have witnessed my resurrection,' I said.

'I know.'

'There's video footage.'

'I know.'

I couldn't keep the exasperation out of my voice. 'Then why are we talking about this? Does Cobain have proof that he's the phoenix?'

'He's got video. If it's fake, it's a good fake,' she said. 'Maybe he's related to you in some way.'

'I'm not the phoenix by birth,' I reminded her. 'It was a spell

12

of sorts that a druid put on me when I was a baby. I'm not like this by virtue of blood.'

Barnes didn't take her eyes off me. 'Is there any chance that the ritual that was enacted to make you the phoenix inadvertently drew on Alan Cobain's power so there are now two of you?'

I stared at her. 'As it seems to bear repeating, I was a baby when it happened. I have no idea how the power works or where it came from. It's not,' I said pointedly, 'something I have any control over.'

'Mmm.'

I folded my arms over my chest, unsure why I was feeling defensive. 'Look, I don't understand why this is an issue. If he's telling the truth – which I very much doubt – and he's a phoenix as well then that's a good thing. There are two of us. I'm not alone.' I pursed my lips. 'Neither is he. We should be celebrating.'

A crease appeared between Barnes's eyebrows. 'Mr Cobain is not celebrating. He's quite ... annoyed that you have supposedly stolen his glory.'

'Glory?' I couldn't keep the disbelief from my voice. 'What glory?'

'I suspect he has designs on being a television presenter, or social media influencer. I don't really understand it myself.'

'Is he alleging that *I'm* the fake?' I asked slowly.

'Either that you're fake or you've stolen some of his power. He's older than you, and he says that he's been the phoenix since the day he was born in 1982. That's eight years before you. I believe that he plans to sue you for stealing from him.'

'What? That's crazy!'

'And,' Barnes continued without missing a beat, 'he also wants to sue the Metropolitan Police for enabling your existence and amplifying it.'

'Amplifying it?' I didn't get it.

'Thereby diminishing his own identity.'

I squeezed my eyes shut. 'This is stupid.'

'Yes.'

'He's a kook, right? He's trying to get attention?'

'He seems serious enough, Emma. He has engaged a solicitor.'

I rolled my eyes. 'That doesn't mean anything.'

'I don't think that he'll go away,' Barnes said carefully. 'This is going to become a thing.'

'A thing,' I said flatly.

She shrugged. 'It happens.'

My mouth tightened. 'Get him to prove it. Get him to die then let's see what happens.'

'Mr Cobain has requested that we shoot him dead so we can witness his resurrection twelve hours later. Obviously, we can't kill a man in order to a test a theory.'

'He could kill himself while you watch.'

Barnes's looked mildly exasperated. 'You know we can't allow a suicide to occur in front of our eyes.'

I drew in a shuddering breath. 'What am I supposed to do about this?'

'I recommend that you take some legal advice. We can help you with that, or you can find your own representation. I just wanted to warn you that there may be some trouble ahead. Both I and the Met Police are going to support you, but things might become a little – fraught.'

I pushed back my hair. 'Can I meet Mr Cobain? Or at least talk to him on the phone? Find out what this is really about?'

'That's not a good idea,' Barnes told me. 'Not with possible legal action on the horizon.'

I cursed aloud.

'Hopefully this will come to nothing, Emma.' Her face

suggested otherwise. 'But it might cause you some problems. You need to be prepared.'

Unbelievable. How was it possible that my week was getting worse instead of better? It wasn't wholly unexpected that somebody like Cobain would eventually crawl out of the woodwork, but I wished he hadn't chosen to do it now. His timing sucked.

I was sure that I could sort it out within minutes if I could talk to him face to face. I'd prove I was the phoenix, he'd admit he was lying, job done. I had much better things to do than worry about a random chancer looking to make a quick buck or get his fifteen minutes of fame.

DSI Barnes stood up and offered me a kind smile. This time it felt genuine. 'Try not to worry about it.' That was easy for her to say.

My stomach lurched, flipping over and over, and I froze. Throwing up in front of DSI Barnes was not on my agenda for today. Or any day.

She raised her eyebrows. 'You're turning green, Emma. Perhaps you should drop by your doctor before your next shift.'

I pushed my hair away from my forehead, suddenly aware of how clammy my skin felt. 'Yeah,' I muttered. 'I might do that.'

I DIDN'T HAVE any enthusiasm for making an appointment with my GP. I wasn't even that ill. It was probably stress – I was hardly living my best life right now. And if it wasn't stress, it was a touch of food poisoning or some nasty little bug that nobody else had caught. A good night's sleep would cure me. And perhaps some peppermint tea.

I looked across the road at the small pharmacy then at

Tallulah. I supposed I could spare five minutes and pick up some medicine. It was better than dwelling on the likes of Alan bloody Cobain.

I crossed the road briskly, continuing to ignore the vamp trio who looked even more out of place here than they had at the library. When I pushed open the pharmacy door, it jingled loudly.

I couldn't remember the last time I'd felt ill; sickness wasn't usually something I had to worry about. I'd always supposed that was a perk of being the phoenix. I scowled as I wondered if my nausea and fatigue were related to being a Cassandra. It made sense because nothing else had altered. If I was cursed not only with seeing the future but also feeling ill, I was liable to throw a genuine tantrum. Or indeed several.

'Good afternoon!'

I smiled weakly at the woman behind the counter before glancing at the shelves. Man, there were a lot of vitamins here.

'Can I help you?' she asked.

I shuffled away from the vitamins towards the painkillers – but I wasn't in pain. I gritted my teeth. 'Yes,' I said. 'I'm looking for something to help with nausea.'

'Certainly. Is it for yourself?'

I nodded.

'Are there any other symptoms? Fever? Headache?'

I considered. 'No, I just feel sick. I might have eaten something dodgy. I have a metallic taste in my mouth.'

'Is the nausea constant?'

'It comes and goes.' I scratched my neck. 'But I'm quite tired. I'm under a lot of stress at the moment though, and I'm not sleeping very well.'

She looked at me kindly. 'How long have you been experiencing the nausea?'

I shrugged. 'A couple of weeks, I suppose.'

The pharmacist didn't look away. 'When was your last period?'

I let out a surprised bark of laughter. 'I'm not—' I began.

Then I stopped.

Wait.

Oh.

The blood drained from my face. 'I'm on the pill,' I whispered. But I'd had a lot on my mind recently and I hadn't been paying attention to my cycle. Dying tended to throw it off track so I wasn't always as aware of it as I should have been.

'The pill is very effective, but no birth control is one hundred percent,' the pharmacist told me.

I was starting to feel nauseous again. 'My breasts are a little tender,' I admitted.

The pharmacist offered a tentative smile. 'Maybe you should try a pregnancy test first,' she suggested.

THREE

I pushed my sweat-dampened hair away from my forehead and stared at the vomit-speckled ceramic. Carrots. Why were there always carrots in puke?

'You know,' Laura said, appearing at the door and handing me a cool cloth and a glass of water, 'it's harder to extract DNA from someone's barf than you might think.'

I dabbed at my skin and gulped down the water before wiping my mouth with the back of my hand and looking up at her. 'Is that your way of telling me it won't matter if I throw up over the next corpse I come across?'

'Oh no, it'll absolutely matter,' she said cheerfully. 'Don't do it.'

Easier said than done. Right now I had more control over my chaotic life than I did over the contents of my stomach – and that was saying something.

'But,' she continued, 'it's not as evidentiarily helpful as other bodily fluids, and it's not found at crime scenes as often as you'd think.' She added after a thoughtful pause, 'I've heard that it's a positive thing in pregnancy, though. Morning sickness is a good indicator that there is less chance of miscarriage.'

I met her eyes. It was less than a day since I'd taken the test and I hadn't mentioned my impending motherhood to anyone. But she wasn't stupid and she was a doctor, a doctor of pathology rather than obstetrics, but still a doctor. I sighed, flushed the toilet and got to my feet. 'It's that obvious?'

She shrugged but I saw the concern in her eyes. 'Lord Horvath,' she began. 'Does—'

I shook my head. 'He doesn't know and it's not why I left him. I only just found out myself.' I dropped my gaze. I'd been staying with Laura since the day Lukas had proposed to me and I'd realised I was a Cassandra. Until now, she hadn't asked any awkward questions and had simply welcomed me into her home. Frankly, she'd been extraordinarily good to me over the last few weeks, but I didn't want to outstay my welcome. 'If I'm in the way here, let me know. I won't take it personally and there are other places I can go.'

Laura's eyes widened. 'Piss off. You can stay as long as you want to. I enjoy the company. You know you're going to have to face him sooner or later, though.' She paused. 'Right?'

Lukas's dark features flashed into my head and I felt a heart-rending stab of pain. Yeah, a baby meant I had to speak to him. I couldn't avoid him now, although it helped that I knew that he'd be the most amazing father no matter what else was going on with me. Even so, I wanted nothing more than to go back to bed, pull the duvet over my head and wish for the rest of the world to go away.

I cricked my neck. 'I'm late for work,' I muttered. 'I ought to go.' At least Supe Squad would give me enough to do that I could forget my current situation for a few hours. I reminded myself that I had to find a solicitor, too. The baby news had put Alan Cobain on the back burner but I doubted he was a problem that would go away.

Laura patted my shoulder. 'I'm always here when you're ready to talk.'

Feeling very small and very pathetic, I looked down at my feet. There was a drop of orange vomit on my shoe. My mouth tightened. 'Thanks,' I mumbled.

Laura gave me a reassuring smile. 'Take care, Emma.'

I brushed my teeth, cleaned my shoe and headed out of Laura's homely flat. The three vamps from the day before had been replaced by another hapless trio. I stared at them from across the street then, with shaky hands, I took out my phone.

Lukas answered on the first ring. 'D'Artagnan.'

I'd rehearsed this conversation over and over and over in my head but I might as well not have bothered. The sound of Lukas's voice sent my brain into meltdown and, instead of saying something, I stood there breathing silence into the receiver like a deranged stalker.

His tone altered. 'Are you alright?' he asked roughly.

I swallowed hard. 'Yes.' The word was little more than a whisper.

'You don't sound alright. Stay there. I'm on my way over to you now.'

That did it. I wasn't ready for a face-to-face conversation. I needed more time. I licked my lips and found the words I needed. 'No!' I pulled a face, realising how I sounded. 'I mean, not yet. I'm fine, Lukas. Honest.'

'Emma...'

'Please, Lukas. Not yet.'

It was his turn to descend into pained silence. Several beats passed before he growled again, 'It's been twenty-three days.'

My shoulders sagged. 'I know.'

'Twenty-three *days*, Emma.'

'I know,' I whispered again.

'I realise my proposal came out of the blue. I'm sorry if it shocked you and you're not ready for that yet. I've tried to give you space.'

'And I appreciate that, I really do.' I took the plunge. 'It's not the proposal, Lukas. That's not why I left.'

'Then what? Why did you run away?'

He didn't hide the pain in his voice but I couldn't answer his question over the phone. 'We need to meet in person and I'll tell you all of it.'

'I'll get my car.'

'No.' I had work to do and so did Lukas. It would be better to wait until the evening when we were both free and there wouldn't be any interruptions. This was already going to be hard enough. 'Tonight. Let's talk tonight.'

'You'll come to Heart?'

I couldn't face his club and all those curious, prying eyes. 'Not there.'

'Home, then?'

I shook my head. I didn't want to meet him there either. 'The graveyard. At Knight's church.'

Lukas was silent for a moment. 'You want to meet on neutral ground? You think I'm going to do something and you need us to meet somewhere safe?'

'No! Of course not. It's just—' I couldn't put it into words. That graveyard was where I'd literally experienced death. It seemed apt that it would also be the place where I'd experience metaphorical death. It felt right. 'If we could just meet there,' I finished lamely.

'Fine.'

'Ten o'clock?'

'I'll be there and waiting.'

I exhaled. 'Thank you. Can you call off your goons? Their presence is getting annoying. I'm not going to run away, and I don't need their protection. You know that.'

His response was curt. 'As you wish.' He paused. 'I love you, Emma.'

I squeezed my eyes shut and pressed the button to end the call. Only then did I whisper back, 'I love you too.'

A warm breeze picked up, rattling a few errant scraps of litter and brushing through my hair. I replaced the phone in my pocket with a heavy heart and watched as one of the vamps answered his phone. A moment later, all three of them peeled away.

Their disappearance didn't make me feel any better; the burden that had settled on my shoulders the moment I'd realised I was a Cassandra only seemed heavier. I wasn't going to be able to escape it. There was no way out – and with a child involved, now I wouldn't be able to give Lukas an escape from it either.

I kicked a nearby lamppost and walked stiffly away.

THERE WEREN'T many parking spots near to Laura's home so I had to walk half a mile or so to reach Tallulah. It should have been a pleasant stroll; the weather was warm and the sun was already shining, despite the early hour, and for once I wasn't being trailed by any vampires. But the beautiful day didn't lift my spirits, it only made me more depressed.

I trudged past a tree and scowled at a little blue tit perched on one of the lower branches as it sang its pretty heart out. I'd shake off my angry fugue by the time I reached the office, but I would allow myself twenty minutes to wallow in my misery before I plastered on a smiley façade that would get me through the rest of the day.

'What's that poor birdie ever done to you?'

I stiffened at the sound of Buffy's lilting voice and stopped, turning to glare at her as she appeared from the other side of the tree. She either didn't notice or didn't care that her presence was ruining my glum start to the day. 'What are you doing here?' I said through gritted teeth.

Her bubble-gum pink lipsticked mouth stretched into an even wider smile. 'It's wonderful to see you too, DC Bellamy.'

I mentally cursed the day I was born, the day Buffy was born and the existence of the entire planet. 'How did you know I was here?' I demanded. 'And what the fuck do you want?'

'I knew you were here because I came looking. And what I want is some advice.' She dipped into a mock curtsey and fluttered her eyelashes.

'You want advice?' I said flatly. 'From me?'

She nodded enthusiastically. 'Yep!'

'Are you planning to commit a crime?'

'No.'

'Have you committed a crime?'

She pretended to consider the question. 'I stole a Mars Bar from a corner shop when I was ten years old.'

'Buffy—'

She beamed. 'Emma.'

I counted to ten in my head. Buffy might not be planning anything illegal but I was beginning to think that I'd happily murder her if she didn't get to the point. Fortunately for both our sakes, she seemed to realise that.

'Okay,' she said. 'The thing is, I need some romantic advice and you're the perfect person to give it.'

I stared at her. For one long, unusual moment words failed me. Buffy continued to grin. 'Buffy,' I said finally, 'this isn't a lonely-hearts column, and I'm the last person who should be doling out advice on anything to do with love.'

She frowned prettily and wagged her finger. 'Romance,' she said. 'Not love. Not yet anyway.' She fluttered her eyelashes.

'Please? I can hardly speak to Lady Sullivan about this sort of thing, and I don't have many friends who can help.'

'I can't begin to imagine why,' I said sarcastically.

She pasted on a doleful expression but I didn't care; I was beyond falling for any of Buffy's tricks. I turned up the collar on my coat and started to walk away. 'Find somebody else,' I said. 'I'm not the person you want for this.'

'But, detective, you are,' she wheedled. 'You truly, truly are.'

Even if I'd wanted to answer her, I didn't get the chance. Before I'd taken another step, a wash of extraordinary dizziness assailed me. There was a loud whooshing in my ears and the sky seemed to darken and slip sideways. My mouth opened and I heard my own words coming at me as if from a long way off, while a series of images flashed with nauseating speed through my head. 'Elementary. Elementary. Elementary. Innocent blood will run.'

As soon as I'd finished speaking, I doubled over and threw up again. No carrots this time; there was only bright yellow bile.

'Ewwww.'

I couldn't deal with Buffy's disgust right now. I retched for a final time and straightened up, pressing my fingertips to my temples. What had I seen? A splash of blood on a grubby pavement, for certain. There had been a glint of something metallic, maybe a knife. And, confusingly, a small flag trodden underfoot by a heavy boot, followed by another flash of sharp metal as a concealed blade slid out from the toe of the boot and slashed upwards.

'Elementary,' I muttered to myself. What did that mean?

'What's going on with you?' she enquired. 'Is being preggers making you crazy? Is this what baby brain is?'

I squinted at her in horror and my stomach dropped to my shoes.

'What? I'm a werewolf – I can smell your hormones from a

mile away.' She tapped her ear. 'I can hear the extra heartbeat, too. Any wolf could. Is the baby why you've left the luscious Lord Horvath?'

Was there anyone in London who didn't know I was pregnant? I hissed in irritation and made a mental note to avoid all werewolves for as long as I possibly could.

It was even more imperative that I spoke to Lukas tonight. I wouldn't put it past any of the clans to break the good news to him allegedly 'by accident'. In fact, if I knew the clan alphas, they'd positively relish the thought. 'If you tell a single soul,' I said, 'including Lady Sullivan then I will—'

Buffy put her hands up. 'Whoa. I won't breathe a word. Promise. Your condition doesn't affect Clan Sullivan so I have no reason to spill the beans.' She grinned happily. 'By staying quiet, does that mean you'll help me with that advice in return?'

I glared at her, spun around and took off down the street.

'Wait,' Buffy called after me. 'Where are you going?'

'Baker Street.'

'Eh?'

'Elementary,' I whispered. My dear Watson. While I was fairly sure I'd read somewhere that Sherlock Holmes never uttered that famous phrase in any of the novels about him, there was no doubt that it belonged to him.

Laura lived very centrally so Baker Street – and the fictional detective's fictional home – was only a few streets away. It would take no time at all to get there and find out what my damned vision was all about. Whether I was already too late remained to be seen.

I forced down the last of my nausea and picked up speed. I needed to get a move on. I put Buffy, Laura, Lukas, the baby, Alan Cobain and everything else out of my head and sprinted as fast as I could.

When I rounded the corner into Baker Street, I saw the usual smattering of early-bird tourists and well-heeled Londoners. It wouldn't take a detective, fictional or otherwise, to tell the difference between the two. The wealthy Londoners, who lived around here and were on their way to work, were wearing sharp suits and shiny shoes, together with tight expressions of distaste at the tourists. The tourists were talking loudly and stopping abruptly at random points along the pavement to take photos or point at buildings. They were dressed far more casually, and even from fifty metres away their excitement was apparent.

What wasn't apparent was any sign of a crime.

'Do you always like to start your day with a crazed run through London?'

I clenched my jaw. 'What are you still doing here?' I demanded. Buffy must have run behind me all the way.

She smiled patiently. 'I told you, I need some advice.'

She was determined, I'd give her that. Sensing that I wasn't going to escape her no matter how hard I tried, I gave in. 'Fine. Come to Supe Squad later today – 2pm. I'll see what I can do then.'

I turned away from her and continued to scan the street. An open-top tour bus trundled past. There was still nothing that looked out of place.

'Great! Thank you!' Buffy blew me a kiss. 'So what's going on? Why the strange chanting and the sudden rush to get here?'

Buffy might keep her promise about not revealing my pregnancy, but she'd definitely tell Lady Sullivan that I was a Cassandra. I wondered bleakly if she'd already worked it out from my involuntary verbal explosion.

'I received a tip-off. Early this morning. I couldn't work out what it referred to and then I realised it was to do with this street.' The best lies are those that stick close to the truth. I'd learned a lot from questioning suspects, both innocent and guilty, over the last year or so. Whether I'd fool Buffy or not was another matter. At least I had to try.

'Elementary?' she asked.

'Yes. And something about innocent blood.' I didn't refer to the images I'd seen flashing though my head. I couldn't explain those.

Buffy's eyes widened. 'So it's a threat.' She seemed more excited than dismayed. 'Well, what are we waiting for? Let's go and check things out! There's a man over there wearing a very suspicious hat. We should interrogate him.'

I hated myself for following her gaze. The man in question was wearing a deerstalker hat and carrying a magnifying glass. 'He's dressed up like Sherlock Holmes, Buffy.'

'Sherlock who?'

I pressed my lips together very hard. 'Listen. I mean this is in the nicest possible way but piss off.'

'Pardon, detective?'

'You're a civilian and this is a potential crime scene.'

She grinned. 'Emphasis on "potential". You can't stop me from being here. I'm simply out for a stroll.'

'Do you want that advice later or not?'

She sucked in her cheeks and considered. I stared at her. Was she actually serious about this romantic advice business? Why on earth would she come to me?

'Fair enough,' she said finally. 'I'll leave you to it.' She wagged her finger. 'But don't die between now and 2pm. I won't accept that as an excuse for you to wriggle out of our agreement.' She moved her finger towards my belly. 'Besides,' she added, 'while you might resurrect in twelve hours, who's to say that your baby will as well?'

I felt a sudden rush of blood to my head and a chill descended down my spine. Bloody hell, she was right. There was no guarantee that any babe in my womb would be protected as I was.

Buffy twirled her fingers in the air. 'Toodle-pip! I'll see you in a few hours.' As she twisted around and skipped away, I gazed after her, my mouth dry. It was only when she disappeared around the corner that I shook myself and refocused my attention on Baker Street. I wasn't the only person in this world with problems – and I had a damned job to do.

FOUR

I marched down Baker Street towards most of the tourists. One of the images I'd seen had been of a fallen flag underneath a black boot; now that I thought more about it, it had been the sort of flag tour guides sometimes used to corral their groups and keep people together. It made sense that tourists would be involved in the forthcoming incident, whatever it might be.

I pulled back my shoulders, ready to do business. 'I've got this,' I muttered aloud. 'And it doesn't matter that I can't let myself die.'

A startled woman pushing a pram stared at me before hastily stepping aside to give me a wide berth. Yep, crazy woman. That was me. Then I glanced into the pram and the blue-eyed child blinking up from its snuggly depths. Huh. Cute kid.

I shook myself and walked on until I was standing next to a cluster of people in front of the Sherlock Holmes museum. I noted two bored-looking teenagers and a boy of about eight or nine years old who was zipping on and off the pavement. He definitely seemed to have already had far too much sugar for the day, even though it wasn't yet nine o'clock. There were also various adults, none of whom appeared to brandishing knives. Not yet, anyway.

I frowned. What if my vision wasn't for the near future? What if it was for an event due to take place tomorrow? Or next week? Or next sodding year?

'The museum isn't open yet,' somebody said helpfully, doubtless registering my expression.

I glanced at the woman and managed a polite smile. 'Thanks.' I must have passed muster as a tourist.

'I know what you're thinking,' she said.

I doubted it. I leaned to my left, checking for anyone suspicious. There was an older man wearing a trench coat that looked like overkill, given the relatively warm weather. I looked him up and down. He could be concealing a weapon.

'You're thinking that Sherlock Holmes lived at 221B Baker Street but this museum is at different number,' the woman continued. 'When Arthur Conan Doyle wrote those books, this part of the street didn't exist – it was added later. And when 221 was added, it was a bank, not a house.' She pointed. 'See?'

I ignored her, my attention still on Mr Trenchcoat. He slowly raised his hands towards the top button of his coat and I stiffened.

The woman either didn't notice that I wasn't interested in what she had to say, or she didn't care. She stepped in front of me, blocking my view of Mr Trenchcoat. 'There's more to Baker Street than Sherlock Holmes,' she said.

I tried to move past her but a cyclist was blocking the way.

'The first Madame Tussaud's museum was located here.'

I pushed myself up on my tiptoes. The man was undoing his coat.

'Dusty Springfield lived here in the 1960s.'

Was he reaching inside his coat? Was he going to pull out a knife? I lurched forward, knocking into the woman. She let out a surprised cry, stumbled and dropped her bag. I finally had a clear line of sight to Mr Trenchcoat and began moving towards him with grim intent.

He shrugged off his coat, folded it over his arm and raised his arm to hail a taxi that was slowly driving past. Goddamnit.

'If you didn't want to listen to what I had to say you could have just told me,' the woman muttered behind me. 'You didn't need to be so rude.'

I turned towards her. She was scooping up a few strewn belongings from her bag. 'I'm sorry,' I said. 'I thought...' I shook my head. 'It doesn't matter. Let me help you.'

I knelt down – then I froze. A few feet away, alongside a half-finished packet of mints and a compact mirror, there was a small flag. 'That's yours?' I asked in a strained voice.

'You're going to make fun of me for having it?' she snapped defensively. 'It's a very useful tool of my trade.' She raised her head long enough to glare at me before reaching for the flag. Before she could grab it, a heavy, black boot stepped onto it. It was a mirror of what I'd seen in my mind less than thirty minutes ago.

My gaze flicked to the mud-encrusted seam between the rubber sole and the leather upper section of the boot and I immediately spied the glint of metal. The boot had a concealed blade controlled by some sort of spring-loaded mechanism. Oh, shit. Here we go.

I wasted no more time. Springing upwards, I barked, 'Police! Stay where you are, sir, and do not move!' I glanced at his deer-stalker hat and realised with dim horror that it was the very same man that Buffy had pointed out. Unbelievable.

The man bared his teeth in a snarl. With one swift movement, he drew out a knife with a lethal-looking edge from the bag slung on his shoulder. A few people nearby spotted the danger, screamed and darted away for cover.

'Drop the weapon!' I shouted.

The man raised the knife and waved it in front of my face. 'Make me!'

Alright then. I reached forward, preparing to grab his wrist, but before I could the woman at my feet stood up and swung her bag. She hit him on the side of his head and he let out a loud roar before turning and swiping the knife at her. The edge of the blade sliced into her cheek and blood welled up.

He shifted his weight and pressed down on his toes. The concealed blade in his boot snapped forward; it looked even more lethal in real life than it had in my vision.

I rushed at him and knocked him down before he could do the woman any more damage. Although he fell, he didn't give up. He raised his leg with the boot blade extended towards me and kicked me on my thigh. I twisted and managed to block the worst of the attack, but the blade still slashed through my trousers and scored my flesh. I hissed with pain.

The man aimed his foot higher and I felt a flash of fear. He was going to kick – and pierce – my belly. I sprang back to avoid the second blow but, as soon as I did, he pulled himself to his feet and turned on the tour guide again. She was frozen, her bag by her feet and her hands at the wound on her face.

The man roared. Brandishing the knife in his hand, he threw himself at her.

I knew the instant the blade slammed into her chest.

There were more screams from the terrified onlookers. I lunged forward yet again, grabbed the man's right arm and hauled him back. While he stared with shock or exultation –or perhaps both – at his bleeding victim and the knife embedded in her body, I threw him to the ground. Staying well away from his feet and the blade that still protruded from the toe of his boot, I flipped him onto his front. I snagged his wrists, ignoring his attempts to free himself, and reached into my pocket for the zip ties I always kept there. Once I had secured his wrists, I hauled him upright and looked over his shoulder at the woman.

The knife in her chest had been plunged in almost to the hilt. Her eyes were wide open and staring up at the sky. Oh no. Oh God, no. But then she blinked once and gurgled a long, difficult breath. She was still alive – she might still make it.

'Call an ambulance!' I shouted. At least two people close by were ahead of me and had their ears pressed to their phones.

'She's going to die,' the man muttered. 'She's going to die. I did it. I killed her.'

I looked at him coldly. 'I am arresting you for attempted murder,' I said. 'You do not have to say anything. But it may harm your defence if you do not mention when questioned something which you later rely on in court.'

'Let me go!' he shrieked in my ear almost drowning out the squeal of the siren from the police car that was hurtling towards us. About fucking time.

A man came running out of the museum door with a first-aid kit. He dropped by the woman's side and started tending to her wounds. Her lips moved as she tried to say something.

I could do little more than watch as I held onto the man. I was aware that it was my presence that had led to her involvement; if I'd not been here, she might not have been hurt. Her little tour flag had fallen to the ground because of me – and that same flag had been part of my Cassandra vision. Had I inadvertently caused this attack? He hadn't pulled the knife until I'd announced myself. Would she have been fine if it weren't for me?

I grimaced. I'd probably never know the answer. What I did

know was that almost everything about this soothsaying business was absolute, utter shit.

'Is it that trouble finds you, or do you find trouble all your own?' DS Grace enquired when he found me in the waiting room at the nearest accident and emergency unit.

He wasn't expecting an answer but, even so, his question sent flares of horror through my body. I must have looked stricken because he patted my shoulder and offered a sympathetic smile. 'It wasn't your fault, Emma.'

He didn't know that. It might well have been my fault – it probably was. No, strike that; it definitely was. My presence in Baker Street had involved the tour guide. My request to Lukas to call off the vampires who were following me had meant that I was alone. And because of my pregnancy, I'd pulled away and given the attacker enough time to stab the tour guide in the chest. It was all my fucking fault.

'The good thing,' Grace said with forced cheeriness, 'is that you get the rest of the week off.'

My eyes widened in alarm. Oh no. Absolutely not. I rose to my feet. 'I'm not taking any time off.'

'I appreciate that you've been given the all-clear by the doctor, but you've been through a traumatic experience.'

'I'm not the one who was stabbed,' I said through gritted teeth. 'I've given my statement and the attacker is in custody. I'm told the victim is in a stable condition and will probably recover. I don't need a holiday.'

The last thing I wanted to do was go back to Laura's house and spend the next minutes, hours and days alone with my damned thoughts. I needed to keep busy. I needed to *do* something.

'You've been on edge for days, Emma. Some time off will do you good.' What Grace left unspoken was that it would probably do everyone in the Supe Squad office some good too if I was away for a while. I guessed I wasn't doing as good a job at maintaining my smiley, everything-is-fine face as I'd thought.

'Owen,' I said softly, 'I need to work. Put me on desk duty. I'll keep away from people – I'll file papers or something. *Any*thing. I want to keep busy.'

He gave me a long look then he sighed. 'There are those cold cases that we've been meaning to look into.'

I nodded vigorously. 'Yes. Yes! I'll look at those. Thank you.' I smiled as brilliantly as I could. When Grace pulled back and frowned slightly instead of returning my smile, I realised that I probably looked more scary than reassuring.

I stood up and removed my forced expression. 'I'll retrieve Tallulah and meet you back at the office.'

He peered at me. 'You're okay to drive?'

'I am.' I met his eyes. 'I'm not going to do anything, or risk anything or anyone else. Truly.' My fingers lightly brushed against my stomach. I couldn't risk myself, either.

Grace finally looked convinced. 'Alright. I'll see you shortly.'

I straightened my clothes and started to follow him out of the hospital. Before I reached the sliding glass doors, my gaze snagged on a newspaper on a chair beside a waiting patient. I swallowed. 'Excuse me?'

The patient looked up at me. From his black eye and the way he was cradling his arm, he'd obviously been having some trouble of his own.

I pointed at the paper. 'Are you finished with that? Do you mind if I have a look?'

He shrugged. 'It's all yours, love.'

'Thanks.' I picked up the paper and unfolded it so I could read the story emblazoned on the front page. The photograph showed a grim-faced man standing next to a blank gravestone. I scanned the headline and the story. Great: Alan Cobain – 'the one and only phoenix' as he was calling himself – was now giving press interviews.

FIVE

I parked Tallulah in front of the Supe Squad building and patted her purple bonnet as I left her. I nodded at Max Vargman, the friendly bellman at the hotel next door, and he grinned at me. 'I hear you've had a busy morning, DC Bellamy.'

'Good news gets around,' I muttered sarcastically under my breath before remembering to play nice. I waved at him in my best friendly fashion. 'You have a good day, Max.'

He saluted. 'Always.'

Stepping into Supe Squad, I took a moment to breathe in the scent of verbena and wolfsbane. It was one of the few Supe Squad traditions that hadn't fallen by the wayside in recent months. We used the herbs in miniscule quantities as a test for the unwary. Only supes could smell them, so it was an easy way of telling worried members of the public, who thought they might be turning furry or growing fangs, that if they couldn't smell anything they were still human.

The smell had seemed strange when I first started working here, but now it enveloped me like a warm hug; it always put me at ease and made me feel at home. The tension stretching across my shoulders started to dissipate. At least here, in this building, I could forget my woes for a short time. Fred and Liza also helped.

I knew that my Supe Squad colleagues were worried about me but I didn't appreciate quite how much until I opened the door. Fred leapt to his feet, abandoned his beloved sofa and gave me a tight hug, and Liza wasted no time in going to the fridge to get me a slice of her finest chocolate cake.

'Thanks, guys,' I murmured and smiled at them. This time my smile was genuine. I shrugged off my coat, reached for the hairbrush on my desk and pulled it through my windswept locks, grimacing at the clump of hair that came out. Pregnant, prophetic and balding. Brilliant.

'Owen's got a meeting at the Talismanic Bank,' Liza told me as I dropped the brush back onto my desk. 'But he told me to pull out those old files for you and leave them on your desk. That's all there is. None of them have been added to the computer system yet, so all you've got is the paper in front of you.'

'Great. Thank you, that's really helpful.' It would have taken me far longer than Liza to work my way through the ancient filing system; she understood its vagaries whereas the rest of us only pretended to.

Tony hadn't liked computers and, while Liza did her best to upload and update the older files, she had other time-consuming jobs to do. Until Grace arrived, Supe Squad had worked under its own set of rules. I was glad that we were dragging ourselves into the twenty-first century but I was painfully aware that it involved a lot of work to do it properly.

I flicked on the kettle; caffeine might make the job easier. Then I hesitated – was caffeine bad for babies? Probably. I grimaced, knelt down and rummaged around the small, grubby cupboard underneath the table. The best I could come up with was an ancient herbal teabag that smelled dubiously of lavender and stale fruit. Better than nothing.

I made the drink, wincing when I took a sip, and sat at my desk. I eyed the pile of folders. Work would help; anything that occupied my mind for the next few hours would be a good thing. Being busy was easier than being idle, particularly when you had a vexing abundance of personal problems to worry about.

Even Fred had learned the value of occupying himself and managed to find something to do: he was slouching on the sofa with a police-issue laptop balanced on his knees using both index fingers to type up a document, although at the rate he was going it would take hours to complete.

I skimmed through the first three files. A spate of burglaries committed against pixies, all of which had occurred more than eight years ago. An unexplained werewolf death from 2019. The disappearance of a gremlin in 2010. Hmm. I took another gulp of the herbal tea, immediately regretted it and set it to one side.

There had been no more reported pixie burglaries and the trail was very, very cold. Whoever had been behind the crimes had probably left the area or moved on to better – and hopefully more legal – things. The unexplained werewolf death was interesting, but it only took one quick phone call to the McGuigan clan to establish that they'd found the culprit themselves and he was currently doing twenty years at the Clink, the prison run by supes and solely for supes. I updated the file before pushing it aside.

In years gone by, the lack of communication between Supe Squad and the supes themselves had been annoying, to say the least. I allowed myself several mutters of pointless frustration, then focused on the gremlin disappearance. This might be something I could get my teeth into.

The gremlin in question was a thirty-one-year-old male. I

checked his date of birth and realised that he was the same age as me; not only that, we shared the same birthday. I was vaguely aware of the birthday paradox – the theory that in a room of twenty-three people, there was a good chance that at least two of them would have the same birthday, but it didn't prevent me from feeling an odd tug of kinship with the vanished gremlin.

I gazed at his photo. Quincy Carmichael was a friendly looking soul. His eyes twinkled and his hair, although tousled, had a rakish, fun air about it. He had the look of someone who'd be a good person to have a party. His last name put me in mind of Phileas Carmichael Esquire, the gremlin solicitor with whom I'd often tangled in the past. There was nothing in the file to suggest they were related, but it seemed likely.

I turned towards Liza, who was chewing on a biro and frowning at her own pile of papers, and cleared my throat. 'Liza, how many gremlins are there in London?'

'Two hundred and thirty-three,' she said without looking up. 'Wait – no. Two hundred and thirty-two. Ma Higgins passed away last month.'

Liza was a wealth of useful information and I had no clue how she retained it all. I nibbled my bottom lip. With so few gremlins in the city, it seemed even more likely that Phileas and Quincy were related. I made a note to check it out and moved on.

According to the files, Quincy had been something of a jack-the-lad, starting and ending different businesses in quick succession. He'd opened a launderette in Lisson Grove that had lasted almost eight months until problems with the washers getting clogged with werewolf fur were too much for him to deal with. He'd sold the operation to a zeta in the Fairfax clan.

He'd then tried his hand at running tours around various supe haunts, no doubt aiming to make a quick buck from curious humans. He was assaulted several times when he tried to take groups of humans into some of the quieter supe establishments where they weren't welcome, so in the end he'd abandoned that idea and moved on to a dating agency specifically for supes.

That hadn't been a bad move; until recently, it had been incredibly difficult for a supe to get a serious date from any of the usual dating websites. However, supe numbers were limited, so poor Quincy had struggled to get enough customers to make his business viable.

At the time he'd disappeared, he'd been dipping his toe into the fake-blood business. He'd been searching not only for ways to provide non-human blood products that offered sustenance to vamps, but also for other fake-blood products that would give humans a similar sort of experience. Food and drink laws were strict, so it sounded as if he'd been skirting the edge of what was legal, but given what I knew of the market and the number of fake-blood 'goodies' that could be purchased in supe shops and online, Quincy Carmichael could have been onto a winner. Unfortunately, he'd vanished before the business gained a real foothold.

There was a lot of information and it would take me time to scour all the details, so I prioritised and scanned the list of people who had been included in the files by my predecessor, Tony. It appeared that Quincy had been as prolific in his love life as he was in his professional life: there were three ex-girlfriends and two ex-boyfriends. Two of the girlfriends had been human.

Tony had written notes about each one, but his handwriting was appalling and it was difficult to decipher more than the odd phrase or two. What was surprising was that he'd gone as far as interviewing Quincy's nearest and dearest. When Tony was the detective in charge, it was unusual for Supe Squad to follow up on supe crimes. Either the supes themselves took over the investigations, as had been the case with the McGuigan werewolf death, or other sections of the Met Police nabbed the cases when it was established that humans were involved. The disappearance of Quincy Carmichael was something of an outlier.

'You were working here in 2010, right?' I asked aloud.

Fred stared at me. 'Boss, in 2010 I was guzzling industrial-strength cider in the park with my mates and trying to put together my entry for the Guinness World Record for the longest bike wheelie.'

'You know your youth is a slap in the face to the rest of us?' Liza said.

'Sorry, grandma.' Fred grinned.

Liza rolled her eyes and answered me. 'Yes, Emma. I was here in 2010.'

'Do you remember Quincy Carmichael?'

She gave a mild snort. Stupid question: of course she remembered him. 'What do you want to know?' she asked.

'Tony did a lot of work on his case. Why was he allowed to?' I tapped my fingers on the file. 'Why didn't the supes look into it?'

Liza put down her biro, and a faint frown lined her fore-head as she thought about it. 'As I recall,' she said finally, 'nobody took his disappearance seriously. He had a reputation for being fickle, and evidence was found at his home that suggested he'd decided to leave the country and head for Spain.'

I flipped through the file again. Ah, yes: his passport was missing, and just before his disappearance he'd purchased a one-way ticket to Barcelona. By bus, not plane. I made another note.

'And,' Liza continued grimly, 'at the time there were bigger things for the supe community to worry about.'

Fred looked up from his laptop, as intrigued as I was by her tone. 'What things?'

'One of the Carr werewolves was found murdered in a house in Soho next to an equally dead – also murdered – vampire.'

I stared at her. Oh.

'Where's the file on *that* cold case?' Fred asked with an inappropriate touch of morbid eagerness.

'There wasn't one – it was out of our hands from the very beginning,' Liza told us. 'The wolves and the vamps took it over and almost ended up at war over it. There were a lot of theories that it was some sort of murder-suicide pact – theories that were thoroughly debunked, I might add. Both sides blamed each other. It was a ... testing time.'

From the way she spoke, I sensed that *testing* was an understatement. She waved a hand at my shocked expression. 'It was before Horvath became Lord, of course.'

'Of course.' Lukas's face flashed into my mind. No matter what happened, he would never let relations with any of the werewolf clans descend into anarchy. He understood the power of diplomacy. Another sharp pain stabbed at my heart and I forced him out of my thoughts. 'Was the culprit ever found?'

'Nope. Not unless the clans or the vamps found the murderer and dealt with him without telling anyone.' She shrugged. 'That's always a possibility.'

I held up Quincy Carmichael's file. 'He vanished at the same time as these murders?'

'Around the same time.' Liza looked slightly amused. 'But before you start thinking he was the killer, he wasn't. As I recall, Carmichael had a cast-iron alibi. I couldn't tell you what it was but I know that Tony was satisfied he'd had nothing to do with the killings.'

I flipped through the file again; there was no mention of the murders in it. Maybe Tony had thought they weren't relevant. I frowned. Quincy Carmichael had last been seen on February 13th, 2010 and reported missing by a friend two days later. He'd not been heard of since. If he had gone to Spain, he'd never returned. Or sent a postcard. Or a text message. Or set up any new Barcelona-based enterprises under his own name. He'd vanished into thin air.

I turned back to his smiling photograph. Alright, I admitted to myself, I was intrigued. This was exactly the cold case I needed.

'Anything else?' Liza enquired.

'I think that's it for now,' I said as the door buzzer sounded. Liza pressed a button on her computer to view the live feed from the camera that Grace had insisted on installing. I simply pushed my chair back and peered out of the window.

Fuck.

'Is that the bloody Sullivan werewolf?' Liza hissed. 'She's so annoying.'

It was too much to hope that Buffy would have forgotten our appointment. I gritted my teeth. This had better not take too long. I stood up reluctantly. Romantic advice, my arse; that canny werewolf was up to something. She always was.

CHAPTER

SIX

'You're still alive!' Buffy beamed. 'Well done!'

Yeah, I was still alive but there was a woman in a hospital bed who had almost died. I bit back my retort. The tour guide and what had happened on Baker Street had nothing to do with Buffy.

'Thanks,' I said drily. I pointed towards the main interview room. 'Would you like to come in and take a seat? I don't have long but I can spare five minutes.'

'You'd better,' Buffy said cheerfully. 'A promise is a promise.' For a moment, I wasn't sure if she was threatening me or not. 'Don't worry, detective,' she continued, 'this won't take long.'

Inside the room, Buffy took the nearest chair and settled in as if she were planning to stay for a while. With a sense of foreboding, I took the chair opposite. 'Listen, Buffy,' I began awkwardly, 'I really don't think I'm the person to be doing this. We don't have that sort of relationship – and even if we did, I don't think I'm a good person to give advice on matters of the heart.'

Her eyes widened. 'Oh, but you are!' she declared fervently. 'You really are. I trust you, detective. You say it like it is and you're very fair. You have experience and you're kind-hearted. You're the perfect person to help me.'

She was trying hard to butter me up but, unfortunately for Buffy, that just ratcheted up my suspicions about her motives. I sighed heavily. 'Go on then. What's the problem?'

When her cheeks coloured, I stared at her. Embarrassment is one of the harder emotions to fake, and there was no doubt that Buffy was genuinely embarrassed. She coughed, then she twitched and drew in a deep breath. 'So there's a guy,' she said, hedging her words, 'who I really like.'

Bloody hell. Now I was the one who was starting to feel embarrassed. I was suddenly tempted to stab myself with the nearest implement to avoid continuing the conversation but sadly all that was to hand was a dirty teaspoon on the table between us.

'I want to ask him out,' she said, 'but I'm a bit afraid.'

Maybe the teaspoon would be enough after all. 'Buffy,' I said, in a strangled voice, 'you're a strong independent woman. Just ask him out. The worst thing he's going to say is no.'

She looked up at me then down at her lap as the words burst out of her. 'He's human!'

'Uh...' I scratched my head. 'That shouldn't make a difference. Should it?'

'I don't always understand humans and their ways. It'd be easy if he was a wolf. Or even just another supe. But he's human and that means—' Her words trailed off.

'Means what?' I asked.

'That I'm out of my depth,' she whispered. 'I can deal with wolf stuff.' She touched her heart with the tips of her fingers. 'But human stuff is much harder. I know it sounds silly but I really like him, and I really want him to like me too.'

I pushed aside my earlier reservations and did my best to be kind. 'Treat him in the same way as you would treat a wolf,' I said. 'Ask him out in the same way you'd ask out a wolf. Honestly, Buffy, humans are not to be feared.'

She twisted her hands together. 'The thing is, there's another woman to consider,' she muttered.

Uh-oh. 'A girlfriend?'

'No.'

My heart sank further. 'A wife? Buffy...'

'No! It's nothing like that.' At my look, her expression altered. 'Honest! She's more like his – mother.'

Now I was thoroughly confused. 'I don't understand.'

'He looks up to her, trusts her. She's like his matriarch, or something.' She sought the right words to explain. 'Kind of like how Lady Sullivan is to me. I want to know if I should ask her permission before I ask him out.'

My astonishment was difficult to conceal. 'Ask her permission?'

'You know. Like how in the olden days a man asked a woman's father for permission to court her. I feel like I should ask this woman for permission to court *him*.'

'Is he an adult?'

'Yeah. Of course.'

'Is he single?'

'Yeah.'

'Then you don't need this woman's permission, Buffy. Just ask him out.'

'What if she doesn't approve of me?' she asked in a small voice.

'You're not going to be dating her,' I said firmly. 'You're going to be dating him.'

'So I should ask him out and not worry about her?'

'Exactly.' I already pitied this poor nameless man – and his matriarch, or whatever she was. They didn't stand a chance with Buffy.

She breathed out. 'Okay. Okay.' She gave me another worried look. 'But what if she tells him that he can't date me?'

I felt a sudden surge of sympathy for her. 'Why would she tell him that?'

She bit her lip. 'Because I'm a wolf.'

'Screw her,' I said. 'It's not up to her. And if this man is worthy of you, he won't care what she thinks.'

She started to nod. 'Okay. Yes, you're right. I should ask him out. I can do it now.'

'You go, girl.'

She beamed. 'Thank you.'

'You're welcome. Let's never do this again.' I stood up as the door opened and Fred popped his head through.

'Hey, boss. I'm heading out for an hour or two, if that's okay?'

'It's fine by me, Fred.'

He smiled and started to withdraw. Before he could leave, Buffy jumped to her feet. 'Wait! Fred, there's something I've been meaning to ask you.'

Hang on a minute...

Fred smiled at her and a genuinely warm twinkle lit his eyes. 'Ask me anything.'

Nuh-uh. No way.

'Buffy—' I began.

She ignored me. 'Would you like to go out with me this evening? I think you're sexy and sweet, and I want to jump your bones at the earliest opportunity. But,' she amended quickly, 'I'm happy to start with a candlelit dinner, if that's more appropriate.'

'Absolutely not!' My tone was harsher than I'd intended, but neither Buffy nor Fred paid me the slightest attention. She was gazing at him hopefully and he was looking back at her with a mixture of embarrassment and delight. The tips of his ears had turned bright pink.

'I would love to have dinner with you,' he said. 'I know a great place not too far from here. If you're happy for me to suggest somewhere, that is.'

Unbelievable. Why wasn't Fred running away and screaming? Not because Buffy was a werewolf, of course, but because Buffy was Buffy.

'Eight o'clock?' she suggested.

'That would be wonderful.' He gazed at her for a few seconds longer, then moved forward and kissed her cheek. 'I'm already looking forward to it.' He left the room without giving me another glance.

As soon as he'd gone, Buffy whirled around. 'It worked!' She hopped from foot to foot as if performing a triumphant dance. 'So, I'm thinking I'll wear my little red dress. It shows off my legs and my cleavage. Somebody told me that it looks like I'm trying too hard and that it's too obvious, but I *want* to be obvious. Fred deserves obvious.'

I frowned. 'His name is PC Hackert. And you cannot go out with him.'

'I have it on very good authority that I have to ignore your wishes,' she said airily. She grinned at me and pull a thin black box from her pocket. 'Voice recorder,' she said smugly. 'Just in case you try to go back on your word. As you've already told me, this isn't up to you. It's up to him and he's already agreed.'

I let out a strangled sound. 'That was before I knew it was Fred you were talking about! He's sweet and kind, and he's the sort of person who falls hard and gets hurt.'

'I'm not going to hurt him, and I know all those things about him already. Those are the reasons I like him.' She paused. 'Well, not *all* the reasons. Have you seen his tight arse?

Of course you have – you work with him. And I bet you've noticed his—'

I growled. 'Buffy!'

She smirked. 'Don't worry, I'll treat him gently. At least to begin with. I don't tend to get out my fluffy handcuffs until at least the third date.' She winked at me. 'Thanks for the help, detective. It's very much appreciated.' And then, before I could say or do anything else, she spun around and left.

I stared after her. I honestly had no idea whether Buffy was playing both Fred and me or whether she was genuine, but I couldn't bear to see Fred get hurt again,. He'd had a dalliance with Scarlett that had caused no end of trouble.

I wondered if he knew that the vampire was getting married and that was part of the reason why he'd said yes to Buffy. I shook my head. No, he wasn't like that. I grimaced and prayed inwardly that this date with Buffy wasn't going to cause more problems. Another broken heart was all we needed.

Resisting the urge to run after Fred and lock him in the Supe Squad broom cupboard for his own safety, I reminded myself that he was indeed an adult and capable of making his own decisions.

I re-focused my attention on Quincy Carmichael. Tony had investigated the case thoroughly, but sometimes the passage of time and a different perspective could offer new insights. Deciding that my best approach was to avoid any more details from the old file and to look into Quincy's disappearance from a fresh angle, I put the folder into my desk drawer and grabbed my coat. The missing gremlin might well be perfectly fine and desperate not to be found, but I was going to find him anyway to ensure both his safety and my peace of mind.

It was colder than before, and I paused outside the Supe Squad building to fasten the buttons on my coat. Max called out a greeting and, in the interests of maintaining a good relationship with our neighbours, I returned it. 'How's your day going, Max?'

'I can't complain, detective. I can't complain at all.' He touched the rim of his black top hat and nodded. 'And when I clock off this evening, I've got an evening out with friends to enjoy. I'm leaving work early for it.'

'Special occasion?'

He suddenly looked a little embarrassed. 'It's my birthday.'

I brightened. 'Happy birthday!'

'Thanks.' He smiled at me. 'It looks like you're having a busy day too. Are you on a case?'

'A cold case,' I told him. 'It's good to get the time to look into historic crimes. The passage of time doesn't mean that the bad guys should get away.'

'With you after them, they should already be running,' Max said warmly. 'Is it a bad one?'

'The case? So far it's a missing person, but there may be more to it.'

'Sounds intriguing.'

'We shall see, Max. We shall see.' I glanced across the street as somebody hurried past with their head down. 'Well, well, well,' I murmured to myself. 'That's handy.'

Max lifted a curious eyebrow. I nodded to indicate that I had to go, then crossed over to intercept the hurrying gremlin. Speaking to Phileas Carmichael had been low on my list of priorities but this was too fortuitous an opportunity to pass up and it probably wouldn't take long.

'Mr Carmichael!'

The solicitor ignored me; in fact, he seemed to pick up speed and do his best to move away from me at a faster pace. Huh. That was weird.

'Phileas!' I ran after him. I wasn't in the mood to let him get away, even if I only wanted to ask him if he was related to Quincy. 'Wait!'

He moved faster. Determined to catch up to him, and curious as to why he didn't want to speak to me, I put on an extra spurt of speed. Realising that I wasn't going to allow him to get away, he finally slowed and turned around. 'DC Bellamy,' he said reluctantly. 'I'm not ready to speak to you yet.'

What did that mean? I frowned at him.

'I am still preparing the relevant documents and I'll be in touch shortly.'

'Documents?'

He squinted at me. 'Pertaining to my client.'

'Mr Carmichael,' I said, 'what client are you talking about?'

His eyes took on a touch of impatience. 'Mr Cobain, of course.'

My mouth dropped open. Barnes had told me that Alan Cobain had sought legal representation but it hadn't occurred to me that he might be using a supe lawyer. 'You're working with Cobain? Why?'

He answered stiffly, 'Identity theft is a serious matter, detective.'

My astonishment only grew. 'You're suggesting that I've stolen Alan Cobain's identity? Seriously?'

Phileas Carmichael raised his finger and wagged it at me as if I were a naughty child. 'You know as well as I do that there is only one phoenix at any time.'

'Yes! It's me!' For fuck's sake.

'Hmm. According to you.'

I couldn't stop myself. 'There's more than enough evidence to prove I'm the phoenix, as I'm sure you know.'

The gremlin solicitor didn't so much as blink. 'There's no legal precedent for someone who has stolen the powers of another supernatural being.' He intoned the words as if he'd been practising them. 'But that doesn't mean such an action is acceptable.'

I threw my hands up. 'Bloody hell, Phileas!'

He looked me owlishly. 'If you wish to communicate further with me or my client, please do so through your own solicitor.' He moved away again.

I hissed under my breath. This was ridiculous – more than ridiculous. I went after him. 'I didn't approach you because of Alan Cobain. I didn't even know you were his solicitor.'

'Well, you know now.' He sniffed.

I gritted my teeth. 'I guess so. I want to ask you about another matter.'

Carmichael sighed heavily and stopped again. 'What is it?' He looked over his shoulder at me with an expression that suggested he was certain that I was using diversionary tactics to learn more about Cobain.

'Two words for you,' I said, tamping down my irritation. 'Quincy. Carmichael.'

Phileas jerked and faced me. The name of the long-missing gremlin was clearly the last thing he'd expected me to mention. 'What about him?'

I straightened my back. 'You know him, then?'

'I did know him, but he's been gone for a long time.' He folded his arms across his chest, creasing his pin-striped suit and messing up his perfectly folded pocket handkerchief. 'He was my nephew.'

Bingo. 'You're talking about him as if he were dead.'

'As I said, detective, Quincy has been gone for many years. His mother – my sister – passed away four years ago. He didn't attend the funeral and he didn't get in touch. If he is alive, he'd do best to stay away.' He gave a derisive snort. 'We don't need him.'

'Why not?'

'He chose to leave and not return. He didn't leave a note or any word about what he'd done, and I strongly believe that his disappearance hastened my sister's death. Quincy is no longer welcome.'

Families are messy things; however, I wasn't going to leave it at that. 'Did you know Quincy was going to leave before he did so? Did he give any indication that he wanted to go away?'

I could see that Phileas's impatience was growing. 'Not that I recall, but the boy was always flighty. He could never stick to one thing.' He glanced at his watch and frowned.

I persisted. 'When was the last time you saw him?'

'The family had Sunday dinner the weekend before he vanished.' Carmichael stepped back. 'Now I really do have to go. The press conference is due to begin any moment and I have to be there.'

'Press conference?'

'Goodbye, DC Bellamy,' he said firmly. He turned away again and marched off. This time I let him go, but my eyes followed his stiff back and swinging arms.

Then my stomach lurched and I leaned over, certain I was about to be sick again. I heaved once, twice, before the moment passed.

When I straightened up, I saw Max watching me with concern from across the street. I waved at him, pretending that everything was fine, then turned on my heel to retrieve Tallulah.

CHAPTER
SEVEN

Given that it was almost thirteen years since Quincy Carmichael had disappeared, there would be no physical remnants of him. Even so, I wanted to visit his old home and places of work and speak to people who might have known him. It was possible that I might unearth some useful details.

Despite his uncle's disgusted dismissal, Quincy's working life intrigued me more than his personal life so I decided to start there. The last business he'd started, manufacturing and selling fake-blood products, was the logical place to begin. As far as I'd been able to glean, Quincy had outsourced the manufacture to a small factory on the furthest corner of Lisson Grove, tucked away from the more residential streets. Quincy might be long gone but the factory still maintained a presence.

I parked outside it, murmured a gentle warning to Tallulah to behave and headed inside.

There was a small, neat reception area with a smartly dressed woman behind the counter, a few healthy-looking plants and a flickering television on silent that was bolted to the wall in the far corner. From beyond the internal door, I could hear the sounds of machinery and people hard at work. I listened for a moment, then approached the receptionist and drew out my warrant card. 'Good afternoon. My name is Detective Constable Emma Bellamy.'

The woman's eyes flared in alarm. I pretended not to notice and consulted my notes. 'I'm hoping to speak to the owner of this factory if he's available. Birch Kale? Is he here today?'

She swallowed. 'I'll check and see. Can I ask what this is in relation to?'

'It's nothing to worry about. I only want to ask him a few questions about someone he used to do business with.'

The receptionist visibly relaxed. I couldn't say for sure why she was so nervous, but I suspected it had something to do with the faint smell of weed that lingered in the air around her. I had far better things to do than chase up recreational pot smokers.

I continued to smile blandly in the hope that she'd continue to relax. Antagonising front-line staff never worked out well.

She edged out from behind her desk and disappeared through the door. As I swivelled around, my eyes fell on the television screen. It was tuned into the news and I watched a reporter outside the Houses of Parliament for a moment or two before the receptionist returned.

'Mr Kale is here,' she said, as if she'd only just discovered his presence and was surprised by it. 'He'll see you in his office. I'll show you the way.'

'Thank you.'

I followed her onto the factory floor. As soon as we were through the door, the noise intensified. The place was smaller than I'd expected, with fewer than a dozen employees bustling around various complicated looking machines. The receptionist led me towards a closed door at the other end of the room, knocked once and entered. 'Mr Kale? This is DC Bellamy.'

Kale was already rising to his feet, his hand outstretched in greeting. 'DC Bellamy. It's lovely to meet you at last. I've heard a lot about you.'

'I guess my reputation precedes me, Mr Kale.' I grinned and shook his hand. 'It's not all true.'

'Oh, I think it probably is. And please, call me Birch.'

It was nice to receive a warm welcome. I looked Birch Kale up and down and decided that I'd definitely not met him before. I didn't know the pixie community as well as I knew the vamps and the werewolves and it was something I needed to remedy; I supposed this was a start.

He gestured towards a chair and I sat down. He did the same and leaned across his desk. 'What can I do for you, detective?'

'I want to ask you a few questions about Quincy Carmichael and your dealings with him.'

Birch Kale let out a low whistle. 'That's a name I've not heard in a long time! Has old Quincy turned up, then?' There was an edge to his words that hinted at both enthusiasm and bitterness.

'I'm afraid not. I'm looking into his disappearance and I thought you might be able to help me out.'

'Oh.' Kale's shoulders dropped a fraction, indicating his disappointment. My gut told me that there was more to his reaction than the desire to see an old colleague again.

I took a gamble, careful not to phrase my next words as a question. 'You didn't part on the best of terms.'

Kale pulled a face. 'You could say that – although we didn't officially part ways. One day he was here and the next...' He waved a hand. 'He left owing me a considerable amount of money. He still does, in fact.'

Ah-ha. Suddenly, Kale's reaction made more sense. 'What happened?'

'He came to me initially with grandiose plans for selling

several lines of blood-esque items. He'd worked on the formulas himself, and he convinced me that there was a market. I was dubious to begin with, but Quincy had a way of persuading people.' He half-smiled. 'He was right, of course. Nowadays the fake-blood-items business is booming, but thirteen years ago not so much. Anyway, he laid down a deposit with a promise to pay the remainder after production. I produced what he wanted and he never paid up.'

'Is that because he disappeared before he could pay, or because he couldn't pay?' It was an important distinction.

'I sent him several reminders before he vanished,' Kale told me. 'And I made it very clear that he wouldn't receive the products he'd ordered until he'd paid me in full. He kept telling me to be patient and that the money was on its way.' He pointed to himself. 'Here I am, a dozen or so years later, still being patient. And still waiting for the money.'

'What happened to the products he'd ordered?'

Kale wrinkled his nose. 'We managed to flog a lot of them to local shops and markets, but we still made a considerable loss. I can have our accounts team dredge up the details for you, if you like.'

'That would be useful. Thank you.'

'No problem.'

I tried a different tack. 'What was Quincy Carmichael like as a person?'

'Very charming, but something of a dreamer. He always struck me as a great romantic at heart. You know that he ran a dating agency before he came to me?'

I nodded.

'I always had the impression that he wanted to be seen as doing something worthy, whether that was helping supes find love or vampires with their blood needs. He liked to think of himself as working for a greater good. He never struck me as crooked, just –incompetent. He bit off more than he could chew.'

'But you think he had money troubles?'

'I know it. I always assumed it was why he upped sticks and vanished. There were too many creditors beating down his door and the easiest thing was to disappear.' Kale met my eyes. 'He wasn't a bad guy, detective. Despite everything, I liked him. If he turned up tomorrow, I'd probably still have a beer with him.' He smiled ruefully. 'Then I'd slap him with my invoice. Hard.'

'I understand that.' I paused. 'Do you know who he was close to at the time?'

The pixie sucked on his bottom lip. 'There was an ex-girlfriend who he still got on well with, I think. She was a vampire. I can't remember her name – Candy, perhaps? I often saw them together. And of course there was poor Simon Carr.'

I registered the last name. 'A werewolf?'

'Yes. Sadly, he was murdered around the same time that Quincy disappeared, together with another vampire.'

Kale had to be talking about the case that Liza had mentioned. Interesting. I sat a little bit straighter. 'They were friends? Simon Carr and Quincy Carmichael?'

'As far as I knew. I saw them together a few times. Quincy said it was a business thing, but I kind of assumed there was more to it. They seemed more like friends than business partners.'

'Did you mention this at the time? Did it come up in the investigation into the murders?'

Kale eyed me shrewdly. 'Where Simon Carr's death was concerned, everything came up. Those murders caused a lot of problems.'

'So I've been hearing,' I murmured.

I ASKED Birch Kale several more questions but nothing of note emerged. He remained helpful and friendly throughout and, when we were done, he walked me out to reception before shaking my hand.

I smiled at the anxious receptionist, who had sprayed herself liberally with some very potent perfume no doubt to disguise the smell of weed, and reached for the door. As I did so, the flickering television caught my eye.

'Fucking hell,' I muttered under my breath.

I gazed at the image of Phileas Carmichael standing next to a large man in a cheap grey suit. Both of them were behind a podium in a room that I immediately recognised as one the larger meeting rooms at the DeVane Hotel. No doubt the large man was Alan Cobain – and this was his damned press conference. It must have been a slow news day, and that was why it was being televised.

I ought to have strode out of the building and ignored it but sometimes I'm my own worst enemy. I asked the receptionist to turn up the volume. She picked up the remote control, eager to do anything that would keep my attention away from her.

Phileas Carmichael's voice boomed from the television screen. 'My client,' he intoned, 'is the phoenix. He has provided video footage to attest to that fact and will demonstrate his abilities if anyone doubts him. That is why we have serious concerns about the Metropolitan Police detective who also claims she is the phoenix. She is in a position of power and authority and is abusing that position by taking Alan's identity away from him.'

One of the off-screen journalists shouted a question. 'Are you saying that this detective is lying about who she is?'

'That is not for me to say at this point,' Carmichael replied. 'It may be the case that there is now more than one phoenix in the world, but it may also be the case that the detective in question somehow took a portion of my client's powers away from him. This possibility is causing him considerable distress. We must remember that nobody is above the law, no matter what their position is. This matter must be investigated further, not only for Alan Cobain's sake but for the public at large.'

I curled my hands into fists. The most frustrating thing was that Phileas Carmichael was right on many counts, especially when it came to my role in the police. I was well aware that many police officers abused their positions in horrifying ways. Nobody should be allowed to act like that, and all complaints had to be thoroughly and immediately investigated and acted upon. It was the only way the police could operate.

Besides, whether I was the phoenix or not, I couldn't claim to be the authority on the matter. I didn't know everything. What if my transformation into the phoenix as a baby had indeed taken power from Alan Cobain? It wouldn't be anyone's fault if that had happened. My parents' druid friend, Miranda, had called upon the power without thought or control when she'd found the three of us dead in our home. Maybe her actions *had* affected Alan Cobain. I couldn't say for sure either way – but if it were true, I didn't know what to do about it. I couldn't give the power back; it definitely didn't work that way.

On the screen, Cobain raised his hand to indicate that he wished to speak. He looked anxious as he cleared his throat. 'I'm not trying to cause anyone any trouble,' he said in a quiet voice that belied his height. 'I just feel as if a part of myself and my identity has been ripped away and my integrity has been called into question. It's costing me my health and my standing in the community. All I want to do is sit down with the detective so we can talk about this and find out what's really going on. I want to get my life back,' he said sadly. 'I wish she'd let me speak to her.'

My eyes narrowed. He was implying that I'd refused to meet

him. I'd spoken to his own damned lawyer an hour or two ago, for goodness' sake. Phileas Carmichael had wanted me to stay away from Cobain, not have a chitchat.

Someone called out another question. 'If you're really the phoenix, show us now. Die now. We'll act as your witnesses. Let's see whether you're really re-born or not.'

Phileas Carmichael glared at him. 'It's no surprise that a vampire would challenge my client. The detective who is claiming to be the phoenix is in a serious relationship with Lord Lukas Horvath, the vampires' leader. This only proves what a mountain of problems Mr Cobain faces in trying to prove his identity. Not only are the police against him but the entire supernatural community is, too.'

For fuck's sake.

A whispered question floated towards me. 'Is that you?' the nervy receptionist asked. 'Are they talking about you? You're the phoenix, right? Your boyfriend is Lord Horvath?'

I glanced over my shoulder at her. Her eyes carried a definite glint of morbid fascination at the scene unfolding in front of her. My back stiffened. 'I couldn't possibly comment,' I said, realising how ridiculous and uptight I sounded.

I clenched my teeth and quickly left the building.

EIGHT

'You had better not be calling me to postpone our meeting this evening, D'Artagnan.' Lukas's voice was silky smooth but I could still hear the throb of desperate pain underlying every word.

'That's not why I'm phoning and you know it, Lukas,' I said as I opened Tallulah's door and threw myself into the driver's seat.

He didn't miss a beat. 'You saw the press conference, then.'

'I saw enough to know that you sent vampires to interrupt it,' I bit out. 'That's not helpful, not even slightly. Alan Cobain is nothing to do with you.'

'On the contrary, D'Artagnan, he's everything to do with me. He's calling supernatural integrity into question and I am duty bound to answer him. It's nothing to do with you.'

'Bullshit.'

Lukas laughed softly. 'Yes, alright, I suppose it is. But I know he's causing you problems and I want to solve them. He's a con artist. All he wants is money.'

'You don't know that for sure. He might be telling the truth.'

'He's not. The man isn't even a supe.'

I gripped the phone more tightly. 'How do you know that?'

'We tested him with wolfsbane and verbena and he didn't smell a thing. This entire public tantrum is some sort of set-up. He's trying to create as much as noise as possible in the hope that you and the police will pay him to slink away quietly. I'm very disappointed that Phileas has gotten involved. I'll be talking to him later.'

'You will not.' My tone was harsher than I intended. 'Lukas, please. Stay out of this.'

'I want to help you, Emma.'

My heart ached when he used my real name and I briefly closed my eyes. 'You'll be helping by not interfering.'

'You know he's trying to goad you into approaching him, then he'll claim that you've attacked him.'

'I'm not planning to approach him.' I wasn't entirely stupid.

'Then he'll claim that you're deliberately avoiding him and use that as proof that he's telling the truth.'

'What if he *is* telling the truth?'

'He's not.'

Regardless of the wolfsbane and verbena test, he might be. I had to consider every possibility. 'Just stay away from him, Lukas. You and all your vampires. Please.'

I heard him sigh. 'Fine, if that's what you wish.'

'It most definitely is.'

His voice changed. 'Are we still on for tonight?'

My hand touched my stomach again. 'Yes. I'll be there.'

'Good.' He sounded satisfied. 'I'll see you then.' He hung up before I could say anything else.

I stared at the phone. Lukas believed that he could solve every problem that came his way, but he still didn't know the truth about me. When he found out that I was now a Cassandra... I shuddered. He'd try and solve that problem too, but I was certain there was no solution. This was my life now, and I had to accept it.

The trouble was that I knew Lukas wouldn't be able to do the same. I shook my head. A few months ago everything had seemed perfect. So much for perfection.

I touched my belly again. At least all was not lost.

ALTHOUGH DARKNESS WAS FALLING by the time I got back to Supe Squad, there were hours to go before I was due to meet Lukas. Max had gone off shift and been replaced by Stubman, his surly, supe- and cop-hating colleague who glared at me as I walked up to the door.

I waved at him and gave him a wide smile in a bid to be as perverse as possible. He growled in response and turned away. Whatever. If that man thought he was a thorn in my side, he ought to get in line – he'd be way back at the end of the queue. Besides, I'd known him for long enough to know that he was all bark and no bite.

I flicked on the light switch as I entered and frowned at the chill in the air. The others must have already left for the day. Liza would be toddling off with Grace to curl up on the sofa like the happy couple they were. Fred would be getting ready for his damned date with Buffy. I cursed aloud for no good reason whatsoever. I was planning to stay here until it was time to meet Lukas. Following up more on Quincy Carmichael would keep me focused and productive.

I wanted to stay warm and comfortable as I worked, so I stomped over to turn up the heating. Then I noted the draught coming from the back of the building so I stomped even more loudly towards the back room, hissing in annoyance when I saw the window was open. That was careless. I slammed it shut and stomped some more until I reached my desk and sat down.

Instead of immediately turning on my computer, I took a moment to sit very still and breathe deeply. Maybe it was hormones, maybe it was stress. Either way, I had to calm down and stop acting like a toddler throwing a tantrum. I was Emma bloody Bellamy. I could deal with this. I could deal with anything.

'Sorry, Jellybean,' I whispered. 'I've been making things hard for you, haven't I? I'm going to stop all that now. I've got you to look after.' I sniffed decisively, then reached for my phone and ordered myself something nutritious to eat while I worked. My jellybean needed me. And so might Quincy Carmichael.

There was every chance that Birch Kale was right: Quincy had left London when his creditors became too much for him. The fact that he'd booked himself onto a Barcelona-bound bus rather than a plane was interesting, though. If he'd flown, he would have been easy to track down and I could have found out if he was on the flight or not. A bus, even an international bus, wasn't quite so easy, especially when the journey had taken place long before Brexit, when European border controls were managed differently.

Why on earth had he sat on a bus for thirty hours when he could have taken a plane and arrived in less than three? I contacted the bus company and left a message, but I knew already that it wouldn't help. I had to think differently if I was going to find evidence that Quincy Carmichael had escaped to Spain.

Drumming my fingers on my desk, I considered the matter. Finally I searched for the phone number I needed and dialled. It connected almost immediately.

'*Buenas noches. Mi nombre es Emma Bellamy.*' I winced. That was about the extent of my Spanish language skills. 'Er...'

'What can I do for you, detective?'

I wasn't surprised that the person on the other end of the line spoke English – our European neighbours are far better at learning languages than we are – but I was surprised that she knew who I was. I hadn't introduced myself as detective. 'You know who I am?'

'Your reputation precedes you. Even if I hadn't already heard of you, your name has been in the news today. The prospect of more than one phoenix has caused something of a stir even here.'

I felt a spasm of annoyance that Alan Cobain's allegations had stretched beyond Britain before remembering that I had resolved to be happy and calm from now on. I breathed in. 'It's not yet clear whether there are two of us or not. It will be ... interesting to find out.'

There was a brief tinkling laugh. 'The word "interesting" covers so many different options, does it not?'

I supposed it did. 'Who exactly am I speaking to?' I asked.

'Oh. My apologies for not introducing myself. I'm Elena.'

I blinked, startled. 'Lady Elena?' She was the head of the Spanish vampires. I'd expected an underling, at best.

'*Sí*. We are not like you Brits. We do not stand on the same ceremonies. And I knew your predecessor, Tony. We chatted sometimes.'

I'd gotten the phone number from Tony's own book so it made sense that it was a direct line. 'It's good to talk to you,' I said honestly. 'The reason I'm calling is because I'm searching for a British gremlin who disappeared several years ago. There is a theory that he ran away to Barcelona.'

'Quincy Carmichael,' Elena said instantly.

Now I was even more startled. 'You remember him?'

'I remember looking for him. It was an unusual situation. Tony asked me to keep a lookout for any English gremlins who landed on Spanish soil. I can assure you that if this particular one came to Spain, he did not make himself known to us. Not then and not since.'

'It was a long time ago. I'm surprised that your memory is so clear.'

Elena paused. 'I remember it because I already knew him,. Before I became head of the vampires here, I used Quincy's services a couple of times when I was visiting London.'

I straightened up. 'His services?'

'Dating services.' Elena sounded rueful. 'Such a thing did not exist in Spain and it was useful to connect with like-minded supes when I travelled.' Her voice took on a more cautious note. 'I dated your Lord Horvath, thanks to Quincy. He was definitely one of the more ... suitable men on Quincy's books. I enjoyed his company.'

'You went out with Lukas?'

She laughed again. 'I am not surprised he didn't mention me to you. Although our time together was pleasant, it was never serious. I always knew he was waiting for his *alma gemela*. I am happy that he found you.'

'*Alma gemela?*'

'His soul mate,' she answered simply.

I swallowed the sudden lump in my throat. Oh. Flustered, I ran a hand through my hair, my fingers catching on a tangle. I reached for my hairbrush to comb it through – and no doubt lose more hair in the process – but the brush wasn't where I'd left it. Liza must have been tidying up again. Absently, I opened the desk drawer to look for it.

'I will tell you what I told Tony at the time,' Elena said. 'Quincy had many loves but his greatest one was London. He would never have left, not for anyone. I am sure of it. I am equally sure that he isn't in Spain.'

Interesting. I closed my desk drawer with more force than I'd intended. 'Around the time he went missing there were two local murders,' I said. 'A vampire and a werewolf were killed. I'm told that Quincy knew one of them. Would you have any reason to think he might have been involved in their deaths?'

She answered instantly. 'Quincy Carmichael was many things to many people, detective, but he was never ever violent. Quincy was not like that.'

I thanked her profusely for her time.

'That is no problem. I would ask for one thing in return, though.'

'What's that?'

'An invitation to your wedding once Lukas has proposed. I would like an excuse to visit London again.'

There was very little I could say to that. I somehow strangled out a polite reply and hung up as quickly as I could.

I leaned back in my chair and used my fingers to tease out the damned tangle in my hair. 'The thing is, Jellybean,' I said aloud, 'other than the payment he made for his bus ticket, there's no evidence that Quincy went to Spain. If somebody hurt him or killed him and wanted to hide his murder, the smart thing to do would be to make it appear that he'd disappeared of his own accord. Somebody else could have bought that ticket.'

I reached for the file to check Quincy's bank statement. Tony had highlighted the bus ticket in yellow and I gazed at the date. The last time anyone had reported seeing Quincy in the flesh had been on the Sunday before he'd vanished, when he'd attended the family dinner that Phileas had mentioned. He'd bought the bus ticket on the Monday afternoon, due to depart the following day.

I stared at the dates, then I tapped on the computer and did a quick Google search. Hmm. The double murder of Simon Carr and the vampire had occurred on the Saturday night. Just because these events had happened during the same weekend, didn't mean they were linked, yet I couldn't shake the niggling thought that there was a connection.

CHAPTER
NINE

It was cold when I finally left for the graveyard. As the appointed hour of my doom approached, the seconds and minutes began to drag by and even searching deeper into Quincy's life stopped distracting me, When I caught myself gazing at the clock for the umpteenth time, I gave up and shrugged on my coat. I'd be early, but it would allow me to calm myself before Lukas arrived. It was time to get the worst over and done with.

Although the graveyard was within walking distance, I took Tallulah; having her close by would allow for a speedy getaway if I needed one. To my surprise, I found a parking space almost directly outside the gates. I turned off the engine and prepared to open the door. As I did, the radio flicked on of its own accord.

'Love takes time,' warbled a songstress, 'and patience but I know you are miiiiiine.'

I frowned and turned it off. It immediately flicked itself back on again.

'I know you'll forgive meeeee...'

I hissed and turned it off again. 'Tallulah,' I warned. 'Stop that.'

The radio whined and started again. 'You are miiiiiine!'

I opened the car door. If Tallulah wanted to sit on her own with the sappy love song playing on the radio in the background, then so be it. I didn't have to sit there and listen to it with her. I left her where she was, with the tune still audible through the car windows, and walked through the iron gates.

It was some months since I'd last been here. I checked in on Reverend Knight occasionally, partly to keep the peace between him and his supe neighbours and partly because I genuinely liked him. However, I'd been avoiding him lately, aware that he was friendly with Lukas as well as me, and any conversation would probably involve well-meaning but painful questions about our relationship.

At least the late hour meant that Knight was probably tucked up in bed with a good book. I didn't want to have to duck behind a gravestone like an idiot to avoid any awkward – albeit well-meaning – nuggets of advice. I was supposed to be an adult, not a small child afraid of a disapproving word or two.

Breathing deeply in a bid to remain calm, I went over to the grave where I'd once been killed and where all this had begun. A faint swirl of mist clung around the top of the headstone, creating an eerie atmosphere; it was textbook horror-film stuff, where the lead character was about to confront the evil villain for the last time in order to save the day – except Lukas was the hero and not the villain. I shoved my hands into my pockets and wondered what that made me.

'Hi, Lukas,' I muttered aloud. 'Good to see you. Just wanted to let you know that the reason I didn't accept your proposal and ran away is that I'm now the very sort of monster that you hate. Oh, and I'm also carrying your baby. Surprise!'

The only answer was the tinny sound of Tallulah's radio, which was still playing. I checked my watch. It was a quarter to ten. He'd be here soon and I could have this over and done with.

I sighed painfully, and then a wave of dizziness washed over me.

No. Not now. Please not now.

The strong smell of burning filled my nostrils. That was new – the visions I'd experienced so far hadn't included smelly portents. An image of flames flashed through my head and I heard distant screaming. A moment later, I saw a writhing body, its arms and legs flailing as the flames took hold.

Words forced their way out of my mouth. 'Ten. Eleven. Fuel will be added to my fire.' As soon as I finished speaking, an ornate sign appeared in my mind's eye. Carmichael Solicitors.

A moment later, I was doubled over and retching onto the grave at my feet.

I choked and spluttered, wrapping my arms around myself until the sensation passed. Ten, eleven. My insides chilled. What if that was the time that this event was going to take place? What if it was only minutes away from happening?

I spat on the ground. I couldn't wait here for Lukas. I had to get to Phileas Carmichael's office as fast as I could. There was still a chance I could stop this.

'I'm sorry,' I whispered into the night air. Lukas would think that I'd backed out at the last minute and run away yet again, but I couldn't ignore what I'd seen.

Whirling around, I ran back through the silent graveyard to Tallulah. I threw myself inside and turned the key to start her engine. She stuttered, refusing to spring into life, and I thumped her dashboard with my fist. 'Not now, Tallulah! There's at least one life at risk!'

I turned the key again. For one long second nothing happened, then her engine roared. Thank goodness. I put her into gear, slammed my foot on the accelerator and took off. I'd been to the gremlin's office before, so I knew where I was going. I could get there in less than ten minutes. I could do this.

Whizzing straight ahead then veering left, I reached for my phone while keeping my eyes on the road. 'Message Lukas!' I yelled at it.

The phone beeped. 'Messaging Lukas,' the automated voice responded. 'What do you want to say?'

A taxi came out of nowhere and swung towards me. I narrowly avoided a collision by spinning to the right, while the taxi driver slammed on his horn. I cursed loudly.

'Fuck off,' the phone chanted at me. 'Is that the message you want to send?'

'No!' I shouted. I ground my teeth and tried again. 'Message Lukas!'

'Messaging Brookers,' the voice said. 'What do you want to say?'

Brookers was my damned dentist. 'No! Not Brookers!' I spun Tallulah's wheel and made it through the next set of traffic lights in the split second before they turned red. Carmichael's street was just ahead.

'Come on,' I muttered. 'Come ON.' As Tallulah obliged and jerked forward, I gave my phone one more shot. 'Message Lukas.'

'Can you repeat that?'

'Message Lukas.'

'I didn't catch that.'

I resisted the temptation to throw the damned phone out of the car window as I pulled up in front of the office entrance. I grabbed my crossbow from the back seat and leapt out. Contacting Lukas would have to wait.

My vision hadn't given me any real clue as to who the arson victim would be, but I didn't need my Cassandra powers to know who was being targeted. I already knew who was in trouble; of course I did. And the words that had spouted forth from inside me were *fuel to MY fire*. This prophecy was related to me.

There was a light on inside the building. I couldn't see anyone through the glass door but somebody had to be in there. I rattled the doorknob but the place was locked up, so I stepped back and scanned the doorway for the intercom button. I pressed it hard until I heard the buzz somewhere inside.

Nobody answered. I checked my watch: it was already five minutes past ten. My stomach was churning. If my interpretation of my vision was accurate, there were only six minutes to go.

I pressed my palms to my forehead and tried to recall what I'd seen. What details had I missed? I tried the door again, banging on it and pressing the buzzer. No shadows appeared, and the dim light inside Carmichael's office didn't flicker.

Panicking wouldn't help anyone. I sucked a long gulp of air into my lungs, stepped back and reached inside Tallulah for my phone. This time I was connected within seconds.

'This is DC Bellamy. I am at premises on Barron Street. I have reason to believe that a crime is about to be committed inside and there is real risk to life. I am breaking the door down to gain entrance and request immediate back-up.' The switchboard operator's response was both rapid and reassuring as I gave him my exact location.

I went back to the door, gathered my strength and kicked it in with one sharp movement, shattering the double glazing and its carefully etched lettering proclaiming Carmichael's services. A heartbeat later I was inside.

I couldn't see anyone. I peered around, noting the closed door in front of me and the bright chink of light underneath it. I moved towards it determinedly, ignoring the crunch of broken glass under my feet but it swung open before I could reach for it and a dark shape lunged at me. I registered the baseball bat and ducked, then raised my crossbow and pointed it straight ahead. 'Police! Don't move!'

Phileas Carmichael was already lifting the bat for a second time. When he saw my face, his jaw went slack with astonishment. 'What the fuck are you doing here?' he spat. 'Did you just break down my bloody door?'

'Where is he? Where is Alan Cobain?'

Shocked understanding flashed across Carmichael's expression. 'I told him that baiting you into approaching him wouldn't work,' he said. 'I guess I was wrong.'

'Phileas! Cobain's in danger! Where the fuck is he?' The gremlin tilted his head in confusion. 'Where *is* he?' I bit out.

I doubt he would have told me if he hadn't heard the wail of sirens heading our way. That was when he seemed to realise I was telling the truth. 'I keep a flat across the road for clients who need it,' he said. 'Alan Cobain is there.'

As he spoke, the flickering glow of nearby flames reflected across the lawyer's face and I heard screaming in the distance. I spun around and saw the fire coming out of the third-floor window of the building opposite us – and the shadowy shape of the writhing figure who was already engulfed by it.

I SAT on the edge of the pavement with a blanket wrapped around me while I stared ahead at nothing. What good were any of these damned visions if I either triggered the events myself or if they occurred too late for me to do anything about them?

'Emma.'

I didn't look up. 'Lukas,' I said dully. I shivered and pulled the blanket tighter around me. Lukas immediately sat down next to me and put an arm across my shoulder, drawing me in close. 'You need to get inside. It's freezing here.'

I didn't want to go anywhere. I wanted to stay there. 'I'm

sorry,' I said. His arm gripped me a fraction tighter. 'I was at the graveyard,' I said. 'I really was there waiting for you. But then I ... I heard about this and had to come.'

'It's fine,' he told me. 'As soon as I got the call about the fire, I knew you'd be here. Don't worry about it, Emma.'

But I had to worry, I couldn't help it. My eyes drifted towards Phileas Carmichael, his head held high as he answered questions from a grim-faced uniformed policeman. Then I heard the trundle of wheels from the gurney and I stiffened as Alan Cobain's shrouded, but no doubt charred, body was wheeled out. He was bundled into the back of the ambulance while Lukas and I watched, neither of us uttering a word.

Heels clicked towards us. I didn't need to look up to know who was approaching but I couldn't help raising my head to check her expression. DSI Barnes gave me a flat look; neither her dark eyes nor her blank face yielded any clues as to what she might be thinking.

'Well,' she said, in a brisk, business-like tone, 'that's one question that will soon be answered. In twelve hours we'll know if Alan Cobain is a phoenix.'

I strongly suspected that Alan Cobain was merely dead. I should have saved him; I should have realised that the image of Carmichael's sign in my prophetic vision had come at an angle. It would have been what Cobain – or his killer – saw from the flat's window in the seconds before the fire was lit.

Next to me, Lukas snorted. 'He's not going to resurrect, DSI Barnes, and you know it.'

Barnes's eyes flicked to him then back to me. 'I need to speak to you alone, DC Bellamy.'

My stomach tightened. I knew what was coming.

Lukas didn't move an inch. 'I'm not going anywhere.'

Barnes didn't say anything, she simply waited. I sighed. 'It's fine, Lukas. Give us five minutes.'

I knew he wanted to argue but I also knew he wouldn't do so in front of DSI Barnes. 'You're sure?' he asked roughly.

I smiled slightly and touched his arm. 'I'm sure. This won't take long.'

A muscle throbbed in his cheek as he stared at me, then he nodded reluctantly and stood up. He stalked across the street to give us some space. As I watched him go, I was aware that his enhanced vampiric senses meant that he could still hear everything Barnes said. I wondered if she realised it too.

'What a shitstorm.' Barnes shook her head, sat down next to me and reached into her pocket to pull out a packet of mints. She offered me one but I shook my head. She popped one into her mouth and began to chew slowly. 'The solicitor says that you smashed in his door before the fire became obvious.'

Here we go. 'Yes,' I said. I wasn't going to deny it.

'How did you know Cobain was in danger?'

I looked away from Barnes and towards Lukas. His head was tilted an inch to one side and, when a serious looking vamp approached him, he waved him away. Then his glittering eyes met mine. Lukas wasn't even pretending not to eavesdrop. But that alone wasn't why I suddenly lied. 'I received a tip-off.'

Barnes eyebrows rose. 'From?'

'An anonymous source.'

'I see. How did they contact you?'

'Phone. I didn't recognise the voice.'

'Male? Female?'

I'd only just begun and I was already losing myself in a quagmire of bad lies. 'It was an automated voice,' I muttered. 'Computerised. It could have been either.'

'And where were you when you received this call?'

That part was easier. 'I was in the graveyard of St Erbin's church. In Soho. I was supposed to meet Lukas there at ten o'clock.'

'Did you meet him? Will he corroborate that?'

'No. I was early and he hadn't arrived.'

'Did anyone else see you there?'

My shoulders dropped an inch. 'No.'

Barnes grimaced. 'You understand why I am asking these questions.'

'I do.'

'And you understand what needs to happen now.'

I nodded. 'I didn't kill Alan Cobain.'

She held up her hands. 'Save it for your official statement.' She gave me a pointed look.

I sighed, pulled out my warrant card and handed it over, followed by my crossbow.

'I'm going to need your phone as well to verify the tip-off you received,' Barnes said.

Shit. I hadn't thought that part through very carefully. I'd make a terrible criminal. 'Uh...'

'Is there a problem, DC Bellamy?'

I handed over my phone and tried to explain. 'The tip-off didn't come through on this phone.'

Barnes didn't blink. 'Which phone was it, then?'

I met her eyes. 'I can't explain that right now.'

'Oh dear.'

I couldn't disagree.

Barnes stood up and dusted herself off. 'We'll need to save this for the actual interview. For now, Detective Constable Bellamy, you are suspended from your duties while the investigation into Alan Cobain's death is ongoing.'

'Okay.' I glanced at her face, wondering if she believed I could have murdered him, though I didn't ask the question. She wouldn't have answered it. Besides, we both knew that anyone was capable of anything under certain circumstances.

'I'll take you to New Scotland Yard myself,' she said.

I wasn't sure if that was a good or a bad thing. I heaved myself to my feet and looked awkwardly at my wrists. 'Do you want to—?'

She clicked her tongue. 'Handcuffs will not be necessary at this point.'

I breathed out. That was something, I supposed.

TEN

L ukas tailed us, his sleek black car less than two metres away at any given time. If he involved himself more directly, there would be serious problems. I made sure he realised that when we finally pulled up outside the police headquarters and got out of Barnes's car.

He parked behind us and also stepped out. 'Go home,' I told him. He folded his arms, leaned against his car and watched me with hooded eyes. 'This is just procedure, Lukas. It's what has to happen.' He still didn't react. 'The only way you can help is by staying out of it.'

He could have been a damned statue. He wasn't even blinking.

I tried again. 'It could take a long time.'

Finally he spoke. 'I'll be here and waiting until you're done.'

Barnes frowned. 'Your relationship with Emma Bellamy is over, Mr Horvath. This smacks of stalking and coercive control.'

'It's Lord Horvath to you,' he said, then he looked at me. 'Is our relationship over, Emma?'

Bloody hell. How was I supposed to answer that? 'Not officially, no.' For Barnes's sake, I added, 'I don't mind if you wait. But don't do anything. Just … wait.'

Lukas bared his fangs. 'I've already proved that I can be very patient.'

'I can have him removed,' Barnes said. 'I don't care who he is, I can make sure he doesn't bother you again.'

'Leave him be.'

'Emma…'

I was going to have to be more specific. I cleared my throat. 'I want him here.'

Barnes nodded reluctantly while Lukas's eyes gleamed with sudden satisfaction. All I could do was run my hands through my hair and sigh. This was a bloody mess. And Alan Cobain was still dead – at least for now.

I'D NEVER BEEN on this side of the interview desk before. Other than my awkward lie to Barnes I'd done nothing wrong, but my palms still felt sweaty and there was a discomfiting twist to my stomach. I hoped I wasn't going to start throwing up again.

I nudged Jon Barber, the human duty solicitor who'd been assigned to me. 'I'm going to need some water,' I said.

He nodded, stood up and knocked on the door until somebody answered. 'Can we get a jug of water in here? And two cups?' He waited until they were passed through then sat down and poured me some.

I took several small sips while he waited. My stomach didn't settle, however, so I swallowed hard and kept a hold of the plastic cup. 'I might vomit any minute now,' I told him. 'It's been known to happen lately.'

Barber didn't miss a beat. 'Are you ill?' he asked. 'Have you taken any drugs?'

'I'm pregnant.' I met his eyes. 'But I'd prefer it if you kept that to yourself.'

'I'm your solicitor, DC Bellamy. You know how this works. I won't tell anyone – though it might be wise of you to inform the lead investigator.'

I shook my head. 'No. Not unless I have to.'

'Very well.' He linked his hands together. Barber projected a calm and reassuring exterior. If circumstances had been different, I might have requested Phileas to be by my side but, as that wasn't possible, I was happy enough with Jon Barber for now. Even if his human ethnicity might cause some problems when he found out the truth.

'DSI Barnes questioned me briefly at the scene,' I told him.

'You should have waited before answering any questions.'

Yeah. Hindsight was great. 'I lied to her.'

Barber winced slightly.

'It's going to come out that I wasn't telling the truth,' I continued.

'Go on.'

'I told her that I received an anonymous phone call that tipped me off about the risk to Alan Cobain's life. That wasn't true. A few weeks ago, I inadvertently gained a new supernatural power. I've started to receive prophetic visions of the future – I'm what's known as a Cassandra. I had a vision that Alan Cobain was going to burn alive.'

Barber stared at me. With shaking hands, he reached for his own glass. This was why a supe solicitor might have been better. 'Ah,' he said. He managed to take a drink without spilling any water. When he finally returned the glass to the table, he eyed me. 'Why didn't you tell her this?'

'It's not something I want to broadcast.' I leaned forward. 'I have no control over the visions. When they come, they're not always easy to interpret. Plus, I don't know if I can alter what I see or if it's already set in stone.'

I took a deep breath. 'I'm a police detective and this a supernatural power that not even supes understand. If it becomes generally known, it will affect my entire career. I'll never receive credit for any work that I do in stopping crimes because people will think I did it through magic and not hard graft. And if I don't manage to stop crimes, they'll think that I'm keeping the visions to myself for my own reasons.'

My mouth twisted. 'There's also every chance that some bigwig in the Met Police or in the government will decide that the best way to use my new power is to lock me permanently in a room and wait for my visions to come, regardless of what prophecies they might involve.'

Barber took a moment before answering. I decided I liked him for that; he wasn't leaping to easy conclusions. 'Most people,' he said carefully, 'would think that a detective who can see the future is a good thing. Your visions might not prevent any crimes from occurring – but equally they might do.'

'Uh-huh.' I nodded. Then I told him what had happened earlier that day on Baker Street.

'You think it was your interference that caused the woman to be stabbed?'

'I do. If I hadn't been there and revealed my identity, it might never have happened.'

'I see. Do you wish to continue keeping this Cassandra power secret?'

Once Barnes knew about it, I could never take the knowledge back, and I still hadn't told Lukas. I wanted more time to think about it first. 'I'd like to keep it to myself unless I absolutely have to divulge it.'

'That may prove problematic.'

No shit. I shrugged to show that I accepted that. 'But I

didn't hurt Alan Cobain,' I said earnestly. 'I've never met the man and I've never spoken to him.'

Barber checked his watch. 'Will he resurrect in nine and a half hours?'

'Honestly?' I said. 'I have no idea.'

There was a knock at the door and DSI Barnes appeared with another detective whose face I vaguely recognised. 'Are you ready?' she enquired.

Barber and I nodded. Barnes sniffed and took one of the chairs opposite us. The other detective did the same and introduced himself as Detective Inspector Michael Katling. From the hard look in his eyes and the way he held himself away from me, it was clear that he wasn't fond of supes. It wouldn't be my first time dealing with a supe-phobic detective but even so I sighed inwardly.

Barnes started the recording, introducing herself and everyone else in the room. She gave me a small smile. 'You have had a long and difficult day, detective. You shouldn't have been on duty after what happened this morning on Baker Street, but I must commend you first for your actions in stopping a violent criminal. If you hadn't been there, it would have been much worse.'

So Barnes was going to play good cop. It wasn't a surprise. 'Thank you,' I said. 'I can assure you that what happened this morning doesn't relate in any way to what happened tonight.' Barber shot me a side glance. I ignored it.

Katling regarded me without blinking. 'What did Alan Cobain say to you the last time he spoke to you?'

Idiot. 'I have never spoken to Alan Cobain.'

'He was compiling a case against you. In fact, over the last twenty-four hours, he has made vigorous efforts to bring his case to light.'

I remained calm. 'I'm aware of that, but it doesn't change the fact that I have never spoken to the man.'

'His solicitor states that you approached him earlier today.'

'I saw Phileas Carmichael in the street and I went to speak to him on another matter. Until then, I had no idea that he was acting for Cobain.'

'I find that very hard to believe.'

I didn't shy away from his gaze. 'Be that as it may, it's the truth.'

'You do realise, DC Bellamy, that even if Alan Cobain resurrects as a result of his phoenix powers, you can still be charged with his murder.'

'Except,' I said distinctly, 'that I didn't murder him.'

Katling pressed ahead. 'But you were at the scene.'

'Technically I wasn't,' I said. 'I was outside the property where Cobain died. I didn't go inside it.'

He leaned back in his chair and watched me. 'So why were you outside the property?'

Barnes shifted in her seat and I glanced at her. 'I received an anonymous tip off that there was going to be trouble.'

'That Alan Cobain was going to be doused in petrol and set alight?'

'No. I was told that there would be trouble. There were hints that there would be a fire. When I realised that the tip-off alluded to Phileas Carmichael's office, I suspected that it might involve Alan Cobain but I had no actual evidence to prove it.'

'You told me that the tip-off came by phone,' Barnes said softly. 'But not *your* phone. We've checked the phone records for Supe Squad. No calls were placed there after three-thirty today. Where did the information come from? How did you receive it?' Her tone was earnest; she wanted me to give her the answer, to prove that I wasn't culpable.

I cleared my throat. Before I could say anything, Jon Barber stepped in. 'DC Bellamy will not answer that at this moment.'

Barnes's eyes widened a fraction; by contrast, Katling appeared to be almost slavering at the mouth with glee. 'Why ever not? The answer could immediately clear her name.'

'She is protecting her source.'

'But I thought the alleged source was anonymous and unknown to her,' Katling zipped back.

Barber was steady in his response. 'At this time, DC Bellamy will give no answer that might reveal their identity. She will say nothing more on the matter.'

'You can trust us, Emma,' Barnes said.

I shook my head; I had no faith in my voice to speak. I couldn't trust them, not in this.

'Do you have any proof that DC Bellamy spoke to the victim?' my solicitor asked, 'Do you have any evidence that she was involved in the arson attack against him?'

'She was outside his flat when he died,' Katling stated.

Barber dismissed him immediately. 'That's circumstantial – and she didn't attempt to conceal her presence. You have nothing.'

'We have motive.'

I held up my hands. 'You've taken swabs. There's no accelerant on my skin. And your supposed motive is flimsy, at best.'

Katling stared at me. 'We shall see about that, Bellamy,' he said finally. 'We shall see.'

CHAPTER ELEVEN

'They have nothing,' Barber said, when the interview finally ended in the wee hours of the morning and we walked out of the station. 'You really don't need to worry.' That was easy for him to say. 'The best-case scenario is that Alan Cobain will wake up in a few hours' time and tell them who actually set him on fire, then you'll be in the clear.'

Unless Alan Cobain didn't wake up, or he had deliberately set himself alight in a bid to frame me. I shook off that second thought. It seemed too far-fetched to consider – and too risky for Cobain.

'They'll keep your phone until it's been fully examined and you'll remain suspended for the time being.' Barber clapped me on the shoulder. 'I suggest you take the next day or two off to relax and get your energy back. You'll be pounding the mean streets of Soho in no time. Those fangy vamps won't know what's hit them!'

It was unfortunate for Barber that Lukas took that moment to walk up to us. 'Uh,' the solicitor stammered. 'What I mean is ... uh ... shit ... uh...'

Lukas smiled professionally. 'Thank you for your help this

evening. I am sure that Emma appreciates your support. I know I do.'

Barber's cheeks were flaming red. 'You … you're welcome.' He glanced at me. 'I'll be in touch as soon as I hear anything more.' He spun on his heel and all but sprinted away.

'You scared him,' I said to Lukas.

He shrugged. 'It wasn't my intention.' He gazed after the fleeing solicitor. 'He seems very young and not particularly capable. I can engage another lawyer for you. Phileas Carmichael isn't the only supe solicitor in town.'

'Actually, I like Barber,' I said. 'He did a good job. I think I'll keep him around.'

Lukas's black eyes grew sharp. 'Are you going to *need* him around?'

I bit my lip. 'That remains to be seen.' An awkward squirm flashed through me. 'Thanks for waiting.'

His gaze held mine. 'I'll always wait for you, D'Artagnan.'

It didn't take a police detective, suspended or otherwise, to understand the double meaning behind his words. 'I know we need to talk, Lukas. There's a great deal I have to explain.'

'That can wait,' he said gruffly. 'You've been up half the night and you look dead on your feet. There will be time later.'

A sudden well of unexpected emotion rose up in my throat.

'What's wrong?' he asked, not disguising his flicker of alarm.

I sniffed. 'Nothing. Everything.'

Lukas spread his arms. 'Would you like a hug?'

So much. It was wrong and I shouldn't have done it, but I threw myself at him, allowing him to wrap his arms around me and hold me tight. I buried my face in his shoulder and, for one long glorious moment, allowed myself to forget everything else. But, as I stopped feeling so sorry for myself, inhaled his deep scent and revelled in the sensation of his hard body next to mine, I became aware of the danger. I pulled away and avoided his gaze. 'Thanks,' I muttered.

He nodded once. 'Come on. I'll give you a lift back to Laura's place.'

'Can I borrow your phone? Mine has been taken into evidence.'

Lukas looked at me curiously but dug it out and tossed it to me. I thanked him and dialled Grace's number. I'd hoped to leave a message but, with sleep weighting his every word, he answered quickly. 'This is Detective Sergeant Grace.'

'Sorry for waking you,' I said.

'Emma?'

'Yeah. I'm calling you on Lukas's phone. You'll probably hear from DS Barnes soon, but I wanted to speak to you first.'

I heard Liza murmur a sleepy question in the background. Grace replied before answering me. 'What's happened?'

'I've been suspended.'

'*What?*'

It was heartening that he sounded outraged, even though he didn't know what I might have done. 'You'll get all the gory details soon,' I told him. 'I'm not sure how long I'll be out, but I wanted to tell you that I've been looking into one of those cold cases you left me. The missing gremlin.' Lukas looked at me.

'From 2010?' Grace asked.

'That's the one. There's a lot about his disappearance that doesn't add up. I really think you should look into it some more. I left my notes on my desk, but if you have questions about it you can still call and ask me. I don't have my phone but I'll pick up a cheap burner tomorrow and send you the number.'

'Okay. What else can I do? What help do you need?'

'I'm dealing with it, Owen. I'll be fine. Investigate the gremlin, though. His case deserves the attention.'

'Emma—'

I knew he wanted to know more about my suspension but I couldn't deal with a re-hash of events just then. I said goodbye, hung up and passed the phone back to Lukas. He returned it to his pocket as we climbed into his car. With a sigh, I settled into the passenger seat. The car smelled of him. It was glorious.

'You were talking about Quincy Carmichael, right?' Lukas asked as he drove away from New Scotland Yard.

'Yes. He went missing the same weekend that there was a nasty double murder.'

Lukas nodded. 'I remember.'

'What happened? With the murder, I mean.'

He sent me a side glance. 'You want to talk about *that* now?'

I might not get another chance. I shrugged.

Lukas ran a hand through his inky-black hair and sighed. 'It was brutal, both the murders and the aftermath.'

'You saw the crime scene?'

His hands tightened on the steering wheel. 'I did. I wasn't Lord then, but I was highly placed and I was tasked with looking into what had happened. We thought we'd find the culprit easily.' He grimaced. 'But nobody was ever found. We didn't even have any credible suspects.'

'I know Simon Carr was the werewolf who was killed, but who was the vampire?'

'Adele Cunningham. She hadn't been a vamp for very long – she was a baby by most standards – but she had a lot of skill for her age. She would have gone far.' He didn't hide the regret or the pain in his voice. It was clear that, even before he'd become Lord, Lukas had taken the death of any vampire personally.

'How did...'

'She was stabbed. They both were.'

'So it must have been a supe,' I said, thinking aloud. No human could have overpowered both a werewolf and a vampire, certainly not with a blade.

'That was the thinking at the time.'

I sensed a 'but'. I waited.

'As far as we could tell,' Lukas went on, 'Simon and Adele had been sleeping together. They were in bed together when they were killed.'

Huh. 'So if they were asleep, it's not beyond the realms of possibility that a human attacked them and killed them before they could defend themselves.'

'It could have happened that way,' he said softly. 'But we couldn't find any human suspects.'

'And Quincy Carmichael?'

Lukas was already shaking his head. 'It wasn't him. I know he disappeared right after the killings, but his alibi for the time of the murders was rock solid. He spent the afternoon getting drunk with Kennedy.'

I started. '*Our* Kennedy?' I asked, referring to the alcohol-sodden satyr who I counted as a real friend.

'Yep. They tore through Soho and Lisson Grove together. Eventually the pair of them ended up in a small bar usually frequented by the Sullivan clan. Kennedy annoyed the wrong werewolf, got into a fight. Quincy got involved and all three of them ended up carted off to the Clink to sober up. When Simon Carr and Adele Cunningham were being stabbed to death, Quincy Carmichael was behind bars.'

That put a different spin on things. 'Were there any real leads into Simon and Adele's deaths?'

'They'd kept their relationship secret, so none of us knew they were together. Given the bloody nature of their killings and the emotional energy their killer must have expended, it looked like a crime of passion. We were convinced that a jealous wolf had killed them when their liaison was discovered. The wolves believed it must have been a cuckolded vampire. There was a lot of finger pointing but absolutely no proof of anything.'

I was tempted to ask him if there was a murder file that I could borrow, but I was suspended from duty. Besides, I'd been tasked with looking for Quincy; a double murder was a totally different prospect, though that didn't mean I'd forget about it. 'Once I'm reinstated and I've found Quincy Carmichael, I'd like to look into their case,' I said.

Lukas laughed, genuinely amused. 'What?' I asked, confused.

'You don't have any doubt that you'll find him, do you? Quincy, I mean.'

'People don't simply vanish into thin air.' I glanced at him. 'I was told that he had an ex-girlfriend who was a vamp – Candy something?'

'Candace. She's still around. I can ask her to contact you.'

'She should speak to Grace, not me, at least until my suspension is lifted.'

'From the way you're peppering me with questions, it doesn't sound as if you're going to let a suspension stop you from investigating.'

That was because I needed to fill the silence between us with something that didn't involve our doomed relationship. I shifted, discomfited again.

Lukas seemed to realise what I was thinking. 'Anyway,' he said, with a wave of his hand, 'from what I remember of Quincy Carmichael and his proclivities, right about now he's probably lying on a tropical beach somewhere with a fruit cocktail.'

'All the more reason to find him then. I could really do with a beach holiday.'

Lukas looked at me, allowing me to catch a glimpse of his very real vulnerability. 'To be honest,' he said, 'so could I.'

∼

I DIDN'T GET out of the car immediately when we arrived at Laura's flat. We sat there with the engine ticking over, neither of us saying a word although both of us were desperate to speak.

Finally I fumbled with my seatbelt and released myself. 'I'll get some sleep,' I said. 'If you want to come around later today, we can have that talk.' The awkwardness that had started to dissipate during the journey had returned. 'If you want to, of course. You don't have to.'

Lukas growled. 'Of course I want to. I love you, Emma. That hasn't changed and it never will. If there's anything I can do that will make you—' He shook his head in frustration. 'No. Let's leave this until later when you've rested.'

'I'll be here,' I said. 'I won't run away this time, I promise.' No matter what damned visions I had, I would sit down and have this conversation with him. I couldn't delay it any longer.

'You could make it easier and come home with me now. You can sleep in the spare room, then we can talk things through when you wake up. You can trust me, Emma.'

Of course I could trust him; I just couldn't trust myself. I reached across and touched his hand with the very tips of my fingers. 'Midday,' I said. 'Right here. Laura will be at work. And I'm suspended, so I won't be going anywhere,' I added ruefully.

Lukas's face tightened. 'In that case, I'll see you here.' He turned his head away to indicate we were done for now.

I had to respect that. I nodded and hastily got out of the car – but I did stand on the pavement and watch him until he'd disappeared in the distance.

TWELVE

I didn't sleep as well or for as long as I should have. After tossing and turning fitfully, I eventually lay flat on my back with my eyes wide open, staring at the ceiling for far too long.

I murmured an apology aloud. 'Sorry, Jellybean. I know I should be resting, but it doesn't look like it's going to happen right now.' I got up and, in lieu of a decent sleep, made myself a healthy breakfast.

Laura had left a scribbled note on the table and I smiled grimly at its contents. She'd been drafted into the morgue early to wait beside Alan Cobain's body and either record his resurrection or perform a post-mortem. Apparently she'd been informed of my connection with his death.

That was a good thing, I decided, despite the obvious conflict of interests. I knew she wouldn't keep me waiting for information, whichever way things went. I ate slowly and, by the time I had washed my plate and glass, there were only twenty minutes to go until Alan Cobain's corpse would reveal his truth.

I drummed my fingers on the table then grabbed my laptop

and searched for his name. There were plenty of news articles about what had happened last night. Although I was referenced, nobody mentioned that I'd been outside the flat where he'd been burned alive. That was positive. But it wasn't last night's events that I was interested in, it was Alan Cobain himself and his supposed phoenix abilities.

I followed the web trail until I found a link to a video from a few months earlier purporting to be of his death and his resurrection. I held my breath and clicked on it.

The quality was poor and I had to squint to make out a lot of it. Cobain had obviously set up the camera himself and nobody else was filming. There was no sound. I watched as he waved a gun around in silence, making a show of loading it to prove that there were live bullets inside. He placed the muzzle in his mouth, pulled the trigger and his body fell backwards onto the floor.

I peered more closely. Due to the angle of the camera, it was impossible to tell if he had actually died. It certainly looked that way but, without a zoom function or a different camera angle, there was no definitive proof. I grimaced.

The video was more than twelve hours long so I fast-forwarded, pausing a few times to check on Cobain's body. There were no signs of life; however, at the twelve-hour point, his foot twitched and smoke started to rise from his stomach. Flames flickered along his arms and his legs then, seconds later, he rose up and gave the camera a wide grin. He mouthed two words. *Ta-da.*

My spirits sank slightly. We were all different, but whenever I was reborn after dying, there were always at least a few seconds of confusion before I remembered who I was and what had happened. There was none of that with Alan Cobain. The video looked real but his reaction didn't.

'I don't want you to be properly dead,' I whispered at the screen. 'I want you to wake up.'

Alan Cobain gave me a happy wave from my computer screen. I sighed and closed the laptop. I didn't know enough about video fakery to determine its authenticity, so all I could do was wait.

I looked at the clock – only five minutes to go. I stood up and started to pace up and down Laura's small kitchen but I'd barely completed three circuits when the doorbell rang. Without thinking, I padded to the door to answer it. As soon as I opened it, I regretted not checking who was there first.

I tried to close it but Buffy was having none of it. 'Morning!' she trilled. She beamed and pushed past me into Laura's flat.

I ground my teeth. 'I didn't say you could come in,' I muttered.

'Come on!' Buffy said. 'You know you want to hear how things went last night with sexy Fred, right?' She winked.

'This isn't a good time, Buffy.'

'You're not doing anything else,' she pointed out. 'I heard you've been suspended so you're not going to work. I thought you might appreciate the distraction.'

Not this sort of distraction. I sighed, but like a fool I gestured to the living room. 'Go on, then. Sit down and tell me what happened.'

Buffy flung herself down on the sofa, grabbed a cushion and hugged it. 'It was amazing. I mean, I knew we were compatible but I hadn't realised *how* compatible. We talked for half the night. We have so much in common! And then, when we stopped talking, and started to kiss...'

I held up my hands. 'Please. No details.'

'But you have to hear this!' Her expression was earnest. 'I felt this fizz. Here.' She touched her belly. 'It was like we were meant to be. I've never felt that way before. It was as if nothing in the world mattered apart from Fred and me.' She nodded resolutely. 'There *is* nothing in the world that matters apart from Fred and me. We're soul mates, there's no other way to explain it. I get it now – this must be how you feel about Horvath. I'd do anything for Fred. I'd lay down my life for him.'

I stared at her. 'You've been on one date.'

'But when you know, you know. Am I right?' She giggled. 'Of course I'm right.' She punched me lightly on the arm. 'You know what it's like. You know all about love too.' She hugged the cushion more tightly. 'I'm never going to give him up, and that's why I know that you should never give up Horvath. Go to him now. You can't lose what the two of you have together.'

No matter what my feelings were on the matter, I was not going to listen to romantic advice from Buffy. 'Okay,' I said briskly. 'You can go now.'

'But I haven't told you about how cute Fred was when I stumbled on the pavement and he rescued me from falling flat on my face.'

'Save it for another time.'

'I need more advice first! Should I call him this morning for our next date? Or should I play hard to get and wait until after lunch?'

I was saved from responding by another ring at the door-bell. 'I'm going to get that,' I said. I pointed at her. 'Don't touch anything.'

Shaking my head, I returned to the front door. This time it was Fred's anxious face that greeted me. Unbelievable.

'Hi, boss.'

'Hi, Fred.'

He didn't smile. 'I heard about what happened. I can't believe the bastards have suspended you. I just wanted to come around first thing and let you know that I've got your back.'

'It's fine, Fred. They have to suspend me until everything has been properly investigated. You know that.'

'It's not right! You didn't kill him.'

'I might have.'

He blinked, then he managed a smile. 'No, you didn't.' He pulled back his shoulders. 'Anyway, if you need anything all you have to do is call me. And I'm going to do everything I can to look into that missing gremlin case while you're away – both Grace and I will. We won't leave any stone unturned. In fact, he's already on it. He called me half an hour ago and thinks he's found something in Tony's notes that might be useful. I'm on my way to Supe Squad and we're going to work on it together. We'll finish what you started.'

His enthusiasm was touching. I bit back my desire to find out exactly what Grace had discovered. I was suspended. This was no longer my case, but I knew I could trust the two of them to investigate it properly. 'Thanks, Fred.'

'You're welcome.' He suddenly looked awkward. 'There's something else.'

There usually was. 'Go on.'

'I had that date last night with Buffy.'

'Mmm.'

He lowered his voice and leaned towards me. 'I really like her, boss.' He swallowed, his Adam's apple bobbing. 'I mean, *really* like her. I want to spend more time with her and I will, no matter what anyone says. I know it might be inappropriate because she's a werewolf but—'

Buffy's voice rang out from behind me. 'There's nothing inappropriate about werewolves.'

Fred stiffened then he blushed. 'Hi, Buffy.'

She moved next to me. 'Hi, Fred.'

I looked from her to him and back again. They were grinning at each other like lovestruck idiots. Heaven help us all.

'Thanks for coming around, Fred,' I said loudly. 'I appreciate your help and support more than you know.'

He didn't look at me. I gave Buffy a nudge and she stepped outside next to him. I yielded to the inevitable. 'Why don't the two of you arrange your next date?' I suggested. 'You could go out tonight.'

'Or we could stay in,' Buffy breathed.

Fred started to nod. 'I like staying in.'

'Me too.'

They grinned at each other some more. Buffy delved into her pocket, pulled out the little handheld recording device and gave it to me. 'I won't be needing this any longer,' she said to me, although her eyes remained on Fred. I huffed quietly but neither of them paid me any attention.

I watched them for another moment then shoved the stupid recorder into my pocket, closed the door and left them to it. If I'd stayed much longer, I suspected I'd witness Fred drooling. They were as bad as each other.

In the kitchen, I checked the time again. If Alan Cobain was going to resurrect, he'd have done it already, but I needed to wait until Laura called me. That would be sensible. I picked up the landline and called the morgue anyway.

I'd expected it would take her a few minutes to come to the phone, but it was passed to her almost immediately. I tried not to jump to any conclusions as I waited to hear the news.

'He's not come back, Emma,' she told me, without preamble. 'Alan Cobain is still dead.'

I exhaled. I wasn't really surprised but I was very, very disappointed. 'Alright.'

'We might have the time of death slightly wrong. He might still—'

'No. I was there. It's been over twelve hours. He's not a phoenix.'

'There's only one,' she said simply.

I rubbed the back of my neck. 'Yes. I guess there is.'

There was a momentary pause. 'There's something else.'

Something about her tone made me stiffen. 'Go on.'

'I shouldn't be telling you this,' Laura said, 'but you're my friend and you deserve to know.'

That sounded ominous. 'What is it?'

'The killer threw petrol over him before setting him alight, petrol that was brought to the premises in a jerry can. The crime scene techs found a few strands of hair stuck to the side of it and asked me to do an initial comparison with Cobain's hair. It's not a match. The working theory is that the hair they found belongs to the killer.'

I immediately brightened. 'That's great! Do the hair strands include the root?' I knew that it would be incredibly difficult to test for DNA if they didn't.

'They do.' Laura still didn't sound happy. 'And they've already gone for testing, so if they match any existing records it shouldn't be too long until we know.'

As far as I was concerned, this was nothing but good news. 'So what's the problem?'

'The hair that was found is straight, dark brown and about twelve inches long from root to tip.'

Oh. I suddenly knew why Laura was anxious. 'My hair is straight, dark brown and about twelve inches long.'

'Yes.'

I drew in a breath. 'I wasn't there, Laura. The hair can't be mine. But the fact it's been found is a good thing – it'll help to clear me.'

My unshaken confidence seemed to reassure her. 'That's what I thought.'

'You were still worried, though,' I said slowly. 'I didn't kill him. I've never met the man.'

'I don't think you killed him, Emma. I'd never think that.' She hesitated once again. 'But other people might jump to conclusions, you know?'

I shrugged: that was on them. I hadn't been inside that flat and I hadn't thrown petrol over Alan Cobain and set him on fire, so the hair strands couldn't be mine. Once they were properly tested that would be proved.

Suddenly I went cold. Except my hairbrush had been missing from my desk last night, and a window left wide open at the back of building. Somebody could have snuck in, taken my brush and—

I shook my head vigorously. No. That was stupid. I was seeing shadows where there were none. 'It's not going to be a problem,' I reiterated. 'Thanks for telling me what's going on. I'll let you get back to work.'

'Take care,' she said. 'And make sure you eat a decent breakfast. You can't exist on nothing more than caffeine, not now.'

'Already done,' I told her. 'I've got this.' Most of it. Okay, some of it. I wrinkled my nose. At least a tiny part. Maybe.

CHAPTER
THIRTEEN

Lukas appeared on Laura's doorstep at exactly midday, and I couldn't help wondering if he'd been waiting around the corner until the appointed hour. I also couldn't help noticing the flash of relief in his black eyes when he saw me. No, I hadn't run away, not this time. I knew I had to face the music.

'Come in,' I said quietly and stepped back. He hovered in the hallway until I motioned towards the living room. He went in and sat on the sofa, then picked up the same cushion that Buffy had been hugging to herself earlier and started to fiddle with it.

'I heard the news,' he said gruffly. 'About Cobain.'

'Yeah.' I sighed.

Lukas raised an eyebrow. 'You're not surprised, are you? You're the only phoenix, Emma. That's the way it works.'

My feelings about it were complicated. 'Whether he was becoming a pain in my arse or not, I certainly didn't want him to die. If he'd resurrected, my name would have been cleared for his murder.' I waved a hand around. 'And there would be someone else to share this weirdness with.'

Lukas snorted. 'Nobody seriously believes you'd kill the

man.' He might be surprised. 'Besides,' he added, 'from what we know of him, he wasn't the sharing type. He was a con artist, nothing more, nothing less. I have no sympathy for him.'

I believed him, but that didn't make me feel any more relaxed about the conversation we were about to have. Swallowing hard, I met his eyes. 'I didn't plan to run away that night.' The words burst out of me as if I couldn't control them. 'When you proposed, I mean. I'd learned something new that made me act like that.'

Lukas didn't move a muscle; even his face suddenly looked as if it were carved out of granite. There were only two feet separating us but it felt like an abyss. 'Something new, D'Artagnan?' His voice roughened. 'Because of something I did?'

'No!' I shook my head. 'God, no, it wasn't you. It was,' my voice faltered as I recognised the cliché, 'it was me,' I finished in a near whisper.

The only evidence that Lukas heard me was a faint tightening around his mouth.

'You remember Zara,' I said, referring to the only other Cassandra I'd ever met.

'Of course I do.'

I dropped my gaze. 'Something happened after she died. I touched her body in that house and I felt something, something like an electric shock.' I raised my head and risked looking at his face again. Confusion flickered across it; of all the things, he must have imagined I would say, he'd never expected this.

I rushed on. I had to tell him now, before I lost my nerve. 'Then later I saw something. Like a – vision. In my head.' I wasn't explaining myself very well. 'I didn't know what it was at the time, but I saw images that later turned out to be your proposal. I saw the future before it happened, Lukas. And it's not the only time. There was an incident on Baker Street yesterday. Plus, the reason I was at Phileas Carmichael's office before

Cobain died was because I'd had a vision that something was going to happen there.' My voice dropped to a whisper. 'I'm a Cassandra. Zara's power must have transferred to me.'

Lukas stared at me as the silence stretched out between us. I felt the familiar return of oily nausea, but this time it wasn't pregnancy induced. Eventually I couldn't stand the silence. 'Are you going to say anything?'

He slowly ran his tongue across his fangs and placed the cushion to one side. 'That's it? That's the reason you left me?'

I blinked, startled at his note of disbelief. 'Did you hear me? I'm a Cassandra. There's no doubt.'

'I heard that part.'

My fingers twisted together. 'I'm sure those vamps you had trailing me told you how much time I spent at the Carlyle Library. I've been through every book I could find, and there's no cure. I'm going to be like this until the day I die! Properly die, I mean.'

He continued to watch me.

'You hate Cassandras, Lukas. You despise them – you've told me that more than once. In fact, you hate anything to do with prophetic visions of the future.'

Lukas leaned back and crossed his legs. A tiny smile lifted the corner of his mouth. 'D'Artagnan,' he drawled, 'there's nothing you could do that would make me hate you. Ever.'

'You say that now but—'

'*Ever*,' he repeated. His smile widened. 'You're right that I don't like the power that Cassandras wield, and yes, I've told you that it terrifies me. But that's because it's the sort of power that can't be trusted unless it's in the right hands. I didn't know Zara, and I was genuinely frightened by the thought that someone whose motivations and morals I couldn't ever properly know possessed that sort of power. But I know *you*, and I can't think of anyone I'd trust more to be a Cassandra. You won't abuse it and you won't use it for your own ends. I trust you. More than I trust myself.' He gave me a satisfied look. 'In fact, I can foresee that you'll do an incredible amount of good with it. I can help you.'

He wasn't getting it. 'You hate what I can do. Sooner or later you'll end up hating me too.'

'Hate is a very strong word. I don't hate anyone. Or anything – except maybe gherkins.'

Unable to help myself, I hissed, 'This isn't the time for jokes!'

Contrition lit his face. 'I'm sorry, but I'm just relieved that this is all it is. I thought it was going to be much worse, that my proposal had made you realise you didn't want to be with me, or I'd done something to scare you off for good. We can deal with this. We can turn it into a positive.'

His use of the word 'we' almost undid me and I choked back an involuntary sob. 'You told me once that nobody should wield that sort of power.'

His expression didn't change. 'Nobody should, but it's a fact of life that some people do. Knowing that you're one of those people actually makes me feel better, not worse.' He raised his eyebrows. 'Remember, I was there after Zara died. Our roles could easily have been reversed. I could have been the person to receive her ... gift instead of you.'

He held my gaze. 'This is not going to be what ends us.' His tone was implacable. He nodded decisively then continued in a more relaxed manner. 'You know, when we first met, I really didn't like the police.'

I nodded; I was aware of that.

'I still don't like the police,' he continued. 'But I love you. Your job is not *you*.'

'A Cassandra isn't a job,' I said quietly. 'I can't leave it. I can't turn it off. I can't bloody control it at all, Lukas.'

'I'm a bloodsucker, Emma.'

I squinted. 'So?'

'You don't like vampires.'

I started. Where did that come from? 'What? That's not true.'

'Let me rephrase that. You don't like that we have to drink blood in order to survive. And you don't like that we're naturally more attractive in order to persuade humans to give us that blood.'

I opened my mouth to protest then I closed it again. Shit. He was right.

'Do you love me?' he asked roughly.

'Of course I love you,' I snapped. 'That's not the problem.'

Lukas folded his arms across his chest, his eyes gleaming with satisfaction. 'I love you too. Nothing else matters. In fact, my love for you will help me overcome any prejudice I have against Cassandras. Everyone wins.'

'It's already causing problems, Lukas. The incident on Baker Street that I mentioned? It might have gone better if I'd not been there. My presence is part of what created the problem in the first place. I saw Alan Cobain's death happening in a vision but I still couldn't stop it. That sort of thing is going to keep happening.'

'Then we'll deal with it when it does,' he said calmly.

'Lukas—'

'I will never hate you. I might not like everything that you do, but that doesn't mean that my feelings for you will change, Emma Bellamy. They certainly won't change because of something outwith your control. I will *always* have your back. I will *always* love you. We belong together. You know it as well as I do.'

I looked into his eyes and I knew, suddenly and fervently, that he was right.

'Will you come home?' he asked quietly. 'Will you let me help you with this?'

My mouth was dry. 'There's something else I've not told you.'

Genuine fear flashed across his face and he stiffened. 'What?'

I drew in a deep breath. Here we go. 'I'm pregnant. I only found out yesterday.'

Lukas's jaw dropped. 'You ... you're ... what?'

I repeated, 'I'm going to have a baby.' I added, somewhat unnecessarily, 'It's yours. *We're* going to have a baby.'

His expression transformed; every part of him radiated delight. 'A baby?' I nodded. He leapt off the sofa and pulled me into his arms. 'A baby,' he breathed. 'We're going to be a family.'

I pressed against him and, because I knew it was true, I said, 'We're already a family.'

Lukas crowed with joy and then he kissed me until every other thought fled my mind. Everything was going to be alright. We were going to get a happy ending.

'Would you like a cold compress?' Lukas asked, handing me a steaming mug of hot chocolate before tucking the blanket closer around me.

I smiled at him. 'No, thank you.'

'How about something to eat?'

'You cooked me a three-course meal less than two hours ago. I'm stuffed full.'

'Do you need another cushion?'

'Lukas,' I said, faintly exasperated, 'I'm fine.'

'I know that. But I want to make sure you're completely comfortable.'

From the other room I heard his phone start to ring. 'I couldn't be more comfortable. Stop fussing. You should answer that, it might be important.'

'Not as important as this.'

If he was going to be like this for the next seven months, we were going to have a problem. 'Lukas, answer the damned phone.'

He rolled his eyes, but at least he did as I asked. I sighed happily and nestled deeper into the sofa. This was great.

Lukas strode back into the room with his phone glued to his ear. 'Are you sure?'

I glanced up, registered the look on his face and frowned. His eyes flicked to me and what I saw in them sent a bolt of alarm rippling through me. I pushed back the blanket and sat up.

'Is anyone inside?' he asked. He spoke quietly but there was a darkness in his voice that terrified me. He listened to the answer, then said, 'We'll leave straightaway.' He hung up and gave me a long, worried look that was completely out of character.

I sprang to my feet. 'What?' I demanded. 'What is it?'

'There's a fire,' he said, without taking his eyes off me. 'A big one.'

'Where?' I swallowed. 'Where is it, Lukas?'

His response was instant. 'Supe Squad.'

FOURTEEN

Lukas didn't argue when I ran to Tallulah instead of waiting for one of his sleek vamp cars to appear. Tallulah was as much a part of Supe Squad as I was, so she had to be there too. I threw myself into the driver's seat while Lukas crammed himself into the passenger seat, and we took off at high speed.

While I put my foot down on the accelerator, Lukas called Fred. 'He's not answering.'

'Try Grace,' I bit out, navigating a turn at high speed.

Lukas located the number. His shoulders relaxed when somebody answered and I breathed out in relief. He turned the phone onto speaker so I could listen in. 'Is DS Grace there? It's Lukas Horvath.'

Liza's voice filled the air. 'No, Lord Horvath. He's gone off to the sticks somewhere with Fred on a case.' She sounded surprised that Lukas was calling but her tone remained professional. I briefly closed my eyes. She hadn't heard yet.

'He's not at Supe Squad?'

'I don't think so, not unless he's returned and is writing up a report before coming home. When he gets back, I can have him phone you.'

Supe Squad was less than a minute away. 'Liza,' I said aloud.

'Emma? You're with Horvath?' Her voice changed; the realisation that something was wrong was starting to hit her.

'Supe Squad is on fire.'

'*What?*'

'We're on our way there now.'

'Is Owen inside the building?' Her voice rose, shaky terror colouring each word. 'Emma, is Owen there?'

'I don't know.'

I heard her gulp. 'Is the fire bad?'

I drove around the final corner. When I saw the scene that greeted us, my mouth dropped open in horror. Clanging sirens screamed from all directions.

'Emma! Is it bad?'

I whispered. 'Yes. Yes, it is. You should get here if you can.'

My eyes travelled across the blazing inferno that was engulfing the whole Supe Squad building. I counted eight fire engines outside. All the buildings nearby, including the neighbouring hotel, had clearly been evacuated. A large crowd of gaping people were being held back by a cordon at the far end of the street while dark smoke billowed to the north.

Lukas's hand reached for mine and squeezed it tightly, then we got out of Tallulah and ran towards the fire. We didn't get very far. 'You have to wait back here,' a uniformed police officer told us as we elbowed our way through to reach the cordon.

'I'm DC Bellamy,' I said. 'That's my building.'

'ID?' he asked.

I reached for my warrant card then remembered I no longer had it. 'I don't have it with me,' I said through gritted teeth.

'I'm Lord Horvath,' Lukas said. 'This area is under supe control and we need to gain access.'

Whether the policeman recognised Lukas or not, he wasn't intimidated. 'You need to let the fire crews do their job. The building in question is run by humans and falls under the remit of the Met police. You have to stay back, sir. You can't help.'

I looked beyond him and spotted two ambulances parked to the left of the fire engines. 'Is anyone in the building?'

'We don't know that yet.'

'Is it arson?'

'Ma'am, I don't have any answers,' he said firmly. 'Take a step back.'

Above the roar of the fire and the screech of the fire alarms and sirens, I heard a growl rumble in Lukas's chest. I placed a hand on his arm to calm him. That was when I heard a mild snort to my right. 'My tiny violin weeps for the loss of Supernatural Squad,' a man's voice said, his sarcasm obvious.

I whirled around and saw Stubman, Max's counterpart who worked the nightshift at the hotel next door. Without thinking, I advanced towards him. 'People might be dying in there,' I spat. 'And you're celebrating!'

The unlikely figure of Lady Sullivan stepped between us. 'Leave it,' she told me. 'He's not worth it.'

I looked from her to the three other werewolf clan alphas who were also in attendance. News of the fire had spread fast and, judging from their expressions, they were all concerned.

Then I saw Buffy, white-faced and shaking. 'Fred could have been in there,' she said.

'He's not?' I asked, urgently.

'He's out with Grace. He called me half an hour ago. He said he was on his way home from somewhere outside London but he was going to be late.'

My shoulders sagged with relief.

A moment later, Liza appeared. 'Owen!' she shrieked. She threw herself towards the cordon. Yet again, the policeman held up his hands, forcing her back.

'He's not there, Liza,' I told her. 'Buffy spoke to Fred thirty minutes ago. They're together. They're not in the city.'

'He's not answering his fucking phone, Emma. He always answers his phone.'

Liza was right: he always did. 'Maybe it needs charging.'

She threw me a scornful look. 'When was the last time he let his phone run out of battery?'

Never. 'Maybe there's no signal,' I said weakly. I looked at Buffy. 'Have you tried calling Fred again?'

'He's not picking up either,' she muttered.

Shit.

Lukas's voice murmured in my ear. 'Emma.'

I glanced across and realised he was pointing to his left. A car had pulled up and DSI Barnes was stepping out. Her expression gave nothing away but her gaze swept the scene, from the raging fire to our group at the cordon. Her eyes fell on me and she nodded before walking over to the policeman, speaking to him briefly and gesturing to Liza and me. 'Only the two of you,' she said. 'The rest of you stay here.'

'DSI Barnes,' Lukas began.

She shook her head. 'This has nothing to do with the vampires, Lord Horvath.' She looked at Lady Sullivan and the others. 'Or the werewolves. What's happening here is not your concern.'

'Supe Squad is our concern,' Lukas snapped.

Lady Fairfax joined him. 'It's as much a part of us as we are of them.'

The others nodded. Under any other circumstances, I'd have been thrilled by their support.

Barnes sniffed. 'I'm sure they appreciate that sentiment, but right now you're not getting through.' She raised her head and marched towards the scene. I sent Lukas an apologetic look then jogged after her with Liza by my side.

'You know I shouldn't be allowing this,' Barnes said in an undertone. 'Not with your suspension.'

'Thank you, ma'am. I appreciate it.'

She flicked a look at Liza and her gaze softened. 'Is Owen Grace inside?'

'He might be.' Liza's voice was suddenly very small.

Barnes' mouth tightened. 'Let's find out. Keep behind me at all times. The fire service have authority here.'

At that point, I was simply relieved to be past the cordon and I'd have agreed to anything. I reached for Liza's hand and together we trailed after Barnes. I kept my eyes fixed on the Supe Squad building; it was being consumed and my horror was growing with the rising flames. It felt almost apocalyptic. And it wasn't only Supe Squad that was in trouble; the fire had spread to the buildings on either side. If any of them survived the night, it would be a miracle.

Barnes was careful to keep well out of the way of the fire crews. She waited calmly at one side, with Liza and I hovering anxiously – and impotently – beside her.

'You could go in,' Liza muttered to me. 'You're the phoenix. Fire is your friend. You can see if Owen and Fred are in there.'

Barnes overheard her. 'Not a chance,' she said. 'She'd be dead by the time she got to the first hallway. Nobody can navigate a fire like that without specialist equipment, and the fact that Emma will resurrect won't help her walk through flames.'

I hated feeling grateful that I didn't have to choose between risking my baby or saving Owen and Fred.

'You could at least try,' Liza said.

Fortunately an approaching paramedic forestalled my reply. 'Three people from the hotel are being treated for mild smoke inhalation,' the young woman told Barnes. 'We don't have any other casualties.'

Yet. I swallowed back my fear. An older man wearing full firefighter's gear joined us and pulled off his helmet. 'The Supe Squad building will be burning for hours, but the worst of the fire is under control.'

'Casualties from inside?' Barnes asked. Both Liza and I held our breath.

'We haven't found anyone.'

Liza couldn't prevent a small cry escaping from her mouth and I exhaled in relief. It looked as if Buffy had been right. Thank God.

'We have found something else though.'

I stiffened and looked at him as DSI Barnes folded her arms. 'Go on.'

'Obviously a full investigation will need to be carried out, and this is only my opinion and not a professional analysis.'

She waved a hand. 'Yes, yes. Go on.'

'From the way the fire spread and the speed at which it took hold, a considerable amount of accelerant was used.'

A chill descended down my spine.

'The fire was deliberate?' Liza whispered.

He nodded. 'It looks that way.'

I stared at the blackened, disintegrating building. Was this my fault? Was this retaliation for what somebody believed I'd done to Alan Cobain? Horrified, I clamped a hand over my mouth.

My thoughts must have been written all over my face. 'It's okay,' Liza said to me. 'It's only a building. Fred and Owen aren't in there.' She gave a shaky laugh. 'Though as soon as I see Owen, I'm going to bloody kill him for not answering his phone.'

The firefighter murmured to Barnes and withdrew. She

turned to us. 'This is a difficult situation, but Liza May is correct – it could be a lot worse. We can't draw any conclusions until a proper investigation is conducted into the fire. Don't forget you remain on suspension, Emma.'

I managed a nod, irritated that she felt the need to continually remind me.

'I know that this fire puts a different complexion on matters,' she added, 'but I do need you to return to New Scotland Yard first thing in the morning. We require a DNA sample from you.' She said it casually, but even so I stiffened. The hair they'd found; that's what this was about.

'I didn't kill Cobain.'

'In which case a DNA test should prove no problem and will help to absolve you of any potential wrongdoing. We received an anonymous call earlier today stating that you were seen arguing with Alan Cobain outside his flat in the hour before his murder.'

I stared at her. 'What? That never happened!'

'Then you have nothing to worry about.' Barnes looked over my shoulder at someone behind me. 'What is it, sergeant?' she asked.

I gritted my teeth as I turned to the police officer .

'Good evening, DSI Barnes,' she said. 'I know this isn't a good time but I thought you'd want to know. We have reports of two Met officers who've been involved in a serious RTC.'

A road traffic collision. I looked at the sergeant and suddenly knew what she was going to say before she said it. It wasn't as a result of my Cassandra powers, but merely dread intuition.

'It happened on the outskirts of the city. Both are alive but in a critical condition. They've been taken to the nearest hospital.'

I closed my eyes.

'We've identified them as PC Frederick Hackert and DS Owen Grace.'

My knees buckled. Beside me Liza raised her head and keened a howl of pure agony.

CHAPTER

FIFTEEN

I t was a small hospital, but busy. The Accident and Emergency waiting room was packed with people waiting to be seen when we rushed through it before being ushered to a quieter area to wait for further news. Both Fred and Owen had been taken to theatre and were being operated on; I sincerely hoped the surgeons were the best in their field.

DSI Barnes had remained at the scene of the fire, so only Liza, Lukas and I were there. I'd already called Fred's parents, who were tearing through the streets of London to get here. Liza had told Grace's sister, but she was in Manchester and couldn't get to the hospital any time soon. The three of us perched on uncomfortable plastic chairs and watched the door as we waited for someone to appear and give us more information.

'You need to eat,' Lukas told me quietly, breaking the pained silence in the small room.

I nodded, distracted. The last thing I felt right then was hungry.

'No, Emma,' he said. 'You *need* to eat. I'll get something from the cafeteria. Liza, do you...?'

She shook her head. 'No.'

Lukas acknowledged her response and left the room. I knew he'd get something for her anyway, though she wouldn't eat it.

She turned to me, her skin pale and drawn against the vivid red of her hair. 'You're back with him then? For good?'

I picked at an invisible thread on my jacket. 'Yes.'

'What happened?'

I sighed; she was going to find out sooner or later. 'I inadvertently acquired a new skill, one that Lukas has had problems with in the past. I left him because I didn't think he'd be able to cope with it, but he's persuaded me that it's going to be fine.'

Liza considered this. 'It will be,' she said finally. 'Anyone can see how much he loves you.' Her voice dropped. 'I feel the same way about Owen. There's nothing that would make me walk away from him.' Her voice hardened. '*Nothing.*'

She was going through hell and I was talking about my love life. 'Would you like a hug?' I asked.

This time she answered instantly. 'No. And I don't want any sympathy from you either, so take that bloody look off your face. Anything like that will push me over the edge.' She glared at me. 'I mean it.'

I nodded. 'Okay.'

Liza looked away, seemingly satisfied. I watched her for a moment or two, then I swallowed. 'Liza, do you know where Owen was? Where he went with Fred, I mean?'

'He said something about an address he'd found in the Quincy Carmichael file that he wanted to check out. He said it was outside London and it would take him a while, but he was in a rush to get there and back before night time. I don't know any more than that.' Her shoulders sagged. 'I should have asked,' she whispered.

I should have found the address when I'd glanced through the file. Shoulda, woulda, coulda. There was a lot of that going around.

We lapsed into silence for several long seconds before Liza raised her head. 'Why's Horvath so desperate for you to eat? He seems even more protective of you than usual.'

Given I'd been standing next to all four werewolf clan alphas at the fire, the entire supernatural world probably knew by now. Also, Liza clearly wanted to talk about something else beyond the horror that Owen and Fred were currently facing. 'I'm pregnant,' I told her.

Her eyes flew to mine. 'Seriously? Congratulations!' Then she grimaced and asked, 'Is it congratulations?'

I half-smiled. 'It is.'

'Then I'm thrilled for you both.' She managed a smile of her own, though it didn't reach her eyes. 'This new power of yours, is it related to the baby?'

'No. I...' I sighed. I could trust her not to go blabbing. 'I'm now a Cassandra,' I admitted.

She started. 'You can see into the future?'

'Occasionally. I don't have much control over it – actually, I don't have *any* control over it. It's part of the reason why I'm in so much trouble over what happened to Alan Cobain.' Although given everything else, being a murder suspect seemed like the least of my worries.

Liza seemed to go even paler. 'Did you see this? Did you know this was going to happen to Fred and Owen?'

'No.' For the first time, I wished that I'd actually had a vision. Even if it was beyond me to change the future that I saw, at least I could have tried. The realisation shocked me.

The door to the small room burst open and Liza and I leapt to our feet, but it wasn't a doctor with news. It was Buffy. 'Where's Fred?' she snarled. Patches of fur were appearing across her face and her eyes were flickering yellow. Damn it; the last thing we needed was a fully transformed werewolf wandering around the hospital.

'He's in surgery,' I told her. 'We don't know anything more.'

'Where are the operating theatres?' She bared her teeth again. 'Never mind, I'll find them myself.' She whirled away, but I grabbed her arm and hauled her back.

'You will do no such thing. You're going to wait here with us and calm down.'

Her breath quickened. 'Are you going to try and compel me, detective?' she sneered.

'Sit the fuck down, Buffy,' Liza said. 'Let the doctors do their job.'

Buffy's narrowed gaze flicked from me to Liza. I waited, preparing to stop her again if she didn't back down. Fortunately for us all, she tossed her head and allowed her emerging wolf to subside. 'Fine,' she said. 'I'll wait.' She paused. 'For now.' She threw herself onto a chair, folded her arms, crossed her legs and huffed loudly.

The business of waiting and watching the seconds tick slowly into minutes and then hours began all over again.

DAWN WAS BREAKING before we finally got some news. I'd been curled up against Lukas, my head on his shoulder and the detritus of the meal he'd brought on the table in front of us. Liza was hunched over, while Buffy had barely moved a muscle since she'd first sat down.

Fred's parents had arrived some time earlier and were sitting together in the corner, clinging to each other's hands as if afraid to let go. Even Owen's sister, Catherine, had arrived to join our slumped, anxious vigil.

When the tired-looking doctor appeared, we all straightened up and forgot our fatigue. I was taut with tension, but I had to know what was happening with Fred and Grace. We all did.

Before the white-coated doctor could open his mouth, there was a loud roaring in my ears and spots flashed in front of my eyes. I gasped and clutched at Lukas's arm, then words started spewing forth before I could stop them. 'Find a penny, wear it in your left shoe and your wish will come true. Throw that penny into the well and a revelation will be beheld.'

My vision swam and my stomach lurched. I sucked in air, blinking hard. Don't be sick, Emma. Don't be sick, don't be sick, don't be sick.

'Are you alright?' The doctor's voice seemed to come from far away.

I tried to focus on him; he still looked blurry, but I was regaining control. I was aware of everyone else in the room staring at me. As Lukas wrapped an arm around my waist and drew me close, I risked a glance at him. His expression was mild, betraying no flicker of disgust or revulsion. 'She's under a lot of stress, doctor,' he said. 'We all are.'

'Of course, of course. I can only imagine how difficult this is for you all.' The doctor smiled uneasily and took a step back, clearly attempting to put more space between himself and me. I couldn't blame him. 'I have some news. I couldn't call it good news – not yet – but it's not bad news either.'

I pushed away what had just happened and held my breath.

'We've had surgical teams working on Frederick and Owen. Both of them remain in a critical condition. Frederick has been placed into an induced coma while he recovers from the worst of his injuries. We've removed his spleen and resolved the issue of internal haemorrhaging, but his body has undergone a massive trauma and the next few days will be vital to his recovery. At this point we're cautiously optimistic, but it will be a long journey.'

Fred's mother gave a choked sob. Buffy went over and hugged her. 'He's strong,' she said. 'Fred will pull through, I know he will.'

'What about Owen?' Liza whispered, standing next to Catherine.

'He has lost a lot of blood but our main concern is that, despite the passenger side of the vehicle taking the brunt of the damage, Owen banged his head quite severely. There's a lot of swelling in his brain. We've stabilised him and he's in intensive care, but I'm afraid that we can't say what will happen. There's a possibility of brain damage, but at this point it's a waiting game. We won't know more until he wakes up. *If* he wakes up.'

Tears rolled unchecked down Liza's cheeks. 'Can I see him?'

'Of course. I can take you to him now. I should warn you that there are a lot of machines and tubes around his body.'

'Can we see Frederick?' his dad asked.

'If you follow me, I'll take you to him, too.'

Buffy clapped her hands together. 'Great! Let's go!'

I glanced at her. 'Buffy.'

She looked my way and I shook my head in warning. This time was for his parents, not for us. She scowled but then she nodded at Fred's mum and dad and stepped back. A moment later only she, Lukas and I were left in the little waiting room. 'It's good, right?' Buffy said, as much to herself as to us. 'It could be a lot worse.'

It could *always* be a lot worse. 'Both of them are tough,' I said. 'They will pull through.' They had to pull through. I needed them.

She looked at me more closely. 'What was that shit you were spouting when the doctor came in? Pennies? Wishes? You sounded like you did when you were harping on about that tip-off for Baker Street.'

I scratched my neck. 'Uh...'

'Don't worry about that now,' Lukas said. 'We have bigger concerns.' His tone was grim. 'These events cannot be coincidental. Somebody is framing you for Alan Cobain's murder and Supernatural Squad is a charred shell. Now the two remaining Supe Squad police officers are half dead. Supe Squad is being targeted.'

'Bad things come in threes,' I said, then nudged Lukas sharply in the ribs. This wasn't the place for this conversation.

'In the space of a day, Supe Squad has been destroyed. Only Liza is left standing, and she's neither an active officer nor is she in any fit state to continue with work,' Lukas persisted.

Buffy's snarl returned. 'You're saying that you think all this has been deliberate?' Her voice rose. 'That somebody tried to kill Fred? *My* Fred? And that they're still out there? What if they try again?'

If she tried to turn into a wolf again, I'd have no choice but to bring her down. I watched her, ready to act.

'I'll arrange for a guard to be put on both their rooms,' Lukas told her, already drawing out his phone to make the arrangements.

'No. The wolves will do this, not the vampires.' She glared at him, as if daring him to disagree, but at least she was controlling her inner beast. Protecting Fred meant that she had an agenda that her werewolf form couldn't help with.

'Call in more werewolves if you wish,' he said mildly.

'I do wish.' Her eyes spat fire at us. 'Wait here.' She gave a menacing wave of her hand. 'I mean it. Don't go anywhere.' Then she stomped out of the room.

As soon as she'd gone, Lukas asked, 'Do you think I'm wrong? Do you think all this is a coincidence?'

Mutely, I shook my head. It felt implausible but it could easily be true. I couldn't be killed so somebody had killed Cobain instead, knowing that my name would emerge as a suspect. Between the strands of hair found at the scene and the anonymous tip-off that was obviously a lie, it was a reasonable theory. And it was compounded by someone consigning Supe Squad to ashes forever and trying to kill Fred and Owen.

'It doesn't make sense,' Lukas muttered. 'You heard the alphas earlier – they were as shocked by the fire as anyone else. Supes have come around to the idea of Supe Squad, and most humans have come to accept supes. Attacking you like this now seems strange timing.'

'Unless whoever did all this wanted to stop what we're doing now.'

'What are you doing? Apart from the investigation into Quincy Carmichael?'

'Nothing,' I said. I met his eyes. 'Quincy's disappearance is our only case at the moment.'

Lukas's expression grew darker. 'What happened before – that was your Cassandra thing, right?'

I nodded warily. 'Yes.'

He reached for his wallet, opened the zip and took out two pennies. 'One for you,' he said, 'and one for me.' He took off his left shoe and placed the penny inside it.

'I'm not sure—' I began.

'What?'

I sighed; I didn't know. I copied him and put my penny into my shoe. 'I didn't see any visions, it was only the words. I have no idea what they mean.'

'I imagine we'll find out in due course.' Lukas gave me a taut smile. 'What do you want to do? They won't let us see Owen or Fred, and anyway neither of them are awake. You're supposed to go back to New Scotland Yard, right?'

I sucked my bottom lip and considered. There was the small matter of my impending DNA test. Until now, I'd been more than prepared to sit out my suspension and do as I was told like the good girl I usually was, but now that scenario wasn't going to work for me. Not since Fred and Owen had also been targeted. Things were different now.

'I need to find out if your theory is correct and then discover who's behind it.' My tone darkened. 'It's the least I can do for Fred and Owen.'

'In that case, let's get out of here and get started,' Lukas said.

'What about Buffy?'

'Do you need her?'

I shook my head.

'Then she can stay here and help guard those two boys,' Lukas said. 'They'll be safe enough with the likes of Buffy outside their doors.'

Something tight and painful clenched at my heart. 'They'd better be alright,' I whispered.

'They will be.' He held out his hand. 'Let's go.'

SIXTEEN

I took a moment to motion to Liza through the tiny glass panel in the door to Grace's room, indicating that Lukas and I were leaving. She looked up from his pale, unmoving body and barely nodded. I'd never seen her look terrified before. I wanted to tell her that everything would be alright but I couldn't. Instead I reached for Lukas's hand and squeezed it hard.

'I'll make sure she's looked after,' he said gruffly. 'I've got several vampires already on the way.'

I nodded, beyond grateful that I had him with me. As we trudged out of the hospital. I shook my head to clear my thoughts. Grace and Fred needed me to be focused. They were my people and I was theirs. Although I was suspended from duties, I wasn't without resources or skills. I knew how the system worked and that made it easy to find the answers I needed with only a few short calls from Lukas's phone.

'The crash site isn't far from here,' I told him as I returned his phone. 'The road has already been re-opened. We should head there first before the morning rush hour makes investigations too difficult. Grace is a careful driver and there's nothing to suggest another vehicle was involved.' My voice hardened. 'But if that's the case, what caused the crash?'

'Somebody might have run them off the road,' Lukas suggested. 'Did your contacts have any idea what happened?'

I shook my head. 'It's too early to tell. There'll be an investigation but it'll probably be low priority. We need to go and see for ourselves.'

I switched on Tallulah's engine and patted her dashboard, murmuring to her briefly about the importance of our journey in case she decided this was a good time to be obstinate. There was no reluctance on her part, and thankfully her radio remained silent. This wasn't the time for tunes and even Tallulah knew it.

Less than ten minutes later, we pulled into a narrow layby next to where I'd been told the crash had occurred. The sky was lightening as dawn approached; although that meant there was now more traffic to contend with, it would make it easier to examine the scene. I hopped out of the car and looked around.

'There aren't any skid marks.' Lukas frowned. 'Are you sure this is the spot?'

'I think so.' I stepped back, moving out of the path of a trundling lorry, then I spotted tracks along the grassy verge at the bottom of the hill we were standing on. I pointed down. 'There's something there.'

We nipped across the road and walked downhill. I saw one short skid mark beside a longer, deeper scratch on the surface of the road. I couldn't work out what had caused that mark.

I narrowed my eyes and glanced towards the verge. Although most of the debris had been cleared away, there were a few remnants of the crash in the grass by the side of the road. I noted some shards of smashed glass and a broken wing mirror that had fallen into a clump of bushes and been missed by the police. I swivelled around, gazing at the slope we'd just jogged down.

'They would have been driving towards this spot,' I said, as much to myself as to Lukas. 'Down the hill so they could join the main road that leads into the city centre.' My gaze followed the flattened grass. 'Another vehicle could have nudged them onto the verge so that they crashed.' I looked more closely. 'But Grace would have taken an evasive manoeuvre. The road is reasonably quiet now, and it would have been even quieter earlier. There are plenty of lampposts around so it wouldn't have been pitch black.'

'Were there any witnesses?'

'No. Apparently someone in one of the houses nearby heard the crash and looked out of their window. They called 999.'

'So there wasn't much of a delay before the emergency services arrived,' Lukas said. 'There wouldn't have been much time for another vehicle to leave the scene.'

'No.' I knelt down and examined the marks in the scrub-like vegetation. I was certainly no crash-scene expert, but it looked as if the car had flipped. Grace and Fred would have had to be moving at an incredible speed in a residential zone for that to happen.

It was possible that somebody had phoned one of them and told them about the fire. Grace could have panicked, put his foot down then lost control, but it seemed unlikely. I was all but certain that he would have been driving.

I pulled a face. It didn't make sense. There wasn't any evidence that anyone else had been involved. Maybe it was merely human error.

'What about the car?' Lukas asked. 'Can we see it? Check the damage for ourselves?'

I nodded. 'That's our next stop.' I gave him a wan smile.

'You might not like the police, Lukas, but you would have made a great detective.'

'I've learned from the best, D'Artagnan.' His tone was light but his expression was sombre. I recognised the emotion because I felt the same way – tenfold.

AT LUKAS'S INSISTENCE, we stopped at a shop to pick up some breakfast on our way to the car pound. I was still slowly chewing the last of a banana when we parked outside and telling myself that, even if the fruit tasted like ash in my mouth, I had to eat and keep my strength up for all our sakes.

As soon as I turned the key and Tallulah's engine fell silent, Lukas tilted his head and his brow furrowed. 'What is it?' I asked.

'Something's wrong,' he muttered.

I stiffened. Before I could speak, he had opened the passenger door and was loping towards the entrance of the pound. My hearing wasn't as good as Lukas's, but when I got out to follow him I heard what had raised his hackles. Beyond the high walls of the police pound, there was the definite sound of growling. Werewolf growling.

Hissing under my breath, I ran after Lukas. The gates were firmly closed and the barbed wire strung across the top of them wouldn't make them an easy climb. It was too early for the entrance to be manned, so there was no chance of persuading someone to let us in.

I cursed and ran for the concrete wall, throwing myself upward until my fingertips curled around the top edge. There was no barbed wire there; the police probably assumed that the walls were too high for anyone to try and climb over them. They would be too high for anyone human, but it wasn't difficult for a supe.

I hauled myself up and glanced at the CCTV camera that most definitely had me in view. There was nothing I could do about it now. I turned my head away before dropping down to the ground on the other side. Seconds later, Lukas joined me. 'If you're going to say that I shouldn't be doing things like this when I'm pregnant,' I began.

He held up his hands. 'I wouldn't dare. I trust you, remember? You know your limits.'

I sniffed, slightly mollified. Then there was another long growl. It didn't sound as menacing as before but it was still worrying – and there was no doubt now that it came from a wolf.

Lukas and I exchanged looks then ran towards the noise.

Buffy had semi-transformed; only her head and her hands were in werewolf form. Her pointed, furry ears were flat against her skull, her sharp teeth were bared and her quivering lips were pulled back to display their full fangy glory. Her claws were outstretched as if she were prepared to pounce and rip out a throat at a moment's notice.

I relaxed slightly. Despite her terrifying appearance, she was still in control of herself. This was a show of intimidation rather than a genuine threat to maim or kill. At that moment, I'd have taken any silver linings I could find. But I still shouted; of course I shouted. 'Buffy!'

Her jaws snapped and the fur around her face melted away. Her muzzle disappeared so she could answer me with decipherable speech. 'Hi, Emma!' she replied cheerfully. She grinned. 'You didn't think you could abandon me that easily, did you?'

I hadn't given it much thought. Buffy was low on my list of important shit to think about. *Very* low. 'What are you doing?' I demanded through gritted teeth.

Her cheeriness didn't subside. 'Enough people arrived to guard my Fred and the other one, Owen Whatsisface, so I left them to it and came here.' She nodded at the remains of Grace's car. 'Alfie is the only one in the building, so it's just as well that I did. He required a little persuasion to do what we need.'

We? I grimaced as I spotted the pair of feet beneath the mangled vehicle in front of us that was barely recognisable as Grace's car. Pain seared through me once again at what had happened to both of my colleagues.

I gave Buffy my nastiest look.

'Step back,' Lukas ordered.

'He's not finished yet.'

There was a cough from under the raised car. 'Actually, I think I've got what you need.'

Buffy beamed. 'Excellent. Out you come, then.'

There was a scraping sound and a moment later the oil-blackened face of a middle-aged man appeared. He wriggled out, slowly got to his feet and wiped his hands on his overalls. Considering what I imagined Buffy had said to him before we'd arrived, his expression was remarkably placid.

'Well, Alfie? What have you learned?' Buffy blinked and tossed her head. Her hands were still in werewolf form.

'My, Grandma,' Alfie said. 'What big claws you have.'

She lunged towards him and swiped the air in front of his face. He took a hasty step backwards, clearly far more nervous than he was trying to appear.

'Stop that, Buffy,' I snapped.

'Alfie needs some encouragement.' She bared her teeth again. 'Don't you, Alfie?'

I looked pointedly at Lukas and he grinned at me. 'With pleasure, my love.' He swooped down on Buffy and hauled her out of the way. She struggled against his grip – but not very hard. After all, she was about to get what she wanted.

'She's got no right to come in 'ere and threaten me,' Alfie said, his London accent growing stronger as his emotions got the better of him. 'I'm only the night manager. I don't do vehicle inspections.'

'But you know how to do them, don't you, Alfie?' Buffy said from inside Lukas's grip. 'What did you learn?'

I turned on her and wagged a finger in her face. 'Not another word. I mean it.' She mimed zipping her mouth closed.

Alfie managed a shaky laugh. I looked at him. 'What *did* you learn?' I asked.

His face immediately fell as he realised I wasn't the saviour he'd been hoping for; from the look in his eyes, he was starting to think that I was the one he should be afraid of. 'The little wolfie was right,' he muttered. 'The accident weren't no accident.'

'I knew it!' Buffy crowed. 'Some bastard cut the brake lines!' So much for not another word.

Alfie rolled his eyes. 'Life ain't like the movies. Cut the brakes on a car and the driver would notice immediately, even if there weren't warning lights coming on. They'd come to a safe stop and haul arse to the nearest garage.' He shook his head. 'Nah. That's not what happened here.'

He pointed to the front of the car. 'The wheel nuts were loosened on all four wheels. Several came off completely on the front tyres, probably after quite a bit of driving, and you can see that the front right wheel is missing. We have it round the back somewhere. It was brought in wi' the car. The nuts are loose on the back wheels as well. Tha's how you can tell it was deliberate. This were sabotage.'

My mouth felt suddenly dry. 'They couldn't have worked their way loose by accident? Or been missed by a garage because of negligence?'

Alfie gave me a flat look. 'No. One wheel nut could be loose by accident or negligence, but not all of them. Besides, these days it's difficult for most people to loosen nuts by themselves. They tend to be fastened on tight. You really need a motorised impact wrench to do it.'

I thought about the long deep scratch I'd seen on the road at the scene of the crash; that would have been made when the wheel came off. Lukas was right, Supe Squad had been deliberately targeted. Somebody was trying to kill us or put us out of the way for good. All of us.

I swayed slightly. Alarmed, Lukas released Buffy and sprang to my side. 'I'm fine,' I whispered. 'I'm just...' My voice trailed off. Shocked? Angry? Confused? All of the above.

'How long would it take for the wheel to fall off?' Buffy asked, her tone harsh as she absorbed the news. 'How many miles would you have to drive before it happened?'

I knew what Buffy was asking: she wanted to know if the sabotage had taken place in front of Supe Squad or at Grace's home, or if the perpetrator had followed Grace and Fred to their destination and loosened the wheel nuts there.

Alfie shrugged. 'Difficult to say. It was probably very recent, though. You'd only be able to drive ten, twenty miles.'

I looked at Buffy; she was no longer focused on Alfie but was hugging herself and looking miserable.

'Do you know where Grace and Fred had been?' Lukas asked me.

'No.' I raised my eyebrows at Buffy. 'Do you?'

She shook her head. 'Fred only said they were past the outskirts of the city. There were cows and sheep – he said it smelled like country and he didn't like it.'

That didn't exactly narrow it down. Shit.

Alfie looked from me to Buffy to Lukas. 'If they used the car's satnav, I can tell you where they went.' He paused and licked his lips. 'If you cross my palm with silver, that is.'

My mouth dropped open. 'This is a police compound and you're asking for a bribe?'

He snorted. 'I ain't no detective. Besides, not all the polis are exactly clean, are they?'

I clamped my mouth shut while Alfie held out his hand. 'Come on then. Pony up.'

'Do you take plastic?' Buffy asked.

'Don't be fucking stupid, lass.'

'I could always rip your throat out instead of bribing you,' she said.

I glared at her. 'You will not. Lukas, do you have any money?'

'Not cash.'

Neither did I – a pound or two maybe, but not enough for Alfie. I didn't often use cash any more. I guessed Lukas could use his vampiric persuasion skills on the man, but somehow that felt as sleazy as offering a bribe.

'I'll take bitcoin,' Alfie suggested.

Lukas pursed his lips. 'I'm a vampire,' he said finally. 'Instead of money, I promise not to bleed you dry. She's a were-wolf and she promises not to eat you. And this one here,' he nudged me, 'is a police detective who's been suspended on suspicion of murder. She promises not to kill you.'

I reminded myself to strangle him later. Threats were not helpful. If I hadn't been a corrupt cop before, I was now. Fuck.

'Nobody is going to hurt you, Alfie.' I splayed my hands. 'Please, can you help us find out who tried to kill our friends by telling us where they were before the accident?'

'Not friends,' Buffy said distinctly. '*Boy*friend.'

'How do I know you weren't the ones trying to kill them in the first place?' Alfie asked suspiciously.

'Because if we were, we wouldn't be here now doing this,' Lukas said patiently,

'Hmm.' Alfie wiped his cheek, smearing the oil that was already there so that it made his skin look even more bruised. He grunted. 'Wait here.'

We watched him trot towards a portacabin. 'Do you think that this is where he calls the real police?' Buffy asked.

'I *am* the real police,' I protested.

'Not now, you're not. You're suspended. And Supe Squad isn't the real police anyway.'

'You're not helping in the slightest,' I told her.

She sniffed. 'I'm getting answers. Anyway, why did it take *you* so long to get here?' There was a note of genuine anger in her voice as if she believed Lukas and I had been slacking.

A dozen irritated responses sprang to mind, none of them helpful. I bit every one of them back and looked at her. We were all on edge. 'We're going to find the bastard who did this, Buffy, I promise you that.' I held her gaze.

She stared back at me and I knew she wanted the argument to escalate. She needed to lash out and she was wrestling with her emotions, her fists clenching and unclenching. Then something in her seemed to ease and her shoulders relaxed. The moment passed and I breathed out.

'Me, you and him?' Buffy asked. I nodded. So did Lukas. 'Does that make us the three musketeers, then?'

Lukas barked a laugh. I gave her an exasperated look, but I was glad that the danger had passed.

The door to the portacabin opened and Alfie reappeared with a tablet in his hands. 'I'll have to be quick,' he said. 'The others will be arriving soon and they're not as nice as I am. They won't be very happy to see you here.'

He was going to help us; suddenly I wanted to throw my arms around his neck and hug him. He powered up the tablet and returned to the mangled metal of Grace's car. Instead of pushing himself underneath it, he squeezed into what was left of the driver's seat, fiddled around for a moment then connected the tablet to a slot in the car's dashboard.

I held my breath and crossed my fingers. *Please work*, I prayed. *Please, please work.*

The seconds ticked into minutes and Alfie grunted several times, his breath misting the shattered windscreen. Finally he smacked his lips in satisfaction and eased himself out. 'I've got an address for you, close to Borehamwood. That's six, maybe seven miles from here.' He tapped the screen of the tablet decisively. 'That's where your friends went. It's the last place logged in the satnav.'

I massaged the back of my neck. Borehamwood hadn't come up in any of the searches I'd done and I couldn't think of a reference to it in Quincy Carmichael's file – and I couldn't go back and check because the damned file had been burnt to ash along with the rest of Supe Squad. I damned Tony in my head for not being more diligent, then instantly felt guilty. Tony was dead, after all.

'Thank you, Alfie,' I said. 'I really appreciate your help.' I stuck my hand out to shake his.

He eyed it and stepped back. 'No offence, like, but if you're really a murderer I'm not touching your hand.'

I wondered why he'd helped us if he thought that. 'I'm not a murderer. And even if I were, criminal intent isn't contagious.'

'Call it suspicion then.' He shoved his hands into his pockets and grinned cheerfully. 'If anyone asks, I'm going to tell them you threatened me.'

I couldn't disagree since it was the truth. Buffy growled but I simply nodded. 'Thank you,' I said, meaning it. 'Somebody did try to kill our friends, and we're going to find out who.'

Alfie glanced us over once more. 'I wouldn't want to be them when you catch up to them,' he said.

I gave him a small humourless smile. Amen to that.

CHAPTER
SEVENTEEN

I offered Buffy a lift in the back of Tallulah but she recoiled as if I'd suggested that she hand over her firstborn. She told me that she wouldn't go near the purple monstrosity ever again, and she'd certainly never get inside it. I guessed I'd finally found the two things that scared Buffy: losing someone she cared about and my battered purple Mini.

She got into her bubble-gum pink Smart car, complete with eyelashes fringing its headlights, and followed us at a distance. While I drove and mumbled to Tallulah to ignore the werewolf, Lukas called the hospital. 'No change,' he reported when he hung up. 'Not in Grace or Fred.'

Pain stabbed at my heart, although I knew that a stable condition was the best we could hope for right now. I remained silent for the rest of the journey. At least Lukas was with me now; at least I wasn't alone.

The location that Alfie had given us wasn't in the town of Borehamwood, it was off a side lane a mile or so from the main road. The lane was narrow, with high hedges on either side that seemed to close in on Tallulah. We might be out of the city and in the countryside, but all I felt was stifling claustrophobia.

Even Lukas seemed relieved when we drove onto a wider road that took us to a cottage. I pulled to a halt, ignoring the small muddy driveway in front of the building in favour of parking on the road. The place looked abandoned.

Buffy's ridiculous car stopped behind us. She lowered her window and yelled, 'Go park in front of the house! There's enough space there for both of us!'

Lukas looked at me and I shook my head. 'No,' I said. I pointed to the driveway. 'There are tread marks there that might tell us something.'

He followed my gaze and his expression cleared when he saw them too. He unfolded his tall frame and got out of Tallulah, and I gave her steering wheel a brief caress before heading after him.

A moment later, Buffy joined us. 'I said that you should park on the driveway in front of the house!'

I ignored her and stepped around the worst of the mud, taking care not to disturb any of the marks in the squidgy earth. 'There's only one set of tyre marks,' I muttered as I examined the ground.

'Yes,' Lukas said, 'but there are three sets of footprints.'

My body tensed. Buffy stopped glaring at me and immediately jogged to Lukas's side. All of three of us stared down. I'd almost missed the footprints. Lukas had keen eyes.

The tyre marks from Grace's car were obvious, then two sets of footprints led both to and from where a car must have parked – undoubtedly Grace's and Fred's. But there were other prints that led from the tarmacked road where we'd parked.

I stared at the third set, which seemed to circle around the heavier tyre marks. They weren't clear enough to get a full print, and there would be no point calling in someone to take a cast in order to match them to a set of shoes, but whoever had made them had stopped at several points around the car.

'Somebody followed them here,' Buffy growled. 'Then when they were inside the cottage having a look around, they sneaked up and loosened the wheel nuts.'

Grace wouldn't have gone inside the cottage – he'd have needed a warrant to do that and he was a by-the-book kind of guy – but otherwise, I had to agree with her.

'Once they'd loosened them,' I said, 'they could have driven away and waited around a corner until Fred and Grace drove back down the lane. The perp could have followed them to make sure the plan worked and they crashed.'

I wondered what would have happened if the car hadn't lost its wheel when it was driving down a hill at speed. Fred and Grace were in a bad way but at least they were both still breathing. For now. Would the bastard who did this have done something even worse if Plan A hadn't worked? I shivered and dismissed the thought; it was almost too much to bear thinking about.

Lukas squeezed my hand briefly in reassurance then walked up the short driveway to the front door. Ivy was crawling up it and there was a faded, hand-painted sign haphazardly nailed next to it. 'The Love Nest,' he read aloud.

Buffy pulled a face. 'Ick.'

Hmm. Quincy Carmichael had run a dating agency for a while. I knew he'd had money troubles, but I wondered if he'd used some of his cash to buy this place as a bolthole. Perhaps he'd given it an ironic name as a nod to his ill-fated former career. It would be easy enough to check. From what Liza had told us, Grace had seen reference to it in the old files that Tony had put together. It was possible Quincy had escaped here instead of Spain when his debts began to catch up to him.

I walked up to the cottage door to join Lukas, taking care not to step in the mud and disturb the marks we'd found. A section of window on the right-hand side seemed to have been cleaned as if someone – possibly Grace – had cleared away the grime in order to peer through. I bent down slightly and looked inside.

The cottage was dark and small, probably with only one bedroom. It had definitely been abandoned for some time judging from its desolate air and the heavy layer of dust that was visible even from the window. I gazed at the shabby, grimy chairs and saw several well-established cobwebs. If Quincy Carmichael had been here, it was a long time ago.

I glanced at the door again. I'd already broken the law by acting while suspended, not to mention what had happened with Alfie. Perhaps I should go the whole hog and kick in the door to get a better view of what was inside. Then I shook my head; I wanted to maintain at least a scrap of integrity if only for a short while longer.

'They didn't go inside the house,' I said aloud. 'But they must have been out of sight when the perp fiddled with the car.' I took a step back, noting the overgrown path at the side of the cottage. 'They must have gone around the back.'

I hadn't even finished speaking when Buffy started marching around the exterior wall. Lukas and I exchanged glances then followed her, picking our way through prickly brambles and bushes to get to the garden on the other side of the house. I sniffed the air, breathing in the overpowering reek of fresh manure. Cows, I thought. And sheep, just as Fred had complained about. But no missing gremlin, and nothing to suggest that coming here was enough reason for someone to try and kill Fred and Grace.

'It's a big garden,' Buffy observed.

I nodded absently. It must have been beautiful once. There was an old apple tree in one corner with the remnants of a rope swing hanging from one of its branches, several unkempt rose bushes and a little bench. Despite its ramshackle state, it would be a good spot for someone who wanted to get away from the city for a weekend. It wasn't far from the centre of London, but it felt rural enough to have been a hundred miles away.

Lukas went towards the back of the garden where a rickety wooden fence was barely standing upright. He stopped before he reached it, looked to his right then called me. 'Emma.' His voice sounded strained.

A trickle of apprehension ran down my spine as I hurried over to him. When I saw what he was looking at, the trickle became a deluge.

Buffy peered curiously over my shoulder. 'What's that?'

'It must be a well.' I stared at the boarded-up hole and the circle of neatly mortared stones beneath it.

'Like a wishing well?'

I met Lukas's eyes; we were both thinking the same thing. My toes curled inside my shoe. The penny I'd placed there at Lukas's suggestion was still under the sole of my foot; if I concentrated, I could feel it through the my sock.

'It's a more utilitarian than a fairy-tale version,' Lukas said. 'But, yes, I believe it's a well.'

Buffy's brow creased. She was far from stupid, and she'd been in the room when I'd had that Cassandra vision. 'Hang on,' she said slowly. 'When we were at the hospital, you said something about a wishing well.'

I stepped forward before she put two and two together. With Lukas's help, I slid the wooden cover away from the top of the well. Several spiders scuttled away as we removed it but I ignored them and dropped to my knees to gaze into the dark depths. An old rope, connected to what I assumed was a bucket, was tied to a rusty hook set in the inner side of the stone wall. I peered past it, attempting to pierce through the gloom.

'Is there anything down there?' Lukas asked.

I could only see darkness. I leaned back, away from the

well's edge and took off my shoe. Feeling like an idiot, I held my breath and tossed the coin in, making a silent wish for Grace and Fred. The coin dropped straight down and disappeared into the darkness. I listened hard and caught a faint clink followed by a muffled splash. My eyes narrowed.

The soft morning light glinted in Lucas's black eyes as he looked at me. He bent down, took off his shoe and removed the coin.

'You don't have to do this,' I whispered. Although it was a small action, it was a direct reaction to my Cassandra vision. No matter how much Lukas said he didn't care about my new skill, accepting the prophecy without question had to be difficult for him.

He offered a crooked smile and threw in his coin. This time the sound was more like a dull thud, as if he'd hit something hard instead of the edge of a metal bucket and water. I bit down hard on the inside of my cheek, then I motioned to Buffy. 'Come and have a sniff,' I said. 'Your sense of smell will pick up any water down there.' Or anything else that might be concealed in those dismal depths.

Buffy stayed where she was, her gaze flicking between Lukas and me. 'Buffy?' I said, with a trace of impatience.

She folded her arms, her expression thoughtful – and calculating. She was clearly trying to work out what was going on. Then her spine stiffened and her eyes widened. Uh-oh. 'I see,' she murmured. 'Now I see.'

Lukas started forward but I put my hand on his arm and shook my head, willing to wait it out while she decided what to do next. After several long seconds, she tossed her head and marched to the lip of the well. 'And you guys tried to ditch me,' she sniffed. 'This is exactly why you need a wolf around.'

She got onto her hands and knees and dipped her head into the well to take a sniff I hoped that her uncharacteristic silence meant she'd decided not to question my prophetic chants and was going to feign ignorance, though I doubted it. Buffy was totally loyal to Lady Sullivan and her clan, and would probably blab at the first opportunity. But I could still hope.

Lukas's mimed shoving Buffy into the well and walking away. I rolled my eyes and he smirked. She straightened up and gave him a suspicious glare. 'If you're thinking what I think you're thinking...' she began.

Lukas put up his hands. 'I have no idea what you mean.' He changed the subject and pointed down the well. 'What can you smell?'

Her answer was simple and immediate. 'Death,' she said. 'I can smell death.'

I reached into my pocket and pulled out a pair of the disposable gloves I always carried. Putting them on, I reached for the rope and tugged hard. Whatever it was connected to was heavy.

'Be careful,' Lukas cautioned. 'The rope is rotting in several places. If it snaps, it'll be impossible for us to bring up whatever's down there without professional help.'

That was probably why Fred and Grace hadn't tried to do it. I had no doubt they had found the well but, in the absence of a search warrant or a werewolf's keen sense of smell, Grace would have erred on the side of caution and planned to return when he was better equipped.

I was willing to throw caution to the wind because circumstances demanded it, but I noted Lukas's words. I raised the rope slowly and tried not to yank too hard. Buffy reached across to help but I muttered her away; I only had one pair of gloves and I couldn't risk any further contamination of the scene, not if this was what I thought it was.

My phoenix skills endowed me with strength and speed; every time I died, I grew stronger. I now had considerable muscle – but the strain of heaving that rope upwards, inch by careful inch, made my arms ache and sweat break out on my brow.

'Jeez. Just how deep does this thing go?' Buffy asked.

I answered her through clenched teeth,. 'Deep.' I heaved some more. Even I could smell it now; the nasty reek of rot, decay and death was filling my nostrils. I squeezed my eyes shut as I yanked on the last few metres of rope. Not long to go now.

Buffy gasped aloud and I sensed Lukas stiffen. I opened my eyes to take a look then stumbled backwards as the ancient bucket and its gruesome contents came into view.

'Don't let the bloody thing fall back down!' Buffy shouted

I hissed under my breath at her, righted myself and moved the loose rope out of the way to grab the bucket's rim and pull it out. The skull inside, with its sparse tufts of matted hair and few remaining scraps of decaying flesh, grinned at me emptily.

CHAPTER EIGHTEEN

I sat on the old, worn garden bench, sucking clear air into my lungs and reminding myself that Laura had told me not to vomit at crime scenes. The combination of morning sickness and physical effort, not to mention the decapitated head, was doing my stomach no favours. I was used to dead bodies by now – hell, I was often a dead body myself – but I didn't often come across rotting body parts.

Lukas handed me a lukewarm bottle of water from the car. 'It's definitely a gremlin,' he said. 'But whether it's Quincy Carmichael or not isn't clear.'

I nodded. Formal identification would have to be via dental records because there wasn't enough of him left for anything else, but there was little doubt that it was Quincy, however. The gremlins were a small community. There were no other recent or historical investigations or reports about dead or missing members.

'Buffy thinks the rest of him is still down at the bottom of the well,' Lukas went on. 'It's only chance that his head ended up in the bucket. He was probably cut up before his body was thrown in.'

How lovely. I swallowed hard and took a sip of the water then wiped my forehead with the back of my sleeve. The fresher air and the liquid were helping. I was going to manage to hold my stomach together after all.

'So years ago somebody murdered Quincy Carmichael and threw him down that well,' I mused aloud. 'They made it look as if he'd just run away. Tony was suspicious and investigated, but eventually concluded that Quincy had indeed run off.'

I took another glug of water and thought about Phileas's reaction to his missing nephew. Even Quincy's family and friends believed he'd simply done a runner. The poor man.

I sighed and continued. 'Then Supe Squad re-opens the case and the killer, who must still be around and be part of the supe community, finds out. He gets scared that his actions will be discovered so he takes drastic steps to halt the investigation.'

Buffy ambled towards us, avoiding the worst of the brambles and nettles. 'How long is it since Quincy Carmichael disappeared?'

'Thirteen years,' I said.

'Some bastard killed that damned gremlin thirteen years ago and then tried to kill my Fred yesterday. What happened in between? Has he been murdering other people and getting away with it?' Sudden fury sparked in her eyes. 'Have you been allowing a fucking serial killer to wander around murdering people for thirteen fucking years, detective?'

Lukas stood up. 'Watch it, wolf.'

'Watch it? Watch *what*? She's the one who's supposed to be the detective! How many people are dead because this wanker wasn't caught thirteen years ago?'

'None of this is Emma's fault.'

Buffy bared her teeth. 'Somebody is to blame!'

Lukas snarled back at her, giving as good as he got. 'Werewolf or not,' he said, 'I am not beyond sinking my fangs into your damned jugular and—'

'Enough.' I got to my feet and inserted myself between them. 'Buffy's question was a good one.' She stuck her tongue out at Lukas. 'But your attitude,' I told her, 'was not.'

She stuck her tongue out at me.

I counted to ten in my head. What I wouldn't give to be here with Fred and Grace. 'Unless the clans are holding out on us,' I looked at Buffy, 'or the vampires,' I looked at Lukas, 'there are no other unexplained disappearances or deaths from the supe community apart from Simon Carr and Adele Cunningham, who were murdered over the same weekend. Whoever killed Quincy could have been targeting humans in the interim years. There are obviously far more humans than there are supes so it'd be far easier to murder a few of them and conceal their deaths. But thirteen years is a long time, and if our killer has been on the go for that long a pattern would have emerged. Somebody would have noticed something.'

'What's your point, detective?' Buffy sneered.

I told myself that patience was a virtue and went on. 'Everyone who's been targeted over the last few days has been targeted for a reason. Alan Cobain was killed because I can't be killed. However, I *can* be suspended if I'm under suspicion for murder.'

Lukas nodded. 'Cobain was nothing more than a convenient victim. You were the real target.' His voice was as hard as granite.

I didn't disagree. 'Then Fred and Grace took up the investigation, found this place and were targeted too. These aren't random acts of violence, there's a very real motive behind each one.' I sucked on my bottom lip. 'We're not dealing with a psychopathic serial killer who has a taste for blood, we're dealing with someone who kills for a specific reason.' I nodded towards the gruesome bucket. 'Quincy Carmichael was killed for a reason. I reckon if we can uncover that reason, we can find our man.'

'You said he was in a lot of debt,' Lukas said. 'If somebody was pissed off that he owed them money...'

'No, I don't think it was that. This killer is methodical. There's logic behind his actions, vicious cold-hearted logic but logic, nonetheless. If you kill the person who owes you money, you'll never get that money back. Quincy was murdered for another reason. We have to find out what that reason was.'

Buffy straightened her back and raised her chin. 'So where do we start?'

'You and Lukas report what you've found here.'

'What? To the police?' she asked, disbelievingly. 'They'll only get in our way. And it's not like we can tell Supe Squad! You don't exist anymore, remember?'

I wasn't likely to forget.

'D'Artagnan is right,' Lukas said.

Buffy scoffed, 'Of course you're going to take her side.'

'We're all on the same side.' He glared at her in a manner that suggested he was less than thrilled by the thought. 'We have to report a body to the authorities and in the absence of Supe Squad, that's the Met Police. They can take charge of retrieving the rest of Carmichael's remains and he'll be identified as supe. Because of the law, the police will then have to step back and not involve themselves any longer. We'll be free to conduct the remainder of the investigation ourselves without further interference.'

His mouth thinned. 'And that means looking again at what happened to Simon Carr and Adele Cunningham. We found no obvious link at the time but things have changed now.'

I was glad we were on the same wavelength. 'Exactly. And while you two are dealing with that, I'll go and take a DNA test.'

Suddenly it was Lukas's turn to protest. 'What? Why would you do that?'

I remained calm. Now that my stomach was no longer churning, it was easier to think clearly. 'I can't avoid it. If I don't turn up to take the test, I'll be under even greater suspicion.'

Lukas frowned. 'And if you take the test and those damned hair strands are somehow a match for yours, you'll be arrested and charged.'

'But it will take a while for the results to come through,' I argued. 'If I take the test, either my name will be cleared or I'll be banged up because the bastard framing me is covering all bases. If I *don't* take the test, I'll definitely be arrested. I need to hedge my bets. This will give us all enough time to find out who's really behind all of this.'

What I didn't add was that it would also give me time to say a proper goodbye to Fred and Grace, if it came to it. I prayed it wouldn't, but I had to be prepared. I suppressed a shiver. 'You two need to watch your backs. You'll be targets now as well.'

'Before the next hour starts, every vampire in London will be searching for anything they can find about Quincy Carmichael,' Lukas declared.

'Every werewolf too,' Buffy added. 'I'll make sure of it. The bastard who hurt my Fred can't kill all of us.'

Anxious happiness gripped at my heart. All for one. And one for all.

Using Lukas's phone, I called Barber and arranged to meet him at New Scotland Yard, then the three of us prepared to part company. Lukas and Buffy were taking her car in one direction and Tallulah and I going the other way.

Before we drove off, we all checked our tyres. I didn't think that Tallulah would allow anyone to sneak up and loosen her wheel nuts, but that didn't mean I wasn't going to check. We didn't know where the bastard behind all this was, and he could still be watching us. Anything was possible.

I tried – and failed – not to smile at the sight of Lukas in Buffy's car. He'd found it cramped in Tallulah; in a bubble-gum pink Smart car, he looked completely ludicrous. It was good to have a moment of genuine amusement amid the darkness.

I sent him a smile through the window and enjoyed his answering scowl. Then I spoke aloud. 'Fred, Owen and Tallulah, I promise you that I'm going to find the bastard behind all of this.' I paused. 'No matter what happens.'

Tallulah's answer was to allow her engine to be started without any chokes or splutters. I lightly touched my stomach. 'You hear that, Jellybean? This is your first important life lesson. We don't give up on our people. Ever.'

I watched Buffy's car disappear into the distance and put my foot down to accelerate. A split second later, I was hammering on the brake. Shit. *Shit.*

Bright flashes of light danced in front of my eyes, then I saw two narrow, glinting yellow eyes staring at me from across a dark pathway. A second later the eyes vanished and I saw my hands stretched behind me, handcuffs securing my wrists. That was followed by the image of a gun, its lethal muzzle turning towards me, and more flashes of light.

My mouth opened. 'Bang!' Sharp pain filled my chest. 'Bang. BANG!' The gun fell and I choked. My chest hurt so much that I couldn't breathe. I couldn't breathe. Oh God – *I couldn't breathe.* I looked down. There was blood trickling down my body, washing across the curve of my stomach and coating it red.

My vision swam as unbidden tears sprang to my eyes. I sucked in air, gripped the steering wheel and pulled as much oxygen as I could into my lungs. This was the first time I'd properly felt a Cassandra vision. I'd seen things and I'd said things before, but I'd never *felt* anything until now .

I rubbed my wrists. No steel cuffs encased them. I reached up and gently pressed my fingertips against my heart. My chest felt sore, as if someone really had squeezed a trigger and shot me, but it hadn't happened and it wasn't real. Not yet.

'Jellybean,' I whispered. Oh, my jellybean.

I wiped away my tears and took a moment to compose myself. I was alone inside Tallulah, and I wasn't in any danger. I gulped another breath into my aching body then I pressed down on the accelerator again and started the drive to New Scotland Yard. Right now there was nothing else I could do.

CHAPTER
NINETEEN

It felt different walking through the glass-fronted doors of the police headquarters now that I was officially suspended from duty. As soon as I strode inside, I felt like everyone was staring at me and judging me.

I bit back the temptation to scream at the top of my voice that I wasn't one of those police officers who blithely committed any number of heinous crimes while pretending to uphold the law. That would only make me look more guilty, not less. Instead, I passed through the metal detectors and waited patiently to be escorted upstairs for my DNA test. Apparently I could no longer be trusted to wander these halls by myself.

I'd hoped – but hadn't expected – that it would be Barnes who would fetch me, and I couldn't help a surge of relief when her familiar face appeared. I knew she'd be fair and she'd look at all the evidence before jumping to any conclusions. And she knew at least some of what was going on.

I got to my feet as Barnes offered a brisk nod of greeting. 'Emma.'

'Ma'am.'

She raised an eyebrow at my meek politeness but didn't

comment. 'I'm receiving regular updates from the hospital. I'm truly sorry for what happened to your colleagues. This is a very worrying situation.' That was the understatement of the year. 'How are you holding up?'

'Fine,' I muttered. Or at least I would be when I found the bastard who was behind this shit.

Her clever eyes narrowed a fraction. 'It seems unlikely that these events are unconnected.'

'Indeed.'

'What are your thoughts?'

'I'm suspended,' I said. 'It's not my place to comment.'

'Hmm.' She frowned. 'It's good that you called in your solicitor. We're going to need to interview you again formally about these latest events.'

I couldn't help myself. 'Is that because you think I killed Alan Cobain, set my office building on fire and arranged for two of my colleagues to almost die in a car crash?'

DSI Barnes stared at me impassively. I sighed. 'Lead the way.'

She remained where she was. 'This is a Met Police matter, not a supe matter. You need to make sure everyone knows that.'

I folded my arms.

'I mean it, Emma. I've spoken to Dr Hawes. Alan Cobain did not resurrect and all indications suggest that he was entirely human. As are DS Owen Grace and PC Frederick Hackert. Plus, the Supe Squad building is Met Police property.'

'Partly funded by the supe community.'

'It's still ours. And it's not only Supe Squad that's been destroyed – the hotel next door has been condemned. You're not the only ones who've been affected by this. I understand that emotions are running high, but these events are for us to investigate. Not the supes. Not Horvath.'

'Yep.' I nodded. 'Sure. Of course. I'll make sure everyone knows that.'

Her lips tightened and I knew she didn't believe me. I wouldn't have believed me, either. Even so, her voice softened. 'I can arrange for some support for you. Whether you're suspended or not, we have counsellors on staff who can—'

'I am fine.'

'Are you?'

I gave a wan smile. There were only so many times I could say the same thing. 'Ma'am, I am just peachy.'

Barnes sighed, but at least she said nothing more.

I SUBMITTED to the DNA swab, then I was directed to an interview room where Jon Barber was waiting. He stood up as I entered but I waved him back to his seat. 'I've been told what's happened,' he said. 'I'm very sorry.'

I appreciated his concern. 'Thank you.'

He pushed a hand through his hair. His grey suit was rumpled and there were shadows under his eyes; he looked as if he'd had less sleep in recent days than I had. However, he still projected the same calm aura. He'd not been scared away by my Cassandra revelation, or by the shocking events of the last twenty-four hours. Although he looked younger than me, I had no doubts about his capabilities.

'Here.' He reached into his briefcase and took out a small black phone. 'It's pretty basic and there's no internet function, but at least I'll be able to call you if I need to.' He gave me a meaningful look. 'The way things are moving, I need to be able to contact you.'

I was the prime suspect in a murder investigation and he

didn't want me to skip town on his watch. I chose not to take offence at the implication and accepted the phone. 'Thanks.'

Barber nodded. 'There's something else,' he said. He picked at an invisible speck of lint on his arm and I suddenly realised that he was still nervous of me and what I could do.

'Go on,' I said warily.

'I looked into the incident you mentioned, the one on Baker Street.'

I stiffened. 'That has no relevance to anything else that's going on.'

Barber held up his hands. 'Hear me out. I've spoken to a few different people and it turns out that the attacker was known to the victim.'

I could have guessed that. I shrugged. 'Okay.'

'The victim used to work with him at the same tour guide company but she had a hand in getting him fired when he started embezzling funds. He held a grudge. His computer has been impounded and it's clear that he's been stalking her for a long time in a bid to get his revenge.' Barber leaned forward. 'As time went on, his hatred towards her grew and he determined to hurt her.'

Jesus. If nothing else, he was now in jail where he belonged.

Barber continued. 'He's been interviewed at length and he's not held anything back. He didn't just want to kill her, he wanted her to suffer too. He'd planned to wait until her tour group arrived – he thought you were part of that group and that's why he approached when he did. He was going to attack everyone in the group before he attacked her. He wanted her to watch while he destroyed her livelihood.' He paused. 'But she survived and she's recovering in hospital. He didn't kill anyone because *you* intervened. You weren't the impetus for his attack – you stopped it from being far worse.'

I wanted to believe him. 'You don't know that for sure.'

'But I do. He didn't just have the knife and the concealed blade in his boot, he was carrying a gun in his bag. He didn't have time to get it out because of you. Your vision saved a bunch of people.'

I stared at him, then licked my lips. My mouth felt as dry as sandpaper. 'You're sure?'

Barber smiled. 'I am.'

Inevitably my mind turned to the vision I'd had before I'd driven here. Was there a way to stop it from happening after all? 'Two of my three colleagues are in intensive care after an accident last night. I received no visions, no prophecies, *nothing*.'

Barber met my eyes. 'Maybe that's because there's nothing you could have done to stop it from happening.' He paused for a long moment. 'It's worth thinking about.'

I leaned back in my chair. Perhaps it was.

Something inside me had eased slightly by the time that Barnes and Katling came into the interview room. I smiled at them both, even DI Katling who was as grim faced as ever. 'I'll answer all your questions with as much detail and honesty as I can,' I said, pre-empting any dark warnings from either of them.

'As you should,' Katling snapped.

Barnes merely smiled. 'Where were you last night between the hours of six and nine?'

Liza must have left Supe Squad at six, and Lukas's phone had rung with news of the fire just after nine. 'I was with my boyfriend, Lukas Horvath,' I told him. 'At our flat.'

If Barnes was surprised at my confirmation that our relationship was back on, she didn't show it. 'We will require a statement from Lord Horvath.'

'I'm sure that won't be a problem,' I replied.

'Did anyone other than your boyfriend see you there? Were

there any visitors to your home who can attest to your alibi?' Katling asked.

'It's a vampire-owned building. Several of them saw us enter.'

Katling's lip curled. 'Several vampires.'

'Yes.'

'Who work for Lord Horvath.'

'Yes.'

'Who's also your boyfriend.'

I sighed. 'Yes.'

'What about any humans? Did any humans see you?'

Barber stepped in. 'Detective Inspector Katling, you seem to be suggesting that any supes who confirm my client's whereabouts cannot be trusted simply because they are supes. Are you aware that prejudice against supes is illegal in this country?'

I didn't miss the flash of fury in Katling's eyes. 'I am not suggesting prejudice against anyone, supernatural or otherwise,' he spat. 'This is about Emma Bellamy's relationship with a supe which might encourage him to lie for her – and encourage him to compel others to lie for her.'

I glanced at Barnes. 'Sounds prejudicial to me.'

DSI Barnes didn't miss a beat. 'Let's move on, shall we? Where were you this morning, Emma?'

'At the hospital, waiting for news about Fred and Owen.'

'You left there not long before seven and you didn't arrive here until four hours later. You're still wearing last night's clothes, so you didn't go home to change. Where have you been in the meantime?'

'I tagged along while Lukas and a werewolf known to us both visited a property on the outskirts of London. They're looking into the disappearance of a gremlin, and the murder of a werewolf and a vampire several years ago. These are all supe cases. They don't involve human police.'

'Supe Squad would have been involved.'

My response was stark. 'Supe Squad is dead in the water.' I lifted my chin. 'In any case, I believe that Lukas is making a report at his nearest police station to ensure that correct procedures are followed.'

Barnes didn't miss a thing. 'Why is he making a report, Emma? What did you find?'

'A dead body.'

Katling rose out of his chair. 'Another body? Another person is dead?'

I stayed where I was. 'He's been dead for a long time. And he's not human.'

'You're suspended,' Barnes reminded me. 'You cannot take an active role in any investigation.'

That was where I was on shaky ground. 'By law, the Supe Squad fire isn't a supe concern and neither is what happened to Grace or Fred or Alan Cobain. None of those matters have anything to do with supes, as you have already pointed out, ma'am. In this case, the reverse is true. The body discovered this morning is not a Met problem, it's a supe problem.'

Katling bristled. 'We'll need a post-mortem to confirm that.'

'And that is why Lukas is reporting what was found,' I said.

'Is this body related to the fire or what happened to Fred and Owen?' Barnes asked quietly.

I prevaricated. 'The body has been undisturbed for many years. Whoever it is, their death is not a new development.'

Barnes would have asked for more detail but Katling was already jumping back in and changing the subject, as if attempting to throw me off balance. 'Did you kill Alan Cobain?'

'No. As I have already stated, I never met Alan Cobain.'

'Did you set fire to the Supe Squad Building?'

'No.'

'Did you run Frederick Hackert and Owen Grace off the road and cause their vehicle to crash?'

My eyes hardened. 'No.'

My solicitor intervened before my temper got the better of me. 'Do you have any evidence at all that Emma Bellamy was involved in any of these incidents?'

'She was at the scene when Cobain was killed.'

'Outside the scene. Not at the scene.'

'There was a phone call made to us that stated she'd been seen arguing with Cobain.'

'An anonymous phone call, an *uncorroborated* anonymous phone call, the details of which my client refutes,' Barber stated. 'She has already answered all these concerns. Do you have any real evidence that she is involved?'

I waited, wondering if Katling was going to mention the hairs that had been found. Given my friendship with Laura, Barnes had to assume that I knew about them. Neither of them said anything.

Barber straightened his tie. 'In that case,' he said, 'we are done here.'

DSI Barnes looked at me. 'Sooner or later you are going to have to decide if you're a supe or if you're a detective.'

I met her eyes. 'Until now, I'd always thought I was both,' I answered quietly.

CHAPTER
TWENTY

There were many things on my to-do list, not least having a shower and getting a change of clothes, but first there was somebody I had to speak to. Given my circumstances I should have asked Buffy or Lukas to do it, but I felt strongly that Phileas Carmichael needed to hear it from me; I owed him that much.

I didn't tell Jon Barber where I was going. The poor man didn't have to know everything.

At first glance, Carmichael's street looked the same as always. There were the same people – mostly supe – going about their day. The bin beside the bus stop was overflowing, the large pothole that had been in the road for months was unchanged, and the usual overzealous pigeons were pattering about the pavement looking for dubious treats.

Even Carmichael's small office appeared no different but, when I glanced towards the flats opposite, the events of recent days were obvious. Two of the windows had been blown out and nothing but taped plastic sheeting was blocking out the worst of the weather. Although the window on the third window remained intact, the glass inside was covered with a sooty film. Crime-scene tape barred the ground-floor entrance.

Passers-by were giving the building a wide berth as if they could be contaminated by mere proximity, but those fears hadn't stopped several other people laying flowers outside the building. I resisted the urge to go over and see what messages had been left. The investigators would be keeping an eye on them on the off-chance that the killer decided it would be funny to leave a note of condolence.

I was the main suspect for Cobain's murder so staying as far from the scene as possible would be wise. I was risking a lot by coming here at all.

I turned away and faced Phileas Carmichael's office. Normally, I'd have walked in and waited until he was free, but that didn't seem right under these circumstances and I hesitated. I couldn't see anybody through the window or the boarded-up door, so I pressed the intercom button. It didn't take long for Phileas to answer. 'The door is already open.' His disembodied voice sounded irritated.

I hunched over the intercom. 'It's me,' I said. 'It's Emma Bellamy.'

I heard a crackle but no words.

I tried harder. 'I need to talk to you. It's not about Alan Cobain, Phileas. I won't mention him at all. It's about Quincy.'

There was a sigh. Then, 'Come on in.'

I opened the door and stepped into the bright, sunny reception area. The faint scent of wolfsbane and verbena tickled my nostrils, causing unexpected tears to well up in my eyes. The smell was so evocative of the Supe Squad offices that it was hard to think of anything else. I gritted my teeth. The last thing Phileas Carmichael needed was my tears.

The interior door opened and the gremlin solicitor appeared, adjusting the cuffs on his perfectly tailored suit. We'd always had a good relationship, but there was no denying the angry, suspicious glare in his narrowed eyes. I wondered if he truly believed that I'd thrown petrol over Alan Cobain and set him alight – or if he had truly believed that Alan Cobain was a phoenix.

'You've found him?' he asked, not bothering to disguise his disdain. 'Let me see if I can guess. Quincy has been found propping up a bar in the Costa del Sol while peddling drugs to stupid tourists.' He raised his eyebrows and glanced at my face. 'No? He's serving ten years for fraud, then.' He sniffed.

I shifted my weight. The easiest way to say it was to come right out with the news. 'We've found a body.'

It took a moment for my words to sink in and at first I thought Phileas hadn't heard me. Then the gremlin started to blink furiously. 'A body? A dead body?' His voice was rising. 'Quincy's body?'

'You know how the process goes,' I told him. 'There's not yet been a formal identification and, given the state of the remains, that may take some time. But it's definitely the body of a gremlin who has lain undiscovered for several years.'

Carmichael staggered back and his arm stretched out for a chair. He grasped the arm rest and sank down. He knew as well as I did that the body had to belong to Quincy. 'I thought he'd done a runner,' he whispered. 'I thought—'

'Everyone thought that,' I said. 'This isn't your fault.'

His eyes snapped to mine. 'I know it's not my fault!' He winced suddenly. 'Sorry. I didn't mean to sound so harsh. I just —' He shook his head. 'I just can't believe it.'

I felt nothing but sympathy for him. 'I'm sorry, Phileas. I truly am.'

'Did he die naturally? Did he kill himself?'

'The body was found down an old well on the outskirts of

London. It was covered over.' In other words, he didn't fall in by accident. Somebody put him there.

His shoulders sagged. 'Quincy was murdered.'

I wetted my lips. 'It appears that way. Lukas is reporting it to the nearest police station and they will start the process of retrieving the remains and identifying them. When it's established that the body is that of a gremlin, control of the investigation will pass back to the supes.'

Phileas's head jerked. 'What about Supe Squad?'

'I'm suspended,' I said gently.

'You're not the only Supe Squad detective. There's that Owen Grace fellow and the young plod – Fred something.'

My next words were shaky. 'They were in a car accident late last night. They're both in a critical condition. And there was a fire at the Supe Squad building. There's nothing left of Supe Squad.'

He stared at me; he obviously hadn't heard the news. 'So who's going to find the bastard who murdered my Quincy? This is your job! You're supposed to be the one who does this! What's the fucking point of Supe Squad if none of you are around to investigate a murder?'

He got to his feet and glared at me, then sat down again. A second later he stood up. 'I don't care if you *are* suspended. You have to find out who did this. Did you kill Cobain?'

If Phileas Carmichael believed that I might have done it, then so would many others. 'No.'

'Well, then.' He looked down before mumbling, 'I didn't really think it was you.'

Uh-huh.

'I didn't!'

'Did you think Cobain was really a phoenix?' I wasn't accusing him, I was simply curious.

His cheeks flushed. 'I thought it was possible.'

I gazed at him. I was certain he was telling the truth – not that I supposed it mattered now.

Phileas toed the edge of a rug and returned to thoughts of his nephew. 'My poor sister. She always thought he'd come back one day. We all did.' He clamped a hand over his mouth and shrank further into himself. 'She died without knowing that it wasn't his fault and that he didn't run away.'

I took the chair opposite so that we were on the same level. 'We found him at a small cottage just north of London,' I said. 'It's called the Love Nest and seems to have been empty for a long time. Have you heard of it? Did Quincy own it?'

Phileas's hands twisted together in his lap. 'I thought he'd sold it to pay off some of his debts. That's what he told me.'

So it had belonged to Quincy at some point, even if it didn't belong to him now. 'What did he use it for?' I asked.

'It was part of his stupid dating agency thing.'

I frowned. 'Like an office?'

'No. Not like that.' His reddened eyes met mine. 'You know what things were like for us a couple of years ago.'

I nodded.

'Well,' he continued, 'they were worse before. A lot of supes never left Soho or Lisson Grove because they didn't feel safe anywhere else. But we were on each other's doorsteps, so we all knew each other's business. You couldn't take a shit without somebody else hearing about it. Part of Quincy's plan for his dating agency was to provide somewhere couples could get away to for a day or two. He made a big deal about offering a confidential service that covered all bases. He said it allowed lovers to get to know one another and have a few test shags – his words, not mine – without the pressure of every other supe in London knowing what they were up to.'

Actually, that wasn't a bad idea.

Phileas noted my expression. 'Quincy wasn't stupid. He had

a knack for finding gaps in the market and exploiting them. There was a time I thought the dating agency idea was the one that would make it. He was more enthusiastic about it than anything he'd done before.'

He ran a hand through his hair. 'But it eventually fell by the wayside like all his other projects. He came to me for a loan to keep it going, but by that point I was tired of bailing him out so I said no. Three weeks later, he'd abandoned the agency in favour of fake-blood products for vampires.'

He looked away. 'We had a big blow-up about it. I told him that the reason he never succeeded at anything was because he jumped from idea to idea. He always gave up too easily, never worked through the tough times to see something through to the other side. For all his clever ideas, Quincy was a quitter at heart.' He pulled a face. 'He almost punched me when I pointed that out to him.'

His eyes filled with sudden tears. 'He's dead. He's actually dead. All these years...' Phileas buried his head in his hands, his grief getting the better of him.

'Is there someone I can call for you?' I asked.

'No. I'll do all that,' he said, his words muffled. He pulled his hands away. 'But you will look for the bastard who did this to him, won't you?'

'I will, Phileas.'

'I'm sorry about Alan Cobain, I truly am. I'll call the police and tell them it wasn't you.'

I smiled sadly. 'It won't make any difference, but I appreciate the thought.'

'The other two from Supe Squad?' he asked. 'Will they be okay?'

It was my turn to look away. 'I don't know. I really don't know.'

IT TOOK a few attempts but I eventually dredged up Liza's phone number from my memory. When she answered, she sounded exhausted. 'I'm going home for a few hours to get some sleep and pick up some bits and pieces for Owen. There's no change,' she said. 'Not in either of them.' Her voice caught and I felt a stab of pain in my heart.

'The pair of them are tough buggers,' I said. 'They'll pull through.' My stomach churned. God, I wished I could trust my own words.

Liza gave a teary sniff. 'Yeah,' she said. 'I'm going to kill Owen when he wakes up for putting me through the wringer like this. And I'm never making another cake for Fred. Not ever. He doesn't deserve it.'

I laughed weakly. We were both putting on a brave face – and we were both aware of the true gravity of the situation. 'I'm going to be using this phone number for the time being,' I told her. 'If you need anything, or if anything changes at all, you call me.'

'I will.'

'I mean it, Liza. Whatever I can do, I will do. For all of you.'

There was a beat of silence. 'A policeman was round earlier, some young fresh-faced bloke who'd barely heard of Supe Squad. He said that they were looking at the car, that it seems somebody deliberately sabotaged Owen's vehicle.'

'Yeah,' I whispered. 'I know.'

'You're looking for the fucker who did this, right?'

'You bet your arse I am. And I'm going to find them.'

She sniffed again. 'Good.'

The faith she injected into that single word almost derailed me. 'Do you have help at the hospital? Did Lukas's vampires arrive?'

'Yes – and a dozen werewolves from all four clans, as well. Nobody's going to get to Owen or Fred. If anyone tries, they'll be ripped apart. These guys aren't playing.'

That was what I wanted to hear. 'If you or Catherine or Fred's parents have any trouble with them—' I began.

'They're being very respectful. Fred's mum and dad are shocked but grateful. Some pixies dropped by earlier with some food, and the ghouls have sent a note. So have the goblins. Everyone wants to help.'

Go the supe community; they were on our side after all. 'I'm glad. You'd better get home and get that rest, Liza.'

'I will. You take care of you too. And that baby.'

I swallowed hard. Then I hung up.

TWENTY-ONE

Although I didn't feel any better emotionally and my damned morning sickness was making an unwelcome return, I was considerably refreshed and energised when I stepped out of the shower an hour later. I towelled off my hair and checked my phone in case any of the people I'd sent my new number to had gotten in touch. There were a few messages of goodwill but nothing important. I was getting dressed and considering my next move just as the front door opened and I heard Lukas call out a greeting.

I padded through the flat and smiled at him. He didn't hesitate but strode over to gather me in his arms. You would have thought it had been days since I'd last seen him instead of a few hours. 'How are you holding up?' he murmured into my ear.

'I'm okay.'

'Would you tell me if you weren't?'

I considered. I'd already decided I wasn't going to tell him about my most recent Cassandra vision. It would worry him far too much, and there was nothing either of us could do about it right now because I didn't know when the attack would happen or who it would involve. I couldn't let anxieties about what was going to come affect what needed to be done now.

'Yes,' I said. 'When I'm not okay, I will tell you.' I wasn't lying. I needed Lukas, and our recent separation had only made me realise how much.

Lukas kissed me and pulled away with a satisfied nod, then he pointed towards the living room. I heard an odd, strangled noise from that direction and my brow furrowed. Lukas's jaw clenched. 'Buffy!' he yelled. 'I told you not to hurt him!'

Uh-oh. My stomach flipped and I hurried through.

I wasn't sure what to expect, but it certainly wasn't a satyr trussed up on the sofa like a turkey with strands of sparkly tinsel hanging from one of his horns. Kennedy reeked of booze; the smell wafted off his body, though his eyes were reasonably clear and focused when he looked at me. 'Bringing police brutality to a new level, are we?' he enquired.

I hissed annoyance under my breath. 'Why is he tied up?' I demanded of both Lukas and Buffy

'He didn't want to come,' Buffy replied with an insouciant shrug. 'Or talk to us.'

I turned to Lukas and glared.

'He was determined to refuse,' Lukas told me, suddenly avoiding my gaze. 'And we all know that time is of the essence, given the DNA test you took this morning.'

I grunted with irritation. Kennedy, meanwhile, began to hum tunelessly before turning to me and grinning. 'They're right,' he said cheerfully. 'I didn't want to come and I don't want to talk. Time spent talking is drinking time lost. I was having fun and these two ruined it. Tell me, have any of you every tried a mushroom cocktail?' He smacked his lips. 'They're quite extraordinary. It's like food and alcohol together – a drink, plus one of your five a day.'

'Five a day?' Buffy looked genuinely confused.

I stared at her. 'You know. Five portions of fruit and veg a day, as per government regulations.'

She pulled a face. 'What? Why is it their business what I put in my mouth? And *five* portions? Are you crazy?'

This was not a conversation I wanted to get into. Instead I nodded at Kennedy. 'Let him go.'

'That's not a very good idea,' Lukas began.

'Let him go.'

Buffy tutted, reached for the ropes and tugged at them.

'I've seen him like this before, Emma,' Lukas warned. 'He's on a bender that won't stop until his body gives way.'

I'd seen drunk Kennedy plenty of times before. In fact, I wasn't sure I'd ever seen him sober.

'I'm a bloody satyr!' he grunted. 'Wine, women and song. It's what I do!'

'It happens every few years,' Lukas said. 'He'll keep going for days until he passes out. Last time, he spent two days in a semi-coma in St Luke's Hospital.'

Kennedy winked at me. 'Don't judge me. It's a satyr thing.'

'A satyr thing, my arse,' I told him. 'You're using it as an excuse to abdicate responsibility for your own well-being.'

He looked unconcerned. 'Personal responsibility is a modern concept that doesn't take into account the pressures of a supernatural existence. I'm all about my own well-being, and my well-being demands vodka. Or gin. Absinthe. Whisky. Hell, even fermented mushrooms will do, as long as they're forty percent proof.'

'Stop talking shite,' Buffy snapped, finally undoing the last knot.

Kennedy smiled at her – then a second later he bolted for the door. Unfortunately his foot caught in one of the luxurious thick rugs that covered the wooden floor and, instead of escaping, he stumbled forward with his legs and arms akimbo. He only narrowly avoided smashing his head against the corner of the glass-topped coffee table.

'Oops,' he burbled as he struggled back up to his feet and tried again to dash for the door. For fuck's sake.

'The rope's for his own good,' Buffy said, jumping forward and looping it around Kennedy's wrists again.

'Hey,' he protested.

'We need to ask you some serious questions, Kennedy,' I said.

He gave me a look filled with alarm. 'Whatever it is, I didn't do it.'

'All I need is fifteen minutes of your time,' I continued. 'Can you give me that?'

He smiled sloppily. 'Anything for you. Come talk to me next week. Tuesday is good.' He pursed his lips. 'Actually, nah. Better make it Wednesday. I'll give you all the time you want then.'

'We need to talk now, Kennedy.'

'I'm busy now.'

I walked around until I was facing him. 'Please.' I needed him to agree before kidnapping and false imprisonment were added to my list of personal failures.

Kennedy blinked at me slowly, looked towards the door then looked back at me. 'Alright,' he said finally. 'But only because it's you. I like you.'

I breathed out. 'Thank you.' I motioned to Buffy.

'He'll try and escape again,' she said. I shook my head. No, he wouldn't. 'Fine. But I'm not running after him again. You can do it.' She released him for a second time.

The satyr grinned at her, winked at me and lurched for the door. Buffy gave me a look as if to say *I told you so*. Kennedy, however, halted and spun around several times like an unbalanced ballerina before facing us once more. 'Fooled ya.' He lowered himself to the floor. 'Go on then, detective. Whaddaya wanna know?'

'You can sit on the sofa, Kennedy.'

'I like the floor.'

I glanced at Lukas. He shrugged. If you can't beat 'em, join 'em. I sat cross-legged on the floor in front of him. 'I need to ask you about Quincy Carmichael,' I said. 'I know the two of you were friends.'

'Quince?' A melancholy smile flickered across Kennedy's face. 'Quince is dead.'

I blinked. Kennedy was the first person I'd spoken to who didn't believe that the entrepreneurial gremlin had run away. 'Why do you say that?' I asked carefully.

He made a show of looking around. 'Because he's not here.'

I sighed. 'Kennedy...'

'If Quince was still alive, he'd be here,' he said. 'He'd be in London. Everyone thinks he ran away, but he wasn't the type to do that. He had his faults but he faced up to his mistakes. Always. And he loved London. He loved being a supe and working to improve things for supes. He's not in Spain, he's dead. I'm sure of it.' He squinted at me. 'But I didn't kill him, if that's what you're thinking. He was my friend. My buddy. My...' he screwed up his face and thumped his chest '...brother from another mother. We were kindred.' His words, although faintly slurred, were heartfelt.

'Did you tell anyone you thought he was dead?'

'Plenty of times. Nobody believed me.' His bottom lip jutted out. 'I went looking for him – I spent weeks trying to find him but there was no sign of him.'

'Did you go to his cottage and look there?' I asked. 'The Love Nest?'

Kennedy leaned forward and took my hands. 'How's that crossbow coming along? Can you use it properly yet?' Once upon a time, Kennedy had taught me how to aim and fire the crossbow correctly. His help had been invaluable, but it had nothing to do with Quincy Carmichael.

'Did you go to the Love Nest?' I persisted.

'Where is your crossbow, anyway?' Kennedy frowned. 'You should have your weapon with you at all times.'

'Kennedy, answer the question.'

'I mean,' he said as if I'd never spoken, 'just because you can't die doesn't mean you can't be hurt. You can't get complacent. You need to live above your ability, not below your capacity.'

Kennedy was certainly living above his capacity for alcohol. Lukas sucked in a breath behind me, obviously preparing to step in and shake Kennedy for answers. I gestured to him to stay quiet. I wasn't going to be side tracked, no matter how hard Kennedy tried. 'Did you go to the Love Nest when you were looking for Quincy?'

'Of course I did,' he finally replied. 'He wasn't there. I looked all around the little house. There was no sign of him.'

'Did you look around the garden?'

As he met my eyes, it seemed to dawn on him why I was asking all these questions. His face fell and his bottom lip trembled. 'You found him, then.'

I hedged my bets. 'We found someone.'

'In the garden?'

I nodded. 'Down the old well at the back. Do you remember if you looked there?'

The satyr stared at me, then he sniffed loudly and several tears rolled unchecked down his cheeks. 'Poor old Quince,' he whispered. 'My poor boy.'

I waited for several moments, giving him the time he needed to compose himself, but I still needed to know if Kennedy had checked the well when he was there. We'd never be able to get a wholly accurate time of death; forensics didn't work that way, and it had been far too long since Quincy Carmichael had died. It would be helpful, though, if we could establish whether the murderer had killed the gremlin at the scene or brought his corpse to the cottage to dispose of later.

Lukas handed Kennedy a handkerchief. Buffy tapped her foot impatiently on the floor but at least she had the sense to remain quiet. We all watched while he dabbed at his tears and blew his nose before nodding slightly to indicate that he was okay to continue. There was a different light in his eyes now, grief providing the clarity that alcohol had temporarily washed away.

'Did you—' I started.

'Check the damned well? Yes, I checked it. Of course I checked it. It was probably the first place I checked. I almost fell down it myself on more than one occasion. I always told Quince he ought to board it over.'

I tried to keep my voice casual. 'Quincy didn't board up the well? He left it uncovered?'

'Yes.'

'How soon after he disappeared did you visit the cottage to look for him?'

Kennedy squinted, trying to remember. 'A couple of days at best,' he said. 'Everyone went crazy once that dead wolf and vamp were found, and a few people had mentioned that it seemed a strange coincidence that Quince had disappeared right after it happened. I wanted to find him and tell him to get back before mild suspicion grew into outright accusation.'

He gave me a pointed look, indicating that he knew I was a prime suspect in Cobain's murder. 'Once a particular name gets bandied about in relation to a crime it can be difficult to shake off the stigma no matter how innocent that person might be.'

Indeed. I hastily pushed away my discomfort at my own

predicament and continued. 'Was the well boarded over when you were at the cottage looking for him?'

His gaze was steady. 'No. And while I may not have the nose of a werewolf, I'm reasonably certain that I'd have smelled the rot if there was a fresh dead body stuffed down it.' Yeah, he was probably right.

Buffy cleared her throat. 'So what does that mean?'

It was Lukas who answered her. 'Quincy Carmichael wasn't killed at the Love Nest. Whoever murdered him killed him elsewhere and dumped him there later. But the killer must have known that the cottage was empty, so they must have known Quincy.'

I nodded grimly. 'What can you tell us about his business dealings, Kennedy? He'd started up a fake-blood business at the time he vanished. Did he know anyone who wouldn't have wanted it to continue for some reason?'

'He had some disagreements with the bloke who helped him make the products. A pixie – Birch Kale, I think.'

I could be proved wrong, but I didn't believe that Kale was involved in Quincy's death. He'd wanted his money back so he'd needed Quincy alive. 'Anyone else?'

Kennedy shrugged.

I glanced at Lukas. 'Fake blood is for the vampire market. Are there any vamps who might have taken umbrage at Quincy's venture?'

There was a defensive flicker in Lukas's black eyes but he took a moment to consider the question seriously. 'I can't think of anyone. It was only thirteen years ago, but nobody at the time believed that fake-blood products would ever be of use, or that they'd ever be lucrative. I guess nobody stopped to consider that humans might be more interested in them than vampires.'

Fair point. 'Who's the biggest manufacturer?'

'You mean who would benefit the most if a fellow competitor disappeared?' Lukas asked. 'This isn't Coca-Cola versus Pepsi. The companies that make these products are small. They do well out of their businesses but they're still niche industries. There isn't a market leader.'

Kennedy licked his lips. 'Can I get a drink?'

'In a minute,' I said.

He sighed heavily. 'There's a limit to how long I can sit here without a vodka chaser because I'm answering questions about a business that Quince didn't even care about.'

My eyes narrowed. 'What do you mean he didn't care about it?'

'I mean that if somebody had wanted to take the fake-blood business away from Quince, he'd probably have given it to them. He only started it to clear his debts from the dating agency. It broke his heart when he couldn't keep that bloody agency going, and he always planned to return to it one day. He wanted to play Cupid and change people's lives, to be invited to weddings and wear a big hat while being lauded for bringing love into the world. He was a terrible business owner with no head for money, but he was also a huge romantic and a true softie at heart. He would have walked away from any disagreement, not provoked a violent fight that got him killed, whether it was business related or otherwise. Whenever I got into trouble and he was around, he always tried to calm things down. He often didn't succeed because I didn't listen to him, and he ended up in trouble because of me several times. But you have to understand that Quince wasn't violent. Me maybe, but Quince never.'

Kennedy's expression was earnest; he was desperate for me to understand that his dead friend was a good guy and what had happened to him couldn't have been his fault. But that wasn't what gave me pause. It was the dating agency; everything always seemed to lead back to it.

'The vampire and the werewolf who were murdered,' I said suddenly. 'Simon Carr and Adele Cunningham. Did they meet via Quincy's dating agency?'

It was Lukas who replied. 'No. It was established at the time that they got to know each other at a local supe yoga class.'

I stared at him. 'Supe yoga?' Why had I not heard about that before? I'd have signed up straight away.

He shrugged. 'It was the in thing for a while. A lot of the wolves liked to do it while they were in animal form.'

Buffy blew air through her teeth. 'It makes downward dog pretty easy to master.'

I transferred my stare to her. '*You* do yoga?'

She cracked her knuckles. 'I like to stay flexible.' Okay, then.

Kennedy coughed and mumbled something so I turned back to him. 'What did you say?'

He mumbled it again. 'She was his client.'

Lukas stiffened. So did I.

'Adele Cunningham? She was a part of Quincy's dating agency?'

Kennedy nodded. 'I only remember because I was with him when her body was found.' He rubbed his neck awkwardly. 'We were in the Clink at the time.' He pulled a face and sighed. 'One of the many times that my actions got Quince into hot water. Anyway, one of the guards told us what had happened, and Quince was really upset. He'd liked Adele a lot.'

'What about Simon Carr?' I asked, suddenly feeling a thrill that we were onto something. 'He knew Quincy, but was he one of his dating agency clients too?'

'I don't know. Quince didn't mention him. He only spoke about Adele.'

I could feel Lukas bristling. 'This never came out at the time,' he growled.

'Quince took confidentiality seriously,' Kennedy said.

'She was murdered!'

'Maybe he would have told you that she'd been one of his clients,' Kennedy said quietly. 'But before he could, he was murdered too.'

This time, we all exchanged glances.

TWENTY-TWO

We walked with Kennedy to the nearest pub. As soon as it came into sight, he all but sprinted inside, as desperate for his next drink as he was to get away from us. All the while I watched him go, my mutterings grew louder. 'I knew in my gut that there was a link between Quincy Carmichael and that double murder. I knew it and I didn't pay enough attention.'

'We're far more to blame than you are,' Lukas said.

'I'm not!' Buffy interrupted. 'I was twelve years old when all that shit happened. It's hardly my fault!'

'I mean the whole supe community is to blame,' Lukas said. 'Everyone looked into Simon and Adele's murders – the wolves and the vamps, not to mention a bunch of others. I don't remember anything about the dating agency coming up and I've been back through the files. You can see them for yourself. There's nothing there.' His mouth thinned. 'But there should have been.'

Buffy folded her arms. 'It's still not *my* fault.'

'Candace,' I said to Lukas, ignoring her pout. 'The vampire

who was Quincy's girlfriend for a while. You were going to ask her to speak to Grace and Fred.'

He jerked his head in agreement. 'I contacted her, but I don't think she managed to get to them before the accident. I'll track her down now and find out what she has to say. Maybe she remembers something about Quincy's dating agency.'

I glanced at Buffy, who still retained the expression of a recalcitrant teenager. 'Can you speak to the Carr Clan? Find out if anyone who knew Simon Carr back then remembers if he was a client as well?'

'I'm not interested in Simon Carr. I'm not even interested in Quincy Carmichael.' Her voice was rising. 'I'm interested in who hurt my Freddie!'

I touched the back of her hand to try and calm her. 'They're probably the same person. If we can find the murderer from thirteen years ago, we can find the bastard who burned down Supe Squad and tried to kill Fred and Grace.'

'And,' Lukas added with a dark growl, 'framed you for murder.'

I nodded. 'That too.'

Buffy sniffed. 'What are you going to do while we're doing the scutwork?'

'More scutwork,' I answered without missing a beat. 'I'm going to hit the streets and find out everything I can about Quincy Carmichael.'

I checked my watch. It was already well past lunchtime and the hours were ticking away. As soon as the DNA check came back on those strands of hair found, I could find myself behind bars. As long I was free, I was going to fight – but time was definitely of the essence.

At least now, however, we had some leads.

~

Despite my snarky response to Buffy, I only had a vague idea where to start. I wanted to know more about Quincy Carmichael because I was convinced that the answer to everything lay with him, but it was thirteen years since he'd been seen on any London streets. The trail wasn't simply cold, it was frozen. It was just as well I liked a challenge.

I headed to Dorset Street. From what I remembered of the now-destroyed files, Quincy had maintained an office there, which he'd used during each of his failed businesses. It was a good location, nestled between Soho and Lisson Grove and close to the smaller enclaves where communities such as the pixies and the goblins often congregated.

I found a parking space at the far end and started to walk, noting the small businesses and shops that still dotted the street. As I moved, I felt several people gaze at me with unashamed curiosity and their stares made my skin prickle. Yeah. Dead woman walking. Shamed detective. Impending disaster. That was me.

I'd just passed a tiny store selling electronic goods when I spotted the cluster of teenagers laughing at the bus stop on the opposite side of the road. They sounded raucous and were clearly enjoying themselves, but their laughter halted abruptly when they noticed me. I resisted the temptation to wave at them and continued on my way.

I didn't get far before one of them called out, 'Oy! Detective!'

I didn't answer to Oy, and right now I couldn't call myself a detective. I kept walking, wondering at what point in this mess I'd allowed my turbulent emotions to get the better of me when it came to dealing with the public.

I nodded at a wizened pixie who was waiting for her tiny Jack Russell terrier to finish sniffing at a lamp post – and that was when I felt someone grip my shoulder.

Instinct took over. I whirled around, clenching my hands into fists and preparing to swing at whoever was about to assault me. When I saw one of the teens blinking at me in white-faced fear, I just managed to pull back my punch in time. 'Creeping up on someone is not a good idea,' I snarled with more force than was necessary.

The teenage boy, who on closer inspection was a goblin, held up his hands and backed away. 'I'm sorry,' he said. 'I called out to you first.'

I was far too fucking jumpy; that was what happened when your entire existence and some of your best friends were targeted by a murderous bastard who was intent on ruining you.

I dropped my shoulders and relaxed. 'No,' I said. '*I'm* sorry. I shouldn't have reacted like that.'

I looked his gangly body up and down. His complexion didn't yet have the lustrous golden sheen that adult goblins possessed. Presumably it didn't matter which line of the supe divide you were born into; when you were a teenager you always suffered from bad skin. A faint line of fuzz lined his upper lip, indicating that he was already well into the latter stages of puberty, and his shining eyes were very earnest.

He shuffled his feet, clearly nervous, especially after I'd yelled at him. 'I just wanted to say that I was sorry to hear about your friends,' he mumbled.

Well, shit. Now I felt even worse.

'And about the building too,' he added. 'My mum works at the Talismanic Bank and she told me that they're putting together a fund to help you rebuild it. Everyone's contributing, not just the goblins.'

The old pixie, whose dog continued to be oblivious to the chatter, piped up. 'It's true,' she said. 'I've donated.' She patted my arm. 'We're with you. And we're all hoping those two boys of yours recover.'

Abruptly, I realised that the people on the street had been staring at me not because they were horrified at what they thought I might have done but because they were horrified at what had happened to Supe Squad. Hot tears welled up in the back of my throat. This was unexpected, *wholly* unexpected.

'Thank you,' I managed. 'Both of you. Thank you. I needed that right now.'

The young goblin's cheeks coloured. The pixie merely nodded briskly. 'You're looking for information about Quincy Carmichael, right?' she asked.

I blinked in surprise. 'Yes.'

She smiled at me. 'Word gets around,' she said. She pointed towards the end of the street. 'He used to work out of number forty-three. I know you'll likely check in there no matter what I say, but the people working there now didn't know Quincy at all. When he disappeared, it was the folk from the cobblers over the road who moved into the premises. They moved again a few years back because they needed somewhere bigger.'

The goblin youth spoke up. 'You should check with the café at the corner as well. It's owned by a goblin couple who've been there for decades. They knew Quincy Carmichael too – they told me he used to go there every day for his lunch.'

All this intel would save me valuable time. I opened my mouth to thank them once again but, before I could, my vision lurched and black spots appeared in front of my eyes. The images came swift and fast, flickering through my brain at lightning speed. The teenage goblin. A bike. A cat running across the road. An old oak tree. A sickening thud echoed through my ears followed by a flash of the boy lying on the ground, his eyes staring sightlessly upwards and a trickle of blood dribbling onto the cracked pavement from the side of his skull.

I staggered to the side and immediately threw up. Squashed chunks of banana infused with bile splattered by my feet. The goblin placed a tentative hand on my back. 'Are you okay?'

I sucked in several shallow gulps of air and waited for the worst of the nausea to pass. When I straightened up and looked across the road, I spotted the bicycle chained to the lamp post behind the bus stop where the goblin's friends were waiting. It was the bike from my vision.

I whirled around and met his eyes. 'Listen to me. This is important.' I pointed at the bike. 'You do not get on that thing *ever* if you are not wearing a helmet.'

He took a step back, clearly confused both by my public vomiting and my abrupt change of subject. 'How...' he stammered. 'How did you know that was my bike?'

I didn't take my eyes from his face. 'Do you hear me? You never cycle anywhere without a helmet. Not ever.'

The young goblin seemed to think I was reprimanding him. 'I usually wear one,' he said. 'I just forgot it this time.' His gaze shifted. 'Okay, maybe I forgot it a few times. My mum's always on at me but—' His voice trailed off and he shrugged.

I wagged my finger in his face. 'You wheel that bike home and don't get back on it until you have that helmet securely fastened to your skull. And you *never* forget it again.' I glared at him. 'Promise me.'

He licked his lips. 'I promise.'

'I mean it,' I said. 'If I find out you've not been wearing it, even once, then—'

He backed further away. 'I'll wear it.' He looked at his friends. 'I should go now. The bus is about to come. I won't get on the bike when I come back. I won't.'

'Good.'

He sent me another anxious look then he ran across the road without checking for traffic. I ground my teeth.

The pixie, whose experience was obviously telling her more than I wanted her to know, gave me a thoughtful look followed by an approving nod. 'I best be on my way, love,' she said. 'We're all thinking of you and your friends.' She tugged on the dog's lead and together they wandered away, just as the goblin's bus finally appeared and he clambered aboard with his mates.

I looked at the bike against the lamppost. I could have walked across and removed it, leaving the kid without it and the mortal danger it presented, but he might have another one at home or he might borrow a friend's bike. He might realise that I'd removed the bike and ride without a helmet out of resentment. Taking the bike away from him wasn't the answer, but the order I'd given him was.

I reached into my bag and found an old receipt and the stub of a pencil covered in fluff. Perfect. I scribbled a note. *No riding without a helmet. I will be watching!* I marched across the road, tucked the note onto the handlebars where he'd be sure to see it and gave a satisfied nod.

Barber seemed certain I'd helped the tour guide who'd been attacked. I'd have to pray that my note would be enough to help the goblin and that my visions weren't flashes of an immutable future.

CHAPTER
TWENTY-THREE

The old pixie was perfectly correct about the premises that Quincy Carmichael's string of businesses used to occupy; the owners of the gift shop that now operated from the space had barely heard of him. I was in and out of there within three minutes flat. The old-fashioned cobblers were more helpful; for one thing, they'd been Quincy's neighbours before they'd taken over the shop – and they were also gremlins.

'I wouldn't say we were close friends,' the proprietor, Reginald Dooley, told me, 'but I knew him well enough. He was polite and well-mannered, even when he was at his lowest. He always made me think of the sort of lad who would flog you slightly stale apples that he'd nicked from somebody's tree, but would help you carry those apples home and peel them for you. He wasn't a bad chap. I always wondered what had happened to him.'

I picked up an old, scuffed shoe from the counter and absently looked it over before returning it to its place. 'Did you see many of his customers when he ran the dating agency?'

'A few. I thought that he didn't have many clients, but my

wife told me that most of them came late at night when it was already dark.' He pursed his lips. 'I guess they were a bit embarrassed to be using a dating agency. I don't know why. It's pretty normal nowadays.'

Beatrice, Reginald's wife, looked up from the leather she was working on. 'A lot of the people who used that agency were looking for something a bit unusual,' she said in a judgmental tone. 'Unnatural couplings, that sort of thing.'

Reginald winced but I seized on her comment. 'Unnatural?'

'You know.' She frowned. 'Inter-species relationships.'

They were still relatively unusual, but I was willing to bet that there had always been couples who found love outside their own species. Robert, the Sullivan beta wolf, had married a pixie and remained deeply in love with her long after their divorce. I knew other long-standing couples who were in so-called mixed marriages and very happy together. Hell, look at me and Lukas. Even so, there would always be people who seized on others' differences and found fault with them.

Reginald sent his wife a death stare and coughed loudly in a very pointed manner. She glared at him, then her expression altered and her eyes widened. 'Oh! Wait, I wasn't talking about you! I don't have a problem with your relationship with Lord Horvath. I don't have a problem with any mixed-supe relationships.' She shook her head. 'What I can't understand is when a human and a supe get together. It doesn't make sense to me. We're too different.'

I reckoned Buffy might have something to say about that, given her sudden but seemingly deep-seated adoration of Fred. 'Quincy Carmichael's dating agency included humans?' I asked.

'Oh yes.' Beatrice nodded vigorously. 'Lots of them.' She shuddered. 'Fucking weird, if you ask me. Humans are inherently weak and inherently judgmental.'

Look who was talking. If Quincy Carmichael had human

clients, it would make this investigation considerably harder. Not only would it widen the pool of suspects but, with no records of his clients, it would be nigh on impossible to track any of them down.

I asked a couple more questions before thanking them for their time. 'Anything to help Supe Squad,' Reginald said, in a tone that suggested he meant it.

Beatrice agreed with him. 'We're very happy to help. Whatever you need.'

I smiled at them, then I looked again at the old shoe on the counter in front of Reginald. 'Actually,' I said suddenly, 'perhaps there is something else you can help with.'

ONCE I'D FINISHED at the cobbler's, I made a beeline for the café. The exterior looked shabby, with peeling paint and several letters missing from the overhead sign, but the interior was warm and welcoming. The décor wouldn't have looked out of place in the seventies and yet it was somehow back in fashion, so the café had a comfortable, bohemian atmosphere. I could see why somebody would come here for lunch every day. In different circumstances, I'd have been tempted to curl up in the far corner and spend the day ordering gigantic cups of steaming hot chocolate while I watched the world go by.

I made a mental note to bring Lukas here if we ever managed to drag ourselves out of this quagmire. I was certain he'd love it. In fact, I realised with a flash of cautious delight, there was more than enough space in that corner for a pram as well. Then I remembered that I might be giving birth in prison and immediately sobered up.

'Oh, aye,' the café owner said, wiping his hands on his apron after coming out of the small kitchen, 'Quincy

Carmichael was here all the time. He wasn't very healthy. He usually had our big fry-ups. Good as they are, they're not the best thing to be eating day in and day out but he loved them. Couldn't get enough of our hash browns.'

'Did you talk to him much?' I asked.

'We passed the time of day, but it wasn't serious stuff. I was surprised when he vanished, but I never thought for a moment that he'd killed that couple. You know, the wolf and the vampire who were murdered around the same time. He wasn't the type.'

Anyone could kill. We just needed the right – or rather the *wrong* – circumstances to combine at the wrong time. We all had a limit beyond which we could be pushed into violent action. Fortunately, most of us never reached that limit – but some people's limits were far lower than others. All the same, I smiled at the café owner. Nobody needed to hear my cynicism, certainly not this fellow. And there was no chance that Quincy had murdered either Simon Carr or Adele Cunningham.

'Did Quincy come here alone?' I asked. 'Or did he bring people with him?'

The man frowned. 'Hmm. He was usually on his own but there was the odd occasion when he'd have somebody with him.'

'Can you remember who?'

'I have a good memory for stuff like that,' he assured me. 'Sometimes he was here with a satyr – Kennedy, I think his name was.' The owner grimaced. 'He usually had a flask with him that he'd sneak out when he thought I wasn't looking. There were a couple of other gremlins from time to time – that solicitor fellow,' that would be Phileas, 'and a woman who I think was Quincy's mother. There was a human male a few times, too.'

I stood a fraction straighter. This was new. 'Do you remember the human's name?'

The café owner shook his head. 'I'm afraid not. I don't think we were ever introduced, and I'm not sure I'd recognise his face if I saw it again. It was a long time ago and my good memory doesn't extend to humans.'

Even if his memory was superlative, I'd have had no idea who the human was. Neither did I have any pictures to show the man, and anyway there was nothing to connect this mystery human to the murders.

'I do remember that he dressed weirdly.'

I frowned. 'The human?'

'Yep. Always looked as if he'd stepped out of a cocktail party a hundred years ago.' He touched his head. 'Big hat. Posh jacket, like you see some people at weddings wearing.'

A top hat and tails. A nervous chill rippled through my bones as I absorbed the information. 'Okay,' I said finally. 'Thanks for your time.'

He smiled at me. 'Here,' he said. 'Have a slice of chocolate cake. It's on the house. Anything for Supe Squad, any time.'

I pressed my lips together very hard as I reached into my pocket, slid out my wallet and found a five-pound note. I left the money on the counter while the café owner gave me a surprised look followed by an appreciative nod. I still had some standards left. Then I took the proffered cake.

My phone rang when I was back on the street. I slid it out of my pocket and recognised Laura's number. I answered it as I munched on the cake and walked back to the small car park where I'd left Tallulah.

'Hey, how are you?' she asked. Her voice caught. 'I've heard what happened to Fred and Owen and the Supe Squad building.'

'I'm alright,' I assured her. 'But they're in a bad way. I'm sorry I've not been in touch, Laura. I'm trying to find out if there's someone behind all this shit.'

'You don't have to apologise to me,' she said. 'I just wanted to make sure you're okay.'

'Then I'm okay.'

'Good.' She sounded relieved, but I sensed that she had something else to say. 'I'm glad you texted me your number earlier.'

I stopped eating and slowed my steps. Laura had news and I suspected that I wasn't going to like whatever she had to say. 'Go on.'

'First of all, I heard it was you who found the body in the well.'

'Yep.' I wasn't surprised that the body had been taken to Laura – in recent months, she'd become the go-to person for any supe-related deaths – but I was surprised that it had been retrieved so quickly. It wasn't a recent death so it wouldn't count as high priority, plus it must have taken considerable effort and equipment to get the remains out of the well.

'I've only done a preliminary examination but I can confirm that the bones are definitely gremlin.'

I sighed. 'I figured as much.'

'We're contacting the gremlin community. I'm happy to continue with a full post-mortem, if that's what they wish, but they might request that we release the remains to them instead.'

I sincerely hoped they opted for the former choice, but it wasn't my call. 'Do you have any idea how he died?'

'I knew you were going to ask me that.'

'I'm not looking for a definitive answer. Your best guess would do.' I held my breath, hoping she had something.

'There are some notches on the rib cage that are too clean to have been caused by rodents gnawing on the bones. I don't know if I'll ever be able to say for sure, but the marks are consistent with a stabbing.'

Adele and Simon were stabbed, and so was the tour guide on Baker Street. It was probably a coincidence, nothing more, but even so it strengthened my growing belief about the link between the murders. 'Thank you,' I said gratefully.

'There's more,' Laura told me. 'I don't know if this will be good news or bad news.'

I swallowed. 'Spill it out.'

'The DNA testing on the strands of hair found at the Cobain murder scene is being expedited. I expect to get the results by midday tomorrow.'

That was less than twenty-four hours away. I had to expect the worst and assume that Cobain's killer had gotten hold of my hair, possibly from my missing hairbrush, and planted it at the scene. There was no doubt that I was being framed for his fiery death.

I thought about the open window at Supe Squad. Somebody could have sneaked inside, but they'd have had to be sure that Supe Squad was empty and it wouldn't have been easy to keep a watch on the building, not with everything else the bastard had been up to lately. I thought about what the café owner had said about the mysterious human in top hat and tails and shifted uncomfortably.

'Emma?' Laura asked hesitantly.

'Thanks for the heads-up,' I said. 'I really do appreciate it.' I bit my lip hard. 'You can't call me again.'

'Pardon?'

I inhaled deeply. 'I promise you that I did not kill Alan Cobain. I didn't hurt Alan Cobain – I've never met Alan Cobain. But somebody wants the world to think I'm culpable and there's a chance that the strands of hair will be a match for my DNA. You're already going to be in trouble for speaking to me, not to mention letting me stay with you.'

'I don't think for one second that you killed him, Emma.'

A ghost of a smile traced across my mouth. 'But others do. You need to protect yourself. I'm sorry that I've dragged you into this mess.'

There was silence. When Laura spoke again, her voice had an edge of defiant huffiness. 'I'm not a mindless automaton. I have my own mind and my own will. Anything I have done, or any information I have passed to you, I decided to do myself. And it's never been a secret that we're friends. I'll submit a full report to my superior with everything we have spoken about, but I will not be ashamed about knowing you or helping you.'

Laura wasn't ashamed but I should be. She deserved far better – her job role deserved better – and, frankly, so did mine. 'You know we can't talk again until all this is resolved,' I said with a heavy heart.

She muttered a curse under her breath. 'Will it be resolved?'

I stared into the distance. It would be if I had anything to say about it.

I mumbled a pained farewell and hung up just as I reached Tallulah. Despite my determination and the support I was receiving from the supe community, there was an ache in the centre of my chest that was doing me no favours.

I wrenched open the driver's door, plonked myself down inside and took a moment to compose myself. Then I pulled on the seatbelt and started Tallulah's engine. The little car coughed and her engine gave a mild splutter, but she certainly didn't roar into life. I gritted my teeth and tried again. This time, I wasn't even rewarded with a cough.

'This is not the time,' I growled. 'We're on a clock. We can't fuck around, Tallulah.'

Still nothing.

I gripped the steering wheel. 'Tallulah, this isn't just about me. Fred and Owen are at death's door and Supe Squad is being rammed out of existence. Both of us will end up in the knacker's yard if we can't fix this.'

I sucked in a desperate breath, turned the key, and again nothing happened. Then, without warning, there was a click and my seatbelt released itself apparently of its own accord. I looked down at the useless length of fabric and my blood chilled. I extricated myself, opened the door and got out.

I popped the hood on Tallulah's bonnet and peered at the engine. Nothing looked amiss, so I closed it again and walked around checking each of the wheels. The wheel nuts were still firmly in place. I wet my lips. A moment later, I lowered myself until my belly was almost to the ground and glanced at Tallulah's undercarriage.

It took me three seconds to spot it.

The slim black box looked innocuous enough, apart from its red blinking light and the fact that it had no place hiding beneath my car. I stretched out my hand before thinking better of it and pulling back. I rolled away, stood up and dusted myself down.

This was a very real – and very dangerous – problem. Fortunately, I knew just the person who could help me with it.

TWENTY-FOUR

There were very few phone numbers I knew off by heart – that's not how the world works any more – but I didn't need to use my memory. Stuffed into my pocket was an invitation to the wedding of the year and I knew Scarlett had included her phone number.

As I stepped away from Tallulah, I scanned the car park and wondered if I was being watched from one of the darkened windows that overlooked it. Many of them were tinted, obscuring the view from any snoopers outside like me. I frowned.

There were only three other parked cars and they were all empty. I wasn't certain but, from what I remembered, they had been there when I'd arrived an hour or so earlier. I pursed my lips then I opened the wedding invitation, located the number and dialled it.

Scarlett's liquid voice filled the line. 'Good afternoon. I don't recognise this number and if this is a scam call, I will hunt you down and slide my single fang into your throat before I drink you dry. However,' she continued in an eerily pleasant tone, 'if I know you and this is a genuine call, then I'm thrilled to chat.'

'Hi Scarlett,' I said. 'It's Emma.'

'Detective!' She sounded genuinely happy to hear my voice. 'How lovely of you to call and how fabulous that things between you and my Lord are getting back to normal.'

Normal wasn't how I'd have described my life right at that moment, but I appreciated the sentiment. 'I've been suspended, Scarlett. I'm not currently working as a detective.'

'I had heard. You have my sincere apologies.' I could still hear the smile in her voice. 'If you would like me to threaten the police commissioner on your behalf, just say the word.'

'That wouldn't be a good idea.'

'You never know until you try,' she chirped.

I was suddenly very glad that Scarlett was on my side instead of against me. 'Everything is under control,' I told her, lying through my teeth but knowing she would get the message to stay out of my business.

'If you say so. Are you phoning to confirm your attendance at my wedding? Or is there something I can do to help with Quincy Carmichael? I know Lord Horvath has us all on the case, but if there's something extra you'd like me to do I'd be very happy to help.'

'Actually,' I said, 'it's not you I'm after. I'm phoning because I'd like to speak to your fiancé.'

'You want to talk to Devereau?'

'Please.'

Her tone altered. 'Why?'

'I could use his expertise.'

'Dev is on the right side of the law these days, more than you are.'

Scarlett wasn't wrong about that. 'It's nothing illegal and it's nothing to do with Devereau himself,' I said. 'It's a problem I'm having that I believe he can advise me on.'

'Hmm.'

I couldn't blame Scarlett for feeling doubtful, but a moment later I heard Devereau Webb's voice. 'DC Bellamy. It's been too long.'

'I'm not DC, Mr Webb. Not at the moment.'

'You'll always be DC to me.' He spoke with only the faintest edge of mockery. Given his history, I couldn't blame him for that.

Rather than dance around the topic, I quickly explained what I'd found underneath Tallulah. As soon as I mentioned it, Devereau Webb's manner became serious. 'It's too small to be explosives,' he said. 'And anyway, we all know there's no point in blowing you up.'

'Uh-huh.'

'Can you take a photo of the device and send it to me?'

I glanced at the small phone that Barber had given me. 'The phone I'm using is not that sophisticated.'

He clicked his tongue. 'Burner, yeah? Pain in the arse. I know what you're going through.' He knew because he used to be a minor crime lord. I wasn't convinced that close friendship was something that either of us wanted to experience, even though I believed we liked and respected each other.

'Well,' he continued, 'you've got two choices. It must be a tracking device of some sort, and a cheap one by the sounds of it. Given the tech available these days it's pretty large, so it's probably an amateur who's attached it to your car and not the Met police gathering intelligence against you and making sure you don't do a runner.'

I was more relieved by that than I cared to admit.

'Although,' Webb cautioned, 'sometimes the police go low-tech when they're trying to be strict with their budgets and they think they can get away with it.'

I grimaced.

'Option one, you can leave the device on your car and use it against whoever is tracking you to throw them off the scent. Turn the tables on them and track *them* instead. Option two, you can yank it off and I'll take a look at it for you. I might be able to trace where it comes from. Do you know how long it's been there?'

Hmm. 'Not long. Whoever planted it must have followed me here and attached it after I parked. Tallulah would have indicated before now if it had been there for longer.'

It was testament to Devereau Webb that he didn't comment about me telling him that my car would have communicated with me. 'So they could still be in the vicinity?' he asked.

'Yes,' I replied grimly.

'Could they be watching you right now?'

I swivelled around. The car park was tucked away from the main street and I caught glimpses of passers-by, but nobody else was visible. However, a lot of windows overlooked this spot and I still couldn't judge if anyone was watching me from any of them. 'It's possible,' I admitted. The back of my neck prickled uncomfortably.

'If they are watching and already know you've found it, you can't use it to draw them out.'

He was right. Option two it was then. 'Can you get over here and take a look at it for me?'

'Do a favour for the police out of the goodness of my were-wolf black heart, you mean?'

'I've been suspended. You're not doing any favours for the police.'

'True.' I heard the grin in his voice. 'Alright, then. It'll take me about half an hour to reach you.'

I checked my watch. 'That'd be great.' I gave him the address.

'See you soon,' Webb purred. He was enjoying himself far too much.

I hung up, patted Tallulah's bonnet and apologised aloud for snapping at her. The tracking device might prove to be the murdering bastard's biggest mistake or it might lead to yet another dead end; either way, I didn't have time to wait idly for Webb to appear. I wasn't going to cool my heels until he showed up, not when I could make myself useful.

I craned my neck for a third time towards the surrounding buildings. At least I could check them out and see if I *was* being watched from one of the tinted windows. Lady Luck hadn't been smiling on Supe Squad lately but maybe she'd be on our side now.

I told Tallulah to be a good girl and wait before I jogged out of the car park. I looped behind the buildings and checked the exterior of each one until I determined that there were three possibilities.

There was an office block, one of those ugly seventies' monstrosities that was more like a giant concrete box than a useful building, a low-rise set of flats and a small shopping centre with windows along one side that looked onto the car park. If I'd wanted to spy on someone, the shopping centre would be the easiest building to use. I headed inside.

It was only two storeys high and seemed to contain small stores that served the local residents rather than big chains that targeted a wider population. There were windows on the ground floor, but the view from most of them was blocked by the wall that separated the centre from the car park. With that in mind, I headed for the trundling escalator so I could check out who was hanging around the first-floor windows.

I marched past some shops, my shoes squeaking on the floor, then I veered left. A passage led towards the public toilets and a bank of windows where I immediately spotted a young woman. There was nobody else around.

Judging by the way she was perched on a narrow seat by

one of the windows and was gently rocking the pram beside her, she'd been there for some time. Her stocky frame and colouring – not to mention the tell-tale tag on her arm indicating that she was zeta – told me that she was a wolf. A sigh of relief escaped me; a supe would be far more likely to speak honestly to me than a human, whether I was suspended or not.

I slowed my steps and approached her gingerly. She glanced up with the exhausted eyes of a new mother, then put her finger to her lips and nodded at the pram. 'I've only just gotten him down,' she whispered.

I stood to the side where the sound of my voice would hopefully be low enough not to disturb the slumbering baby werewolf. 'I'm Emma,' I said. 'I'm—'

'I know who you are. Everyone knows who you are.' She wasn't being rude, merely matter of fact.

I smiled ruefully in acknowledgment of her words. 'Have you been here for long?' I asked. 'In this spot, I mean?'

She removed her hand from the pram and squinted at me, obviously puzzled by the question.

'I'm looking for someone,' I explained. I glanced out of the window. I could see most of the car park from here but only Tallulah's rear was visible. Hmm. 'They might have been hanging around here and looking out of the window.'

Her eyes widened. 'Is this to do with that missing gremlin?' she asked, forgetting to lower her voice. 'And that human who was set on fire last week?'

The baby stirred and emitted a tiny grumble that was probably the cutest thing I'd ever heard. His mother flinched with alarm. 'Sorry, bud,' she whispered, reaching out with a practised hand to resume rocking the pram.

'Have you seen anyone?' I asked, deliberately not answering her questions.

She shook her head. 'No. I've been here for almost forty

minutes. I nipped into the bookshop round the corner but he began wailing his head off. He might be small and cute, but he sounds like a banshee when he gets going. I took him out of the shop and brought him here to settle him down. It's my fault. It was almost time for his nap anyway.'

She looked in the pram. 'Isn't that right, my little bruiser?' she cooed, smiling at her slumbering son. She brushed away a curling lock of hair from his face, then her nose wrinkled and she glanced back at me. 'Actually,' she admitted guiltily, 'I've been focused on him. Somebody might have passed by, but I probably wouldn't have noticed them unless they'd blown a trumpet in my face.'

That might have been true, but the bastard behind all this wouldn't have risked hanging around. He might have come here first, but he wouldn't have remained. He certainly wasn't watching from here now; in any case, the angle wasn't quite right for surveillance.

'Thank you,' I said. 'I appreciate the help.' I looked into the pram. 'He's a lovely baby.'

A besotted grin lit up her expression. 'He's hard work but he's more than worth all the sleepless nights and screaming fits. You'll see when yours comes along.'

I jerked. I'd temporarily forgotten about werewolves' ability to sense foetal heartbeats.

'She sounds healthy,' the woman said.

'She?' Could she really tell?

Her grin widened. 'I could be wrong, but I reckon it's a girl. Congratulations either way.'

Sudden warmth suffused me. 'Thank you. And thanks for your time.'

I moved away and looked out of the window again but this time I wasn't checking the car park. There were two more build-ings to investigate. While I could only see the corner of the ugly office block from this vantage point, the low-rise flats were visible. From here, I could see into the shadowy stairwell, which hadn't been possible from the car park. If somebody could get inside the building, they could probably use the stairwell windows to spy *into* the car park...

I peered more closely, searching for anybody standing still and staring out. I couldn't spot anyone but they could be further back where they'd be less visible. That building would be my next stop; there should be plenty of time to scope out the public areas before Devereau Webb appeared.

As I smiled again at the woman and turned to go, a suggestion of movement from the flats caught my attention. My eyes flicked to the right and I saw that one of the windows was opening. One of the residents must be letting in some fresh air. It was highly unlikely that any of the inhabitants of that building was my target because I'd only parked in that tiny car park out of convenience.

I took a step back as a head emerged from the window and leaned out to look straight down at Tallulah. When I saw the narrowed eyes and familiar dark scowl, I went completely still. It was Stubman, the night-time bellman from the hotel next to Supe Squad.

CHAPTER

TWENTY-FIVE

It had to be a coincidence; after all, Stubman had to live *somewhere*. But it seemed strange that somebody with such an undisguised hatred for supes lived deep within the supe community. It was also strange that he'd chosen to work in a hotel in that same supe community.

I thought about the open window I'd discovered at Supe Squad only a few hours hours before Alan Cobain was killed. Stubman's job meant that he'd have been in the perfect position to know about the window. He could have climbed in during his break and picked off a few strands of hair from the brush I kept in my desk drawer. He'd also have known when the Supe Squad office was empty because he could watch all our comings and goings. And his uniform was a top hat and tails – just like the café owner had described when he'd mentioned the human who'd been seen with Quincy.

I told myself that I was clutching at straws; there was no actual evidence of anything illegal. All the same, when I looked out of the shopping centre window at the disgust Stubman was displaying towards Tallulah, a chill shuddered through me. If nothing else, his presence merited further investigation.

I ran out of the shopping centre and thudded along the same path I'd looped around before. When I reached the front of the block of flats, I paused at the main door and studied the labelled row of buzzers to the right of it. The entrance was supposed to be blocked to anyone who didn't have a key or who wasn't buzzed through, but the wooden wedge propping the door open suggested that security wasn't taken very seriously. Anybody could stroll in.

I ran my eyes down the buzzers again. There were only flat numbers, not residents' names, so it was impossible to learn if Stubman actually lived here. I nudged open the door slightly so I could slip inside and immediately saw the slim letterboxes along one side of the tiny lobby. Stubman's name was third from the bottom. Flat 2D.

I set my mouth in a grim line, then I spun away from the tiny lift and headed for the stairs.

Nobody was in the stairwell. Instead of going directly to Stubman's flat, I took the time to go up and down the whole staircase to make sure nobody was lurking behind any of the exit doors. Despite the large windows and the clean floors, the air smelled stale – it appeared that the residents of this building usually opted for the lift. But there was a good view of Tallulah. She was sitting in the same spot where I'd left her and there was no sign yet of Devereau Webb. I reckoned the view from flat 2D would be even better.

I returned to the second floor, just as my phone rang. Lukas. He'd probably found Candace and was calling to update me with the information she'd provided. Instead of answering, I sent him a quick text; my burner phone possessed a message function, if nothing else. *Can't talk now. Will call back in 15 mins.* Then, *Love you.*

I opened the door and walked down the corridor until I found 2D. My phone buzzed as Lukas texted back. *Love you more*. I smiled, pocketed the phone and rapped sharply on the door to Stubman's flat. Come out, come out, wherever you are.

There was no answer. I frowned and knocked again. Still nothing. Irritated, I pressed my ear against the wood and listened. Had Stubman somehow seen me coming? Was he hiding inside? I strained my ears but I couldn't hear so much as a whisper from beyond the door.

I pulled back and gazed at the lock. I could break the door down. Once upon a time, I wouldn't have possessed the strength to manage such a feat without the right equipment to hand, but my phoenix powers meant that now I had more than enough power to kick it open. But I didn't have a warrant, I was suspended from my job, and without anything other than coincidental circumstance, there was nothing to tie Stubman to anything illegal.

I hissed under my breath and padded back down the corridor to the stairwell, then peered out of the large window to see if I could glimpse Stubman still glaring out at Tallulah.

He wasn't in his flat any longer – he was outside on ground level in the car park itself. I could see the top of his shiny head from here. I grimaced. While I'd been checking the stairs and taking my time, Stubman must have exited his flat and used the lift. I'd missed him by minutes.

My stomach churned at the thought that he was deliberately avoiding me. I watched as he trudged along the pavement and paused to pick up something from the ground. He hefted it in his hand and then his stance changed. He turned, drew back his hand and threw the object towards Tallulah. A stone – the bastard was throwing a stone at my little car. He knew too much about her to get too close but there was no denying what he'd done.

The stone smacked into Tallulah's rear windscreen. I couldn't see if it had done any damage but I no longer cared. I stopped wasting time turning over my suspicious thoughts and took off, hurtling down the stairs to catch up with him.

I ran at full pelt, taking several steps at a leap more than once. When I finally reached the ground floor, I threw myself at the entrance door. Unfortunately, I was too focused on my target and not what was immediately in front of me, and I collided with a woman carrying two heavy bags of shopping. She let out a surprised oof and dropped the bags. Apples and oranges rolled down the narrow pavement outside the building. Shit.

'Sorry!' I darted for the escaping fruit, scooped it up and returned it to one of her bags.

'You should bloody watch where you're going!'

'You're right. I'm sorry,' I said again, handing her a tin of tomatoes. She snatched it from me and I splayed my hands out in contrition. Then, before she could berate me some more, I wheeled around her stiff, angry body and started running again.

Stubman was no longer in the car park. I left Tallulah where she was and darted to the main road, emerging through the narrow street until I had a clear view. I glanced up and down. There were bobbing heads and passing cars everywhere, but then I saw Stubman walking briskly across the road with his hands in his pockets. From the pace he was maintaining, he was in a hurry. I wasn't going to let him run away. I inhaled deeply and ran after him.

He disappeared down a side street as I reached the crossing. Reminding myself that I no longer had only myself to look after, and that getting hit by a passing car wasn't a good idea, I waited with growing frustration for a break in the traffic. It seemed to take forever but finally the lights changed. I sprinted across the road and turned into the same street Stubman had disappeared down moments earlier.

There was no sign of him. My feet came to a stuttering halt.

There were several small businesses lining the street: a tattoo artist with some intriguing designs displayed in the window; a swanky hotel called the Bell Plaza; a barber's, and a dusty-looking antique shop. Small roads branched off to the left and right. I wove in and out of the passers-by, glancing through the shop windows and peering down the streets, but I couldn't see Stubman anywhere.

The more time passed, the more convinced I was that he was trying to hide from me. Naturally, that only increased my determination to find him. I paused to peer down one of the wider streets and pushed myself onto my toes to get a better view over the heads of the passers-by. As I did so, I heard a loud crash from somewhere behind me.

I spun around to look. Directly in front of me was a dark alleyway. Of course there was. It was squeezed between two buildings and barely a metre wide. Rubbish bins and discarded piles of wooden pallets blocked some of the view. I pursed my lips; it was an ideal hiding place. I'd probably have walked right past it if I hadn't heard the crash.

I started moving down it, stepping carefully over the litter and shimmying past the pallets that almost blocked my path. The alleyway seemed to be blocked off by a wall, a dead end. If Stubman had swung down here because he wanted to hide from me, I'd find him. And soon.

As I began to march more quickly, my phone buzzed in my pocket. I ignored it and kept my focus on what was ahead. That supe-hating bastard couldn't run forever.

There was even more rubbish near the end of the alleyway and I had to squeeze around it to avoid snagging my trousers on rusty nails and sharp spikes of wood that jutted out dangerously. Suddenly my foot landed in a grubby puddle, soaking my shoe. Cursing, I glanced down – and spotted an old leather wallet nestled against a pile of discarded aluminium tins.

I bent down to scoop it up and take a closer look. When my fingers brushed against the leather, I sensed movement behind me – and I knew with sinking horror that I'd fallen for the oldest trick in the book. A split second later, before I could tense my body in preparation, something swung down on the back of my head. A flash of bright, white, blinding pain pierced my skull before the world spun and everything went black.

DAMP WAS SEEPING through my trousers and chilling my skin, and the throbbing pain in my head was almost unbearable. I groaned aloud, turned on my back and opened my eyes. I sucked in a breath at the sight of a blurry face peering down at me. So I hadn't been shot yet, then and this wasn't the Cassandra vision I'd seen earlier. Relief flooded through me.

Then I reacted and slammed my hands into my would-be assailant's cheekbone.

'For fuck's sake!' he snarled.

I blinked, swallowed and sat up. Oh. 'Shit. Sorry.' I waved a hand in front of my eyes, willing my vision to return properly. As the world around me sharpened, Devereau Webb's face swam into view.

'That's no way to greet your knight in shining armour,' he told me. 'Scarlett will kill me if I've got a black eye when she walks down the aisle.'

I grimaced. 'I didn't realise it was you.' When I reached up and touched the back of my head, my fingers came away bloody. Whoever had hit me had thrown all their energy into the blow. I hissed with pain, then accepted Webb's wary offer of a hand to help me to my feet.

'I'm amazed that anybody managed to bring you down when you've got a right hook like that,' Devereau Webb drawled.

'They sneaked up behind me,' I muttered, embarrassed.

'You didn't see who it was?'

I shook my head, then immediately regretted it because it only made the pain in my skull worse.

'You ought to take more care,' he chided. 'You can't take risks when you're pregnant.'

My answering glare was so ferocious that he released my hand and stepped backwards, obviously afraid I'd punch him again. Good. 'How did you find me?'

'I followed your scent.' Webb flashed a sudden smile. 'One of the many advantages I have discovered of becoming furry.'

I nodded in understanding then I stopped. 'What else do you smell?'

'I take it you mean beyond rotting food and damp wood.'

'I mean can you scent anything of the person who attacked me?'

'There is a lingering ... perfume in the air,' Webb said, 'which is oddly familiar.'

I stiffened. 'Familiar in what way?'

He shrugged with an ease that set my teeth on edge. 'It's human,' he admitted. 'And a human I've smelled before.' He raised his eyebrows. 'Unless I'm mistaken I recognise the scent from around Supe Squad.'

'*Inside* Supe Squad?'

'No. I can't smell anything in there, thanks to that damned verbena and wolfsbane that you use.' Webb paused. 'Did use. I'm guessing you can't smell anything there now apart from barbecue.'

I scowled at him but he only grinned again. When he sobered up, he said, 'The scent is familiar to one I've noticed outside the Supe Squad building, but I could be wrong. It's faint, and a lot of humans smell the same to me, so don't go thinking that anything I say will stand up in a court of law.'

I didn't need it to; he'd already told me more than enough. It was Stubman who'd attacked me. Alistair Stubman was behind all of this; he had to be. I nodded. 'Thank you.'

Webb gave me a crooked smile and pointed to the back of my head. 'You should get that looked at in a hospital, you know. You could have concussion.'

'I'm fine,' I muttered. I glanced down at the spot where I'd fallen. There was no longer any sign of the wallet. My mouth tightened as I turned to head out of the alleyway. 'I don't have time for concussion.'

He chuckled and started to follow me. 'If you say so, detective constable.'

'I'm...'

'...suspended. Yeah.'

I shot him an irritated look over my shoulder. 'Did you come straight here? Or did you manage to get the device from Tallulah?'

He pulled out the slim black box from inside his coat and waved it at me. 'I removed it first, then I came looking for you.' He bowed dramatically. 'You're welcome.'

'Thank you.'

Webb grinned again. 'Unfortunately it's a fairly standard device. You can get them off the internet very cheaply. I'll ask around a few places that I know sell them, but I don't think you'll get much joy.'

'It doesn't matter any more. I already know who I'm looking for.' Stubman had revealed his hand by attacking me and he was going to pay for what he'd done. In spades.

'You should probably answer that,' Webb told me.

'Answer what?' Then I realised my phone was buzzing in my

pocket. Bugger it – maybe I did have mild concussion after all. I pulled it out, expecting to see Lukas's number on the display, but it wasn't Lukas who was calling. It was Liza.

The pain in my head vanished in an instant but my stomach dropped to my shoes and fear tensed every muscle in my body. I pressed the answer button with shaking fingers, praying this wasn't going to be bad news. 'Liza?' I whispered.

'Hi, Emma. I thought I should call – I thought you'd want to know.'

I swallowed hard. 'What is it?'

'Owen is awake. And he's talking.'

CHAPTER
TWENTY-SIX

Devereau Webb crammed himself into Tallulah's driver seat and drove me to the hospital. I told her to behave and that having a werewolf at her wheel was only a temporary state of affairs. Fortunately, she obeyed; maybe she'd decided that Webb was acceptable because he'd removed the offending tracker from her underbelly. Or maybe I was only imagining that she possessed any sentience. Either way, we arrived within an hour.

'You can come in,' I said to the erstwhile crime lord, deciding to ignore what DSI Barnes would say about the company I was keeping. When the chips were down, you suddenly realised who was on your side and who wasn't. Devereau Webb, for all his faults, was with me and mine.

'Nah,' he said with an easy smile. 'I'll grab a taxi and see what I can find out about this thing.' He waved the tracking device. 'I have some ... friends who might be able to help.'

My hackles rose. 'It's probably better if you don't involve any of your friends from the other side of the law, Mr Webb.'

His smile grew. 'These friends are different.'

'Different how?'

He tapped the side of his nose. 'I could tell you, but then I'd have to kill you.'

I rolled my eyes, then paused and looked at him more closely. Wait a minute.

Webb pretended not to notice my sudden interest. 'I'll see you later. There's only so much time I can spend in public in the company of a detective constable before my street cred is damaged permanently.'

Sometimes ignorance was bliss, so I left him to his secrets and raised an eyebrow instead. 'You know I'm coming to your wedding, right?' Webb only smirked.

I waved him off and trudged into the hospital. The back of my skull was no longer bleeding but my hair was matted with blood, and the pain was still bad enough to be a concern. I was walking wounded, but that was a far cry from the state that Fred and Grace were in.

Lukas and Buffy were still in the same waiting room, together with Liza. She looked pale and exhausted but considerably happier and more relaxed than the last time I'd seen her.

Lukas stiffened as I walked in and his nostrils flared as he sensed my blood. Buffy obviously noticed it as well and her eyes widened. I gave her a warning shake of my head. We were here for Fred and Grace; my head wound could wait.

I hugged Liza and she reciprocated, although her nose wrinkled and she told me that I smelled like a rubbish dump. I managed a smile, then we got down to what was important. 'How is he?' I asked.

Liza gave me a tired smile. 'Better than expected,' she said. 'And there are no signs of any brain damage. It'll be a long road to recovery, but he'll pull through.'

'My Fred hasn't woken up yet,' Buffy broke in, her voice louder than necessary.

I could see the pain and anxiety in her eyes. 'Is there anything new from the doctors?' I asked.

She twisted her fingers together. 'They said he needs more time before they bring him out of his induced coma. He's stable and that's what's important.'

I breathed out. Finally, there was some good news. It was about fucking time.

'Owen's sister and Fred's parents have gone home to get some sleep,' Liza told me. 'But Owen's awake now and he's asking for you.'

Lukas folded his arms across his chest. 'You need to see a doctor first, Emma.'

I shook my head. 'After I've spoken to Grace.'

Sparks lit his black eyes. 'Your head—'

Liza looked alarmed. I waved them both away with a determined hand. 'Grace first,' I reiterated.

Lukas set his jaw in a tense line but he knew better than to argue with me. He stepped back, allowing Liza and I to head out of the waiting room and across to Grace's room.

Two werewolves from the McGuigan clan were standing outside the door, alongside two vampires. Such a large supe presence was probably overkill but I was glad to see them. All four nodded at me in greeting and I returned the gesture.

Liza opened Grace's door and beckoned me inside. 'I'll wait here,' she said. I flashed her a quick, grateful smile and went in.

His doctors may well have been pleased with his progress, but Detective Sergeant Owen Grace looked terrible. He was lying on the hospital bed, beeping machines next to him and far too many tubes for my liking. His skin was pale and waxy and his eyes were shut.

When I approached, his eyelids flickered open and a tiny smile raised the corners of his mouth. 'Emma,' he whispered.

'Hey,' I said softly. I pulled up a chair and sat next to his bed.

'You had us all worried. It's good to see you back in the land of the living.'

He coughed slightly. 'What ... I ... wouldn't ... give,' he croaked, 'to be the ... phoenix ... right ... about ... now.'

He was making a good point; I had no right to complain about my supernatural lot when I didn't have to worry about ending up confined to a bed at death's door. Then I touched my belly and felt the weight of responsibility settle back onto my shoulders.

'Liza told me ... this ... was ... deliberate,' Grace said. 'Somebody ... did ... this ... deliberately. The same ... somebody ... who ... killed ... Carmichael.'

'I think it was Stubman, the night bellman from the hotel next to Supe Squad,' I said. 'I don't have any real evidence but all the signs point to him.'

Even his condition couldn't prevent shock from flashing across Grace's face. He coughed again. 'There are files,' he managed. 'From Carmichael.'

I leaned in. 'What?'

'When ... Carmichael ... disappeared, his mother ... cleared out his things ... from his flat and .... his business.' He licked his cracked lips. The effort of speaking was clearly difficult, but the determination in his eyes told me that he was going to talk even if it destroyed him. 'She took his business files. Look there. There might be something you can use.'

In theory it was a good idea, but I knew from Phileas that Quincy Carmichael's mother had died so it was doubtful that any of the gremlin's files still existed. I nodded anyway; this wasn't the time for a long debate or conversation. 'I'll look into it,' I promised. 'You just concentrate on getting better. We need you to get better.' My voice was shakier than I'd intended. I reached for Grace's hand and squeezed it gently. '*I* need you.'

His eyelids fluttered and he wheezed. As if on cue, a nurse

bustled into the room, glanced at me and straightened her back. 'Alrighty, then!' she said in a cheerful voice. 'That's enough for now. Owen needs to rest.'

I stood up, but Grace wasn't done. 'Emma,' he whispered.

I turned back. 'Yes?'

He raised his head an inch off the pillow and his eyes met mine. 'Don't let Supe Squad sink. It's up to you to keep it alive.' He paused. 'No matter what.'

I swallowed hard. 'I will,' I told him. 'I promise.'

Grace sank back. 'Good,' he murmured. 'Supe Squad needs you now more than ever.' Then his eyes closed once more as he succumbed to sleep.

LUKAS WAS PACING up and down the small hospital cubicle. 'That prejudiced fuck of a bellman?' he snarled. 'He's the bastard behind all this?'

'All the signs point towards him. I don't know why he'd have killed Quincy or Adele Cunningham and Simon Carr all those years ago, but he's always despised supes. And he certainly had the opportunity to firebomb the Supe Squad building and get evidence to frame me for Alan Cobain's murder.'

'I'll rip his throat out with my bare hands.' Lukas was vibrating with fury – but he wasn't the one I was worried about. That honour went to Buffy, who was standing silently in the corner, her normally expressive face set in a blank mask.

'First of all,' I said for her sake as much as Lukas's, 'we don't have proof. We need to question Stubman and find out more. Secondly, he's human. Even if Supe Squad were operational, he wouldn't automatically fall under our jurisdiction. Any attempt to hurt him, kidnap him or do *anything* to him is wholly illegal.'

'He doesn't deserve automatic protection because he's human,' Lukas growled.

'No,' I agreed. 'But he does deserve the benefit of the doubt until we can prove otherwise. I've already left a message for Phileas Carmichael in case he knows if Quincy's files still exist and there's something useful in them. But no matter what evidence we find or what Stubman admits to, we cannot hurt him.' I looked at Buffy. 'I mean that.'

She sniffed but she didn't say anything.

'I'll get my people out looking for him straight away,' Lukas said.

'They can't—' I began.

'Don't worry. They won't hurt him,' he told me. His eyes flashed. 'But they won't let him get away, either.'

I sighed. I'd have to hope that Stubman didn't put up a fight when the vamps got to him. Despite Lukas's words, things wouldn't go well if Stubman resisted.

'I spoke to Candace,' he told me.

I raised my eyebrows. 'Did she have anything useful to say?'

Lukas's face was dark. 'Adele was definitely one of Quincy's clients. Candace said Quincy had been worried about her because one of his other clients who'd dated her wasn't keen about taking no for an answer. This client had apparently decided that they were destined to be together whether she agreed or not.'

Shit. This was it; this was why all this had started. 'Who was this client?' A name could seal the deal as far as Stubman's guilt was concerned.

'Candace didn't know. All she knew was that he was human.'

'Why didn't this come up at the time? After Adele was killed, I mean?'

Lukas's voice was taut with anger. 'Candace told me that

she'd mentioned it but, between Quincy's disappearance and the troublesome client being human, her information wasn't taken seriously enough.'

He met my eyes. 'If Supe Squad had been investigating, maybe it would have been. I checked back through the old investigation files and it was barely mentioned. After Quincy disappeared, the focus was on whether he was the murderer. When it was established that he wasn't, the dating agency was dropped as a line of investigation.'

He was right: that would not have happened if Supe Squad had been in charge at the time, but it wasn't appropriate to say so. Anyway, hindsight is always twenty-twenty.

I turned to Buffy. 'Did you find out anything about Simon Carr?'

She took a while before answering. 'Yeah,' she said shortly. 'He was friends with Quincy but he never used his dating agency. He really did meet Adele at yoga.'

I opened my mouth to ask another question, but before I could a white-coated doctor pulled back the curtain and smiled. 'Good afternoon! I hear we have a nasty head wound that needs attention.'

Buffy straightened her back. 'I'll leave you to it,' she said and left without another word.

I smiled back at the cheery doctor and gave Lukas a meaningful look. 'Don't let her race off after Stubman,' I warned. 'Keep an eye on her.'

Lukas frowned but nodded and went after her, while I hopped onto the narrow examination bed.

The doctor introduced herself and manoeuvred around to examine my head. She sucked in her breath. 'You're talking without any issues and your pupils aren't dilated, so any concussion is likely to be mild. But you might have fractured your skull,' she warned. 'We should do an X-ray to be sure.'

'How long will that take?'

'We're quite backed up, so it'll be a few hours.'

I shook my head. Nah. 'Stitch me up, doc. I'll come back later for that X-ray.'

'That's not a very good idea.' She clicked her tongue. 'You can't be too careful with head wounds.'

It probably wasn't a good idea to run off from the one place where I'd be safe, especially given my condition and the echoes of my last Cassandra vision that were still bouncing around my head. My next death could well be imminent.

My stomach lurched without warning, as if my jellybean were suddenly reminding me of her presence. After my conversation with the young werewolf mother, I was already thinking of her as a girl. Lukas's vampires would find Stubman; I should do as the doctor said and stay here to make sure my jellybean and I were okay.

This was all very new to me, and I wasn't used to having to worry about my health. I considered my options, sighed and eventually conceded. 'Alright then.'

'It's for the best.' The doctor patted my shoulder. 'Wait here and I'll make sure you're booked in. I'll be back later.'

Once she had gone, I reached up and gingerly touched the back of my head. The pain was less than it had been and my thoughts felt clear and unfuzzy. That had to be good, right? But I should still err on the side of caution. I could wait for the X-ray without breaking my promise to Grace about Supe Squad. It would be tomorrow morning before the DNA results came back and potentially implicated me in Cobain's murder, so there was still plenty of time to resolve all this shit.

I dropped my shoulders and felt my eyes drift shut. I should use my time wisely and get some rest while I could. I allowed a moment to marvel at myself for being so responsible, then I lay down and curled up as if I were a child.

TWENTY-SEVEN

When I opened my eyes again, a warm blanket had been draped over me and I was no longer alone. Lukas was sitting in the chair next to the bed, staring at me intently. 'Hey, you,' he said softly. 'You've been out for the count.'

I rubbed my face, sat up and yawned. 'The X-ray?'

'The doctor popped in earlier and said it'll be another hour or two before they can fit you in. The hospital is very busy.'

I grimaced. After that sleep, I felt considerably better and an X-ray was starting to feel like over-kill. 'What time is it?'

'Just after 11pm.'

Alarm lit through me. 'We've been here for hours!'

'You needed the rest, Emma,' he chided gently.

Even so, that was a lot more time than I'd been willing to waste. 'Where's Buffy?'

'They woke up Fred and she's with him.' He tapped his mouth. 'I think she genuinely cares for him, you know.'

'Is Fred—?' I held my breath.

'He's okay.' Lukas smiled. 'He's doing well.'

I exhaled with relief, then I leaned across and gave him a

tight hug. He wrapped his arms around me and held me. 'I needed that,' I mumbled.

'It's been a rocky road,' he said. 'But everything is beginning to work out.'

The sudden image from my Cassandra vision of the gun firing at me flashed into my head. Not yet it wasn't. I burrowed deeper into Lukas's arms. 'Are you alright?' he asked, concerned.

I knew that I should tell him, but he'd wrap me in cotton wool. And even if he did, the prediction would probably still come true. I had to let events play out as they must. Even so, I stayed where I was for several moments, drawing as much comfort from Lukas as I could. 'I'm great,' I told the crook of his shoulder. 'Do you think I can see Fred?'

He pulled back and smiled. 'Let's find out.'

He took my hand and we wandered down the hallway until we eventually found Fred's room. I peered through the window at his thin figure in the dimly lit bed. Buffy was there, focused on the book in her hands; it looked as if she were reading aloud to him. Wonders would never cease.

She must have felt my gaze because she looked up. As soon as she saw us, she put down the book, sprang to her feet and came out to speak to us. 'He's sleeping now,' she said. 'But he was talking earlier.' She offered me a genuine smile. 'I think he's going to be okay.'

Thank fuck. 'That's great news.'

She nodded happily, just as one of Lukas's vampires approached. He cleared his throat pointedly and we all turned to look at him. The vamp, who was dressed remarkably formally for a hospital, adjusted his tie. 'We've found him.'

I jerked. 'Stubman?'

The smile on Buffy's face disappeared; patches of angry fur were already breaking out all over her skin. 'Where is he?'

The vampire flicked a nervous look at Lukas, but he nodded and motioned to him to continue. 'He's at his flat. We located him on one of the streets nearby and tracked him back there. He's pinned down. He's not going anywhere.'

A trickle of unease ran down my spine. Why had he gone home? Even if he'd hit me hard enough to kill me, Stubman knew that I wouldn't stay dead. Why would he blithely return to the one place where we'd be sure to find him?

I opened my mouth to voice my concerns but Buffy was already sprinting down the hospital corridor. 'Stop!' I yelled. Of course, she ignored me.

'She won't get near him,' the vampire said. 'We've got Stubman penned in.' He was underestimating what Buffy was capable of.

I shook my head in dismay and pulled out my phone. 'What's Lady Sullivan's direct number?'

Lukas stared at me.

'Lukas, she's the only person who can rein Buffy in,' I protested.

'My vampires can hold back one werewolf.'

It wasn't just one werewolf, though: it was Buffy. I met his eyes. 'Are you absolutely sure about that?'

His gaze slid away from me, then he pulled a face and recited Lady Sullivan's number. I jabbed in the numbers and waited, listening to the phone ring and ring and ring. Damn it. 'She's not picking up.'

'It's her personal number. Only a few people know it and it's only ever used in an emergency. She always picks up this one.'

Maybe this time she knew who was calling and why. 'Perhaps,' I said, 'Buffy is calling in the furry cavalry, and instead of one werewolf trying to get at Stubman there will be an entire clan.' I paused. 'Or four.'

Lukas didn't hesitate. 'Warn them,' he snapped at the suited vampire. 'I'll go there right now.'

'I'm coming too.'

He glared at me. 'You need an X-ray.'

'I'm fine.' And I was; I was almost sure of it.

'Emma...'

'Instead of wasting time arguing about it, let's just go,' I said.

Lukas exhaled hard with frustration, but then we were both running down the corridor in the same direction that Buffy had gone.

EVEN AT THAT time of night, it took far longer than I liked to get back to Stubman's building. Tallulah seemed to recognise the urgency but even her determination, coupled with Lukas's foot pressed to the accelerator, didn't help much.

As soon as we turned onto the main street which led to Stubman's building, I knew we had problems. Werewolves were streaming in from all directions. Some remained in human form but plenty of them had already transformed into their animal bodies. I spotted members from all four clans and, up ahead, a large collection of grim-faced vampires ready to meet them. Yep. My worst fears were about to be realised.

Humans lived here as well as supes. All it would take was one frightened human to place one 999 call and we'd end up with armed police to contend with, too. None of this was going to help anyone, least of all me.

'Your vampires need to back off,' I said to Lukas urgently.

'If they do, there will be nothing to prevent those were-wolves storming the building and ripping Stubman to shreds before you can ask him a single question,' he said reasonably,

I passed a hand over my face. For fuck's sake. 'The wolves have just as much self-control as the vampires – not to mention that we're all on the same side, Lukas.' I glanced at his face and caught a flash of guilt. He nodded.

'Park here.' I pointed to the side of the road. It was a double yellow line but getting to the tiny car park would waste time. 'I'll deal with this.'

'I'm right with you, Emma,' Lukas said quietly. 'I'll follow your lead.'

So at least I would have some back-up that I could count on. I patted his shoulder then jumped out of the car. I ran past several large clusters of approaching wolves until I reached Stubman's building, where the showdown was about to take place.

Lukas took up position in front of the vampires to make sure that none of them did anything rash, and I jumped into the small space between them and the werewolves. All four clan alphas were there. I couldn't see Buffy, but I had to assume she was there too. I sincerely hoped she hadn't found a way into the building to confront Stubman on her own.

I pulled back my shoulders, raised my chin and cleared my throat. 'Everyone needs to disperse immediately and go home.' I amplified my voice so nobody could miss the order.

Lady Fairfax, who was dressed in a tight black dress, tottering stilettos and full-make-up as if she were out to party the night away, stepped forward. 'My dear,' she declared. 'We are only here to back you up.'

By her side, Lord McGuigan nodded fervently. In contrast to Lady Fairfax, he appeared to be wearing pyjamas beneath his long coat, as if he'd been disturbed from his sleep. 'Supe Squad is practically non-existent now. You need our support and we are happy to give it to you.'

'Emma already has the vampires' support,' Lukas said. I

shot him an annoyed look. That wasn't helpful. 'We are all on the same side here,' he added. 'We all want the same thing.'

I exhaled. Thank you, Lukas.

Lady Carr, the oldest werewolf alpha, sniffed. 'That man in there is responsible for the murder of one of my people. I have every right to be here.'

Several of the vamps started to protest. 'He killed a vampire too! He murdered Adele!' one of them yelled.

I hoped we wouldn't descend into total anarchy. The werewolves and the vampires had worked together at the hospital to keep Fred and Owen safe in a way that had genuinely warmed my heart. Although I had no doubt that their intentions were pure, here it was a different story. It was time for what little remained of Supe Squad to take control, suspended from duty or otherwise.

I held up my hands and the shouting from both sides subsided. Start with a compliment, Emma. Keep them on side. 'You have no idea how much your support means to me,' I called out. 'I know that for many years Supernatural Squad was a thorn in your side, but I can see that has changed and I, for one, am very glad that it has. It gives me genuine optimism for our future.'

One of the werewolves let out a brief howl. Another yelled, 'Damn right!'

That was the carrot. Now for the stick. 'There is a suspect inside that building who needs to be questioned. Not threatened or bullied, but interviewed properly. He is human, and that means none of you can be involved.'

'You've been suspended,' Lady Sullivan murmured. 'That means you can't be involved either.'

I was glad she'd kept her voice low because she was right; I shouldn't be here any more than anyone else. No matter what happened with the Cobain investigation, I deserved to lose my warrant card for good.

'Either you all respect Supe Squad and what we do for the supernatural community or you don't,' I said. 'Either you trust that I have your best interests at heart or you don't. If you don't, then the police will take over from this point. Let's face it,' I waved a hand at both belligerent groups, 'they're probably already on their way, thanks to all of this. Let me deal with this as it should have been dealt with thirteen years ago and we can achieve the justice that you deserve. Anything else will only cause more problems.'

Lord McGuigan turned to Lady Carr. 'To be fair,' he said, 'she did kill that other human last week, so we can probably trust her brand of justice.'

For fuck's sake. 'I didn't kill him,' I snapped. 'And I'm not going to kill anyone in this building, either.'

Several of the wolves turned their heads as the wail of distant sirens filled the air. The police – the real police who weren't suspended from duty like me – were heading towards us. My stomach sank. Time was running out.

A lone voice piped up: Buffy. As if things couldn't get any worse. 'We can't trust the police,' she said. 'We've never been able to trust the police.'

Goddamnit.

'But,' she continued, raising her finger to point at me, 'we can trust Supe Squad. We can trust *her*.'

My mouth dropped open. Lady Sullivan gave Buffy a hard look and something unspoken passed between them.

'Eight vampires,' Lukas said, 'and eight werewolves. Two for each clan. We remain here to make sure that Emma's suspect doesn't flee. Everyone else leaves now.' He looked over my head to the clan alphas. 'Buffy is right. We can trust Emma – and we can trust each other.'

I half-expected more discussion but, to my surprise, all four clan alphas bowed their heads in agreement. 'Do not let us down,' Lady Carr muttered.

Lady Sullivan met my eyes. 'She won't.' Vampires and were-wolves melted away, and within seconds only sixteen supes remained.

The sirens were getting louder. 'You deal with Stubman,' Lukas said. 'Talk to him and find out if he's really our man. We'll keep the police out of your way unless he needs to be arrested.'

I breathed out. Okay.

I glanced at Buffy, wondering if I should repay the favour and invite her to join me. It didn't feel like a good idea, but perhaps she could help. 'No,' she said, reading my mind. 'You can't trust me, not with that wanker. Do it alone.'

I swallowed, then turned and jogged towards the front door of Stubman's building.

TWENTY-EIGHT

Someone, no doubt an enterprising werewolf or vampire, had made sure the lift was shut down so there was no chance that Stubman would slip past me this time. The only way up or down was the staircase.

Despite the late hour, I reckoned he was well aware of what was happening outside. He was used to working nights and was probably still awake, and he couldn't be oblivious to a near riot on his doorstep. He had to know I was coming. Whether this would end up with Stubman pulling a gun and fulfilling my earlier prophecy remained to be seen.

I touched my belly. 'Let's hope not, Jellybean,' I whispered. Let's hope not.

I took the stairs two at a time until I reached Stubman's floor. There were chinks of light from underneath the doors of some of the flats; other people had clearly been disturbed by the commotion outside. I trusted they'd be sensible enough to remain inside their homes.

I jogged down the silent corridor until I reached the right door, raised my fist and knocked loudly. Would Stubman answer this time? To my surprise, he did.

He was dressed casually; it was strange seeing him out of his usual uniform and in grey jogging bottoms and a T-shirt instead of top hat and tails. I looked him up and down carefully, trying to decide if he had a gun concealed on his body. Unless it was tucked down the back of his trousers, it didn't look possible. All the same, I remained wary.

'Hi there,' I said softly. 'Remember me?'

He didn't blink; instead he raised a derisive eyebrow. 'Are you here to arrest me?' he asked. 'Or kill me?'

I didn't miss a beat. 'Why would I do either of those things?' If this was where he confessed outright to his crimes, it was going to be far easier than I'd thought it would be.

'A little bird told me that I was in the frame for torching your building.' He snorted. 'Never mind that I'm now without a job because of that fucking fire. Never mind that I was busy working at the time and I could quite easily have been burned alive, too.'

He splayed his hands. 'No. Go and blame the human for the supes' fuck-up.' His mouth turned down. 'You didn't have to wait until the middle of the night to show up – and you didn't need to bring an army with you.'

'I've sent most of them away,' I said.

'Not all of them.' He peered around the doorway into the empty corridor. 'How many vampires are down there waiting to bleed me dry?'

'I'm alone, Mr Stubman. Everyone else is outside.'

'So you *are* going to kill me, then. You've made sure there won't be any witnesses.'

I stared at him. He really did hate the police. 'I'm not here to hurt you. I only want to ask you a few questions.'

'Is that what you told Alan Cobain when you set him on fire?'

'I didn't hurt Alan Cobain,' I said, still watching him very carefully.

He shrugged. 'If you say so.'

Nothing about this was going as I'd expected. Stubman looked both frightened and defiant, but he didn't look guilty. 'Where were you between three and four o'clock this afternoon, Mr Stubman?'

His answer was swift. 'I was here. I didn't leave my flat all day.'

Bingo. I'd caught him in a lie. But people lied to the police for all sorts of reasons, especially when their feelings were as strong as Stubman's. 'That's not true, though, is it? I saw you outside this building.'

He scowled. 'Then why the fuck did you ask me where I was if you already knew?'

I pressed him for an answer. 'Where did you go?'

He folded his arms defensively across his chest. 'None of your business.'

'Mr Stubman—'

He huffed loudly. 'Fine. I had a phone call, alright? One of the hotels nearby called me and said that they'd heard about the fire. They said they might have work for me, so I went to speak to the manager.'

'Which hotel?'

'It doesn't matter,' he muttered.

'Which hotel?' I repeated.

'The Bell Plaza. But it doesn't matter because it wasn't true. There was no job and they said they hadn't called me. It was somebody playing a sick joke.' His eyes narrowed. 'Maybe it was you.'

I didn't take my eyes off him. 'You're saying that somebody pretending to be from the Bell Plaza Hotel called you up and told you they wanted to interview you, so you left your home to speak to them? And when you got there, there was no job?'

'That's what I just fucking said, right? Are you hard of hearing?'

I kept my face blank and changed the subject. 'Tell me about the night of the fire.'

'I already went through this with the real police.'

I waited. He glared at me. 'Nothing much happened that night. It was a typical shift. The hotel was quiet. We had some guests check in late so I went inside to help them with their bags. When I came back out, there was smoke everywhere and the fire alarms were going off. I didn't see anyone walking around with petrol canisters.' He sneered. 'But if I had seen them, I'd have helped them. I'd have lit the match myself.'

I was puzzled. Despite Stubman's antagonistic attitude, everything he'd told me was verifiable: the hotel guests he'd helped at the start of the Supe Squad fire, the Bell Plaza he'd visited today supposedly in pursuit of a new job. It didn't add up.

The knot of suspicion in my stomach was growing but I didn't have all of the puzzle pieces – and those I had were not fitting together. 'What about the night before the fire?'

'What about it?'

I leaned forward on my toes. It was the night Alan Cobain had been set alight. I wanted to know where Stubman had been when that had happened. If he'd been at work, he couldn't have killed Cobain. 'Humour me.'

Stubman sighed. 'Fine. My shift started earlier than usual because Max asked me to fill in for him. It was his birthday and he wanted to leave early so he could start partying. I don't know why he bothered – apparently he turned up late to his own celebrations.' His lip curled. 'Whatever. And before you say anything, no, I wasn't annoyed that I wasn't invited. I was happy to fill in for him. I take my job seriously.' His eyes narrowed, daring me to disagree.

I kept a straight face. The fact that he'd mentioned his lack of an invitation suggested that Stubman was very pissed off about it. I hadn't realised he and Max were friends; they were very, very different.

Stubman continued. 'One of the guests complained about their room and I had to move their suitcases to a different suite. Another guest gave me a decent tip. Nothing else interesting happened.' He glared at me some more. 'What else do you need? Do you want to know where I was when JFK was shot? Or if I faked the moon landings?'

He wasn't old enough. I pulled back and thought about what he'd said.

'Fucking supes,' Stubman spat suddenly. 'And fucking police. I hate the lot of you.' He spun on his heel and marched back inside his flat, though he didn't close the door.

I hesitated for a beat then followed him in. He had plonked himself in the centre of a sagging sofa and was fiddling with something underneath a cushion. I looked around. There was a television in the corner, displaying flickering pictures of an old black-and-white film. The walls were bare of any pictures and there was very little furniture. It was completely soulless, as if Stubman had only just moved in and was still waiting to unpack his belongings.

'How long have you lived here?' I asked.

'What does that have to do with anything?'

I shrugged and sat down gingerly on the single wooden chair next to the sofa; judging by the rings marking its wooden seat, it was normally used as a side table.

'I moved in 2010,' he said. 'About thirteen years ago.'

I sat up straighter. 'Which month?'

Stubman squinted. 'Which month did I move in? September, I think.'

Adele Cunningham and Simon Carr had been murdered in August. That was when Quincy Carmichael had disappeared, too. And Quincy's old business premises were only a stone's throw away.

'Why here?' I asked him. 'This is a supe community. You don't like supes.'

His eyes shifted. 'I got a good deal because I sublet it off a friend. I wouldn't get anywhere else in London like this for the same price. Not even close.'

'Who's the friend?'

Stubman's face twisted with fury. 'Come after me all you like, but you're not coming after my people too.'

'I'm not coming after you. I only want to understand.'

'Understand what?'

I kept my voice gentle. 'The hotel you work at is in the supe community, right next to Supe Squad.'

'I don't work there any more, do I? The building's been condemned. The hotel has gone because of you and your lot,' he spat.

Again I waited. It worked. After several seconds passed, Stubman filled in the silence. 'I didn't plan things this way, but beggars can't be fucking choosers, can they? I wanted to be in the police. The bellman job was supposed to be a stopgap but then the Met decided I wasn't suitable.'

He scowled, directing his angry gaze towards me as if that were my fault. 'I thought I'd go to evening school and get better grades to do something else, but I started working nights and...' His voice trailed off. 'Here I am fifteen years later, still stuck in the same dead-end job – and even that no longer exists.'

His shoulders slumped an inch. He raised his eyes to mine

with bitter defiance. 'I'm a failure, alright? I've failed at everything. Including life.' He was not in a good place emotionally.

I licked my lips. 'Why do you hate supes so much?'

This time he didn't hesitate before answering. 'Because you lot think you're so fucking superior. You think because you've got money and strength and power that you're better than the rest of us. You're no better than I am! Just because I don't have the right connections, or I wasn't born into the right family, doesn't make me less of a person than you are. This is my country. It's *my* city. You lot don't belong here.'

I stared at him, suddenly understanding a little more. Despite his best efforts, his life hadn't gone the way he'd wanted it to. All around him he saw supes who, in his eyes, had everything they could possibly wish for while he had a shabby bare flat, a crappy job and very few prospects.

'Do you know any gremlins?' I asked.

'What? No.'

'Did you know a gremlin called Quincy Carmichael?'

'I just told you I don't know any gremlins. What kind of stupid name is Quincy, anyway?'

'What about Adele Cunningham? Or Simon Carr?'

Stubman stared at me blankly. I tried again. 'Have you ever been to Borehamwood? Or a cottage nearby?'

He wrinkled his nose. 'Where?'

'Have you ever thought about joining a supe dating agency?'

'You're fucking nuts. You know that, right?' He shook his head. 'Let's just get this over and done with. Do it already.'

'Mr Stubman—'

He yanked his hand out from underneath the cushion. I froze, gazing at the black gun he'd pulled out. It was identical to the one in my Cassandra vision. 'Do it,' he snarled. 'Kill me.'

I kept my voice as calm and even as I could. 'Put the gun down, Mr Stubman.'

'Why? You're not afraid of it. I could shoot you in the head a hundred times over and you wouldn't die.' His lip curled. 'I know all about you and what you're capable of.'

Uh-huh. He didn't know everything. 'I'm not here to hurt you.'

'Bullshit. I know why you're here. I've been told.'

I didn't move a muscle. 'Told by whom?'

'He warned me,' Stubman said, his eyes flicking from side to side. 'He told me I should run while I could. But I'm not afraid of you. I'm not afraid of any of you. I ain't running.'

From the way his hands were trembling, he was very fucking afraid. I fought back every instinct and leaned back against the wooden chair, crossing my legs and leaving my hands loosely clasped in my lap. 'Who told you to run?' I asked. 'Who told you that you were in danger?'

Stubman scoffed and brandished the gun towards me. 'Name, rank and serial number. That's all you're getting. I don't care what you do to me.'

I watched him for another moment or two. It wasn't paranoia if they were really out to get you. I ran my tongue over my teeth. 'I'm going to take my phone out of my pocket,' I said. 'I need to make a call.'

'Got a case of the willies, have you? Going to get your fanged boyfriend to finish the deed?'

'No,' I said simply. I moved slowly, doing everything I could to demonstrate to Stubman that I wasn't threatening him and I wasn't about to pull out a weapon. I slid out my phone, taking my eyes off the shaking bellman only long enough to find the number I needed, then I pressed the button to call.

Buffy answered instantly. 'What is it? What's wrong? Have you got him? Has he confessed?' Then, 'Is the fucker dead?'

Stubman flinched and I cursed inwardly at Buffy's choice of

words. 'I have one question for you,' I said. 'And I need you to answer honestly. It's important.'

'What?'

'The truth, Buffy. I mean it.'

'For fuck's sake. Yes, I'll tell you the truth. What do you want to know?'

I drew in a breath. 'Did you tell Lady Sullivan that Stubman was here?'

'No.'

'Did you tell *anyone* that Stubman was here?'

'I was a bit too busy getting myself here,' she snapped. 'I didn't stop to chat along the way.'

'Then why were all the clans here? Who told them that our main suspect was at this address?'

'I don't fucking know!'

I counted to ten in my head. 'Can you find out?'

'Why? You know, the real police are here now and they're being very pushy. You're not the only one in a difficult situation.'

'Please, Buffy,' I said. 'It's very important.' I licked my lips. 'In fact, it's a matter of life and death.'

On the sofa, Stubman jerked. I eyed the gun hoping he had the damned safety catch on.

'It's always life and death where you're concerned,' she grumbled. 'But fine. Give me a second.'

Her voice vanished. I heard some murmuring in the background but it was too faint to make out any words. Stubman's nostrils flared. He stared at the gun in his hand. I wondered what the hell was going through his head.

Then Buffy returned to the line. 'There was a tip-off,' she said flatly. 'Somebody called the Carr clan and told them that Simon's killer was here. They gave Stubman's name.'

It was interesting that the call had been placed to the Carr clan, who were arguably the most invested of all the werewolves. We'd made the link between Simon, Adele, Quincy and the more recent events, but apart from Lukas, Buffy and I, the only other person who would know of such a link would be the perpetrator. 'I'm guessing,' I said drily, 'that the caller didn't leave their name.'

'You guess right,' Buffy answered. 'It was a man with a London accent, that's all they know. The operator who took the message told Lady Carr, and she called in the other clans. Hey presto.' She paused. 'What does this mean?'

I didn't answer her question. 'Thanks, Buffy. I'll talk to you again soon.' I hung up, then I eyed Stubman. 'Put the gun down,' I said. 'We both know you're not going to shoot me.'

'I haven't done anything wrong,' he said.

I nodded. 'I know. Put the gun down.'

His movements were jerky, but he did as I asked and dropped the weapon onto the floor with a thud.

'Do you know why I'm the main suspect for Alan Cobain's death?' I asked conversationally. Stubman stared at me. 'It's because somebody left an anonymous tip-off that I was there just before he was killed. Somebody left an anonymous tip-off with the werewolves about you. Do you know who might have done that?'

He didn't answer.

'I reckon,' I said, 'that it's probably the same person who lured you out of here this afternoon and who knocked me unconscious when I tried to follow you.'

Stubman blinked several times.

'They wanted me to think that you were the one who did it. They wanted to leave a trail of breadcrumbs because they needed somebody to take the fall. It had worked for them before, so they thought it would work for them this time.'

Stubman was the perfect patsy. A few well-placed whispers

would stir his paranoia into thinking that the supes he hated so much were coming for him. It would have been easy to make him believe that we would attack first and ask questions later. His only recourse was to run and be hunted down, or to defend himself to the death.

But whoever had tipped him off hadn't reckoned on Stubman's true nature. Yes, he hated supes, and yes, he wore that hatred on his sleeve, but deep down he wasn't a violent man and he had no reason to fight back. He had been a defeated man long before any of this had happened.

'Whoever gave you that gun was someone you thought you could trust, but who actually wanted to frame you for murder,' I told him. 'And they wanted you to die before you could protest your innocence. If you had run, the werewolves and the vampires would have run after you. They'd have found you and,' I added, because I knew it was true, 'they'd probably have killed you, whether they meant to or not.'

Stubman's eyes flashed towards the weapon again. His jaw was working; he didn't want to believe me but he was starting to.

'Is the person who gave you the gun the same person who sublets you this place?' It would make a kind of twisted sense. If Stubman's landlord had lived here thirteen years ago, he could well have met Quincy Carmichael thanks to their proximity. He wouldn't have risked hanging around and being implicated in Quincy's disappearance or the murders of Adele and Simon, but he would have wanted to keep a close eye on events. A trusted tenant was a great way to do just that.

Stubman swallowed. 'I—'

My phone rang, interrupting him. He jumped and I swore. Then I saw the caller ID and instead of declining the call, I answered it. I raised a hand to Stubman to request his patience.

'Phileas,' I said. 'I hope you're calling at this late hour because you have something interesting to tell me.'

The gremlin solicitor sounded gruff. 'I got your message earlier. When my sister died, I cleared out her house and put her things in storage. I always meant to get around to sorting them out but I never did.'

I tapped my fingers. 'Did those things include files from Quincy's old businesses?'

'They did.'

'The dating agency?'

'Yes.'

'Is there a list of clients who used Quincy's agency?'

'Hang on.' There was a shuffling of paper. 'Yes. I have it here.'

'Can you see the name Alistair Stubman there?'

Disgust lit Stubman's eyes.

'No,' Quincy said. 'There's no-one with that name.'

I wasn't surprised. I raised an eyebrow at Stubman. Hmmm. He didn't strike me as the kind of man who had a lot of friends, but he did know a few people. In fact, his job as a bellman meant that he knew a lot of people – and there was one person in particular that he *definitely* knew.

I took a gamble. 'What about the name Max Vargman?'

Stubman stiffened and his gaze landed on the fallen gun once again. This time he stared at it as if it were about to rise up of its own accord and shoot him.

There was more shuffling from the phone. 'Yeah,' Phileas grunted. My heart missed a beat. Shit. The gamble paid off. 'That name is here.' His voice altered. 'Who is he?'

Max was the one I'd told that I was looking into cold cases. He was the one who'd watched me accost Phileas Carmichael on the street to ask about his nephew. He was the one who knew that Stubman was volatile. He was the one who also worked next door to Supe Squad and could have finagled access to the building. He was the one who might have met Quincy Carmichael in the café down the road while wearing a top hat and tails. And he was the one who'd given me an alibi and told me he was leaving work early on the night of the fire because it was his birthday party – and then arrived late.

I ran a hand through my hair. I still didn't have all the puzzle pieces, but I was getting closer. 'He's the man who killed your nephew,' I told Phileas.

I ended the call. Stubman stood up then sat down. A moment later he stood up again. 'Max,' he whispered. The betrayal in his eyes told me everything.

I was right, I was sure of it, but I didn't have the evidence I needed. Not yet. 'Is Max your landlord?'

Stubman nodded. Yes.

'Did he give you that gun?'

The pale-faced bellman didn't respond but he didn't deny it.

'Is it Max,' I asked, 'who told you that the supes were coming for you and that you had to run?'

He looked away, then he gave a tiny nod.

'Mr Stubman?' I leaned down and reached for the gun so I could check it was properly loaded. 'I need you to do me a favour.'

TWENTY-NINE

I t wasn't easy sneaking back out of the building. I couldn't afford to let anybody catch a glimpse of me, and I certainly couldn't afford any of the police noticing me. Everything rested on getting away without being spotted.

I ended up breaking one of the windows on the ground floor of the stairwell and gingerly clambering out so I could scoot through the car park and keep well away from the main entrance. I crossed the road, keeping my body low and in the shadows to avoid being seen.

Fortunately, the police officers were engaged with the loud argument taking place between the werewolves and the vampires. Lukas, in particular, was doing an excellent job of yelling epithets at Buffy while she was responding with energetic insults. I wondered if they were completely faking their mutual antagonism. Probably not.

As soon as I launched myself into Tallulah's driving seat, I checked the time. There were still a few minutes to go. I sat for a moment, then I made a phone call. 'I'm sorry, Lady Elena, for disturbing you at this late hour,' I said,

She laughed musically. 'I'm a vampire, darling. The night is yet young.' I could hear the smile in her voice. 'Are you calling to invite me to that wedding of yours?'

I pulled a face. 'Not yet. I wanted to ask you again about your experiences with Quincy Carmichael's dating agency. When we spoke before, you said that Lukas was one of the more suitable men you dated when you came to London. Does that mean that the others were unsuitable?'

'That's an interesting question after so many years.'

'Please,' I said, 'indulge me.'

'There were a few … uncomfortable moments. There was a werewolf who was very insistent on marking his territory everywhere we went – that caused some problems. And a human who became most aggressive when I told him that I didn't think we had a future. As I recall, he seemed to think I was deliberately humiliating him when I turned him down, instead of simply making an informed choice.'

'Uh-huh. Can you remember his name?'

'Hmm.' Elena paused. 'It began with an M. Mark maybe?'

'Could it have been Max?' I asked. 'Max Vargman?'

'Yes,' she said slowly. 'I think that might have been him.'

I checked my watch again. It was almost time. 'Thank you, Lady Elena.'

'No problem.'

I tossed the phone onto the passenger seat and buckled my seatbelt, then I wound down the window and waited. It didn't take long. Against all reasonable expectations Stubman had come through – and he was right on time.

I'd been concerned that the commotion outside Stubman's building would mean that nobody would notice, but I needn't have worried. The sound of three gunshots fired in quick succession was impossible to miss. There were several alarmed shouts and screams, whether from the supes or the police I couldn't tell, but it didn't particularly matter.

I put Tallulah into gear and drove off. Five seconds later my phone rang again as I'd expected. In fact, Lukas was perfectly on cue.

'Emma!' He sounded breathless and panicked in a way I'd never heard him before. I'd debated calling him before all this happened, but he was in a public place and I didn't want to tip my hand to anyone else.

'Are you alone?' I asked, speeding away from the scene.

'Buffy's here. We're coming up the stairs to you now. Are you alright? Did he shoot you?'

I put as much force into my voice as I could. I needed Lukas to calm down and listen to me. 'Stop. Don't go any further. I am fine. You have to listen.'

'What?' He still sounded frantic. 'What's going on?'

'I need the police to think that I've shot Stubman and disappeared with his body.'

Lukas's voice rose. 'You need *what*?'

I heard Buffy's voice float over. 'Has she killed the bastard?'

'Stubman is fine. He should be hiding in a cleaning cupboard on the next floor up. But everyone has to believe that I've either killed him or he's about to be killed.'

'*What?*'

I remained calm. 'There's no body, so you'll have to improvise.'

'Emma—'

'Stubman was being set up, Lukas. If the real killer thinks that I fell for his ploy and got rid of Stubman, he'll stay where he is. If he thinks for a moment that we've not been fooled then he'll run.' I drew a breath. 'I have to catch him. He's responsible for at least four deaths and he tried to kill Fred and Owen. He burned Supe Squad. He can't get away.'

'It's not Stubman? He didn't do any of this?'

'Nope. He's an ornery supe-hating wanker, but he's not a murderer.'

Lukas swore aloud. 'If he's not the killer, then who is?'

'Max.'

There was a beat of silence. 'The other bellman?'

'Yes.'

'The friendly one?'

'Yes.'

'The one who always smiles and says hello and helps you out?'

'Yes.' I sighed. 'Unfortunately there's nothing in the rule book that says murderers have to look evil and act like bastards. The worst ones are kind, thoughtful and everyone's friend.'

Lukas swore again.

'I need you to do this, Lukas. Make everyone think I killed Stubman until I've brought Max down. It's the best way to ensure he doesn't escape.'

'You're already the main suspect in one murder, Emma. If the police think you killed Stubman, they won't stop until they get you. They won't hesitate to shoot you and the baby—'

'I had a vision about this. Don't worry.'

'You saw this future?'

'Yep.'

'It's going to turn out okay?'

I grimaced. 'Mmmm.' Time to end this call. 'I have to concentrate on driving. I'll talk to you again soon.'

This time, I threw the phone out of Tallulah's window; I wouldn't be needing it again. A moment later, I put my foot down on the accelerator.

~

Stubman had given me Max's address. He didn't live in a block of flats close to supernatural action, far from it. Max now resided in a tidy two-up, two-down in the quiet London suburb of Hillingdon. Perhaps he'd felt the need to distance himself from his actions as much as possible, only using his job and Stubman to keep an eye on things in case his name ever came up. He was a canny bastard – and far more conniving than I ever could have imagined.

Judging by the lights on at his house and the shadows moving around behind the curtains, he was also wide awake, even though he was a day worker and it was now almost two o'clock in the morning. He was waiting to hear if his plans for Stubman had worked. I was sure of it.

I circled around the block and examined both the front of Max's house and the shrouded rear, which included a small fenced-off garden. I debated sneaking in from the back and taking him by surprise, but I already knew what was going to happen. I'd seen it in my vision. Besides, I wasn't the criminal here and there were smarter ways to confront him. I had a plan – of sorts. I'd just have to pray it worked and I didn't end up with my brains splattered against a beige suburban wall.

I started down the narrow garden path leading to Max's front door. I'd barely taken two steps when the security light from the neighbouring house flashed on and I sensed movement to my left. I froze and turned, immediately spotting the two shining yellow eyes fixed on me. A fox.

I expelled a rush of breath from my lungs. I'd seen those eyes in my Cassandra vision and I knew what would happen next. This was where everything ended; strangely, the thought spurred me on instead of holding me back.

The fox remained stock-still for another second before twisting around, jumping over the low hedge to the rear and disappearing into the night. I doffed an imaginary cap in its direction, then I strode the final few metres to Max's door and rang the bell.

Unsurprisingly, it took him a long time to answer; after all, it was the wee hours of the morning. As I saw the curtains in the window twitch and heard footsteps approach, I rearranged my face into what I hoped was an appropriate expression. A moment later, the lock was unlatched and the door opened an inch. Max's tense face peered out.

'Max!' I exclaimed. 'I'm so relieved you're awake! I didn't want to disturb you but I didn't know where else to go. I know it's late but I desperately need to talk to you.'

Some of his tension seemed to ease. He opened the door wider and blinked at me. 'Detective! What on earth are you doing here?'

I waved my hands helplessly. 'It's a long story but it's to do with your colleague, Stubman. It's imperative that I find him as quickly as possible.' I watched his face, waiting to see if his expression would betray him but there wasn't a single flicker to reveal his guilt. He'd been playing a role for far too long and he was far too skilful at it.

'Alistair?' He clapped his hands to his face in a display of concern. 'My goodness. Is he in danger?'

Yeah, he was good. 'Possibly,' I said, hoping my ability matched his. 'But others might be in danger from him.'

Max stepped back. 'You'd better come in.'

I pressed my palms together in gratitude. 'Thank you, Max. Thank you so much.'

Without a single backward glance, I entered the lion's well-disguised den.

The interior smelled homely and pleasant, with a faint floral scent that was fresh without being overpowering. As I followed Max through the warm hallway and into his living room, taking in the clean and tidy décor, doubts crept in. I gazed at the painting on the wall of a bucolic country scene. Maybe he was nothing more than a nice, ordinary bloke who lived in a nice, ordinary house. Maybe Max wasn't the killer I was looking for.

'Can I get you a drink?' he asked.

'It's the middle of the night – you don't have to play host,' I said. 'You're already doing more than anyone should.' I bit my bottom lip. 'Do you have Stubman's phone number?'

He nodded. 'I do. Would you like it? Or would you like me to call him?'

'It might be better if you tried,' I said. 'He'll be more likely to answer if he recognises the phone number.'

Max gave a worried smile and picked up his phone from the coffee table, using face recognition to unlock the screen and locate Stubman's number. I stepped closer to him. It wasn't lost on me that it took him only a second to find it; it was in his recent contact list. Of course it was. He'd called Stubman several times over the last few days.

He pressed the green call button and both of us waited. I already knew that Stubman wouldn't answer but Max frowned and waved the phone in my direction. 'He's not picking up. He might be asleep.'

I looked doubtful. 'Sure. Yes. He might be.'

'Have you tried his flat? He doesn't live that far away from Supe Squad.'

'Oh,' I said innocently. 'Have you been to his home?'

Max was too smart to be caught out like that. 'I have,' he said. He twisted his hands together. 'I can give you his address.' He paused. 'What...' He paused and swallowed. 'What's he done?'

I grimaced. 'I shouldn't tell you.'

'Okay.' He dipped his head. 'Okay.'

'He assaulted me earlier today.' I let the words tumble out in a rush. 'He's the one who set fire to Supe Squad. I think he also tampered with Grace's car and caused a terrible accident.' My voice dropped. 'And he's killed people. Supes. Three of them.'

Max's eyes widened. 'Are you sure?'

'I think so,' I whispered.

'He's never liked supes,' Max said. 'He's never been very keen on the police, either. I didn't think he'd ever kill anyone but he can be ... violent. When he gets into a rage, he's a dangerous man. He's scared me quite a few times.'

Liar. 'You've never mentioned anything like that.'

He fidgeted. 'I didn't want to get him into trouble. He's had a hard life. He's only trying to get by.' He looked away. 'That's what I thought.' His head jerked back to mine. 'Does he know you're onto him? Does he know you're here?'

I shook my head. 'Oh no. He couldn't possibly know that.'

'Does anyone know you're here?'

My stomach flipped but I maintained the same expression. 'No. I can't tell anyone where I am or what I'm doing because I'm about to be arrested for murder.' I added hastily, 'But I didn't kill anyone! I think Stubman framed me.'

'Jesus.'

I licked my lips. 'Yeah. My whole life is falling apart, Max. The only way I can fix it is if I can find Alistair Stubman and get him to confess. But it has to be soon or it will be too late.'

'Wow. That's...' He shook his head. 'Wow. I'm so sorry.' He nodded towards another room. 'I'll get a pen and write down his address. Are you sure I can't get you a drink?'

'Maybe a cup of tea?' I asked.

'Of course. I'll put the kettle on.'

I smiled gratefully. 'Thank you, Max.'

He turned on his heel and left me alone. I put my hands in my pockets and wandered over to an oak side table where there was a small potted plant next to a few junk-mail envelopes. The plant was in an odd position to the left of the table with a blank space to the right. The asymmetrical placing was awkward, as if something were missing.

I glanced over my shoulder. The kettle was starting to boil, which would mask any noises I made. I held my breath, silently told my jellybean to stay strong and reached for the little drawer underneath the table top.

I slid it open. When I saw what was in there, I stepped back. I was right; it had been Max all along.

There were only two items in the drawer. One was a framed photo of Adele Cunningham smiling at the camera with Max's arm around her. The other was my hairbrush.

CHAPTER

THIRTY

With shaking hands, I closed the drawer again. When I turned around, I half-expected Max to be standing in front of me with a gun in his hand but he was still in the kitchen. I could hear him bustling around, clinking cups.

I placed a hand on my stomach and briefly closed my eyes. 'It'll be okay, Jellybean,' I murmured. 'I've got this.' I pulled back my shoulders and marched into Max's kitchen. It was time to end this dance.

Max, however, had his phone glued to his ear. He was still one step ahead of me. 'You have to help me,' he whispered into the receiver. 'She says she's already killed other people and I think she's going to hurt me. She's got a gun. Please hurry. I don't know what to do.'

I cleared my throat. Max jumped and spun around. 'I have to go,' he muttered into the phone, then he hung up and stared at me.

'You called the police,' I said flatly.

He gave me a panicked look but I could tell from his stance that he was anything but anxious. 'You've come knocking on my door in the middle of the night. You said that you're about to arrested for murder. You can't blame me for being concerned. I'm sorry.'

'You told them I have a gun.'

'Only because I wanted them to come quickly!' he blustered. 'I shouldn't have done that – I'll tell them the truth when they get here. I'm really sorry, Emma. I don't want to get you into trouble but I'm a bit scared of you. You said nobody else knows you're here...'

I folded my arms. Even now, he was determined to lie his way out of this; he even sounded credible. 'Why would you be scared of little old me, Max?' I asked softly. 'We know each other. I've seen you almost every day for the last two years. I thought we were friends.'

'We are!'

'No.' I shook my head. 'We're not. You see, I couldn't possibly be friends with someone who stabbed a vampire and a werewolf in their sleep thirteen years ago. Someone who murdered the gremlin who'd introduced him to the vampire and threw his body down a well. Neither could I be friends with the sort of person who would kill an innocent man to frame me for his murder, firebomb a police building, tamper with a police car, assault me and pin the blame for it all on a colleague.'

We stared at each other. Behind him, the kettle rumbled as it reached boiling point, sending out clouds of steam, then it clicked off.

Max sighed and ran a hand through his hair then he shrugged. 'It's not my fault,' he said simply. 'If you hadn't re-opened that damned cold case into Quincy Carmichael then none of this would have happened. You should have stayed away from ancient history.'

Adrenaline surged through my body. He'd admitted it. He'd

admitted it *all*. 'Ancient history? You murdered four people, Max.'

His face darkened. 'I was a different person back then. I'm not like that now.' Except, of course, he clearly was.

'Why?' I asked. 'Why Adele and Simon? Everything else you've done was to cover up their murders, but why did you kill them in the first place?'

'I'm not like that now,' he said again.

Two could play the repetition game. 'Why did you kill them?'

Max muttered under his breath. 'I used to have a thing for vampires, alright? Just like you.'

I was *nothing* like him.

'I joined Quincy's dating agency to meet some.' He sniffed defiantly. 'There are more vamps than you might think who want to get involved with humans. They can feed from us and shag us – it's win-win for them. And us. You know what it's like, you get it.'

'Sure,' I lied, desperate to play for time until the police arrived as well as hear the truth, at least as far as Max believed it. 'I completely understand.'

Relief flashed in his eyes. 'Good. You see? We're still friends after all.'

Uh-huh. 'So you met Adele via Quincy?'

'Yeah. We hit it off and we had a good thing going, but she didn't want anyone else to know she was dating a human so she kept it quiet.' He bared his teeth in a snarl 'At least, that's what Adele told me. Then I found out she didn't want to go public because she was dating other men as well, playing me for a fool. I confronted her and it all went wrong. The werewolf she was with attacked me. I defended myself and Adele got in the way. It was an accident – I didn't *mean* to hurt her. Or the wolf. I only wanted them to know how much they'd hurt me, humiliated me. I didn't set out to kill them. I'm not a psychopath.'

Except he'd confronted them with a knife rather than words. And the only way a human like Max could have over-powered a wolf and a vampire was if they were asleep. He'd killed them in cold blood.

'So you're the victim in all this?'

'Yes!' He peered at me. 'Wait. You don't believe me.'

'Of course I believe you,' I soothed. 'I know you.'

Too late. 'Nah.'

He glared before reaching behind him to the counter top. A second later, a gun was in his hands. It was identical to the one he'd foisted upon Stubman – maybe you got two for the price of one in the illegal arms trade.

'Sorry, detective.' He raised the muzzle. 'I'm going to need a little time to get my story straight and make sure everyone believes me. At least you won't be permanently dead, so it's not like I'm really hurting you. Twelve hours while you resurrect will be enough time to make sure everyone hears what I want them to hear. It'll give me time to produce the evidence that'll keep me in the clear.'

He looked at me earnestly, as if he still thought we could be friends. 'It's not personal. It's really not.'

I didn't panic. 'I wouldn't do that if I were you.' I shoved my hand into my pocket and yanked out Buffy's voice recorder, which had been there since she'd given it to me days before. A tiny red light was blinking on it. 'I've recorded our conversation and this little thing is connected to the internet. By now your confession is secure in the cloud, ready for everyone to hear. You just confessed to the world, Max. Those police you called in aren't coming for me, they're coming for you.'

As if on cue, blue flashing lights appeared through the kitchen window. Max's nostrils flared; for the first time since this shitty business had begun, he wasn't in control – and he knew it. He hadn't planned for this and he didn't know how to react.

Max only had one course of action left, and his hand tensed. As my phoenix skills kicked in, I threw myself to the left. The gun fired, shattering the glass-fronted oven that I'd been standing in front of.

The police outside obviously heard the shot because there were loud shouts followed by a thump on the door. They'd be inside in seconds. There was no time for Max to explain away what he'd done, no time to wipe clean the gun or plant evidence on me. He whirled around, threw open his back door and ran – but he was still armed and he was still dangerous.

Avoiding the shards of glass around me, I picked myself up from the floor. There was another loud thud as the police tried to break down the front door, but I didn't have time to wait for them.

I sprinted outside after Max. It was dark and, despite my brief reconnaissance, the area was unfamiliar. If I'd been wholly human, he'd have had the advantage, but I was the phoenix. The one-and-only phoenix. And I was going to bring him down.

I leapt over the low garden hedge, twisting my head left and then right just in time to glimpse Max's back as he disappeared around a distant corner. He moved fast for a middle-aged human and I wondered if he'd been preparing for this.

I thundered after him, splashing in dirty puddles and soaking my trousers. I reached the same corner and wheeled around. Shit. Now where was he? I frowned at the silent street until I caught a faint quiver from a bush less than twenty metres away. He'd decided to hide. That wouldn't help him.

I smiled grimly and focused on the trembling leaves. A second later, before I could take more than two steps towards them, a loud voice boomed, 'Police! Stop! Put your hands behind your head!'

For fuck's sake. Not now. Some enterprising officer had taken it upon himself to leave his colleagues to deal with the carnage in Max's house while he investigated the streets nearby. It was a smart move on his part, but it didn't help me in the slightest.

I knew better than to resist. I came to a stuttering halt and lifted my hands. 'I'm DC Emma Bellamy,' I said, keeping my voice as calm as possible. 'I'm in pursuit of a suspect who I believe is hiding in bushes just over there. He's armed.' I started to turn my head to look at the officer.

He barked out an order. 'Don't move!'

I pulled a face but did as he commanded. Instead of turning to look at him, I trained my eyes on the clump of bushes. This was only a minor setback; Max wouldn't get away.

'You've been suspended, DC Bellamy,' the officer said. 'There's already a warrant out for your arrest.'

My stomach dropped. Damn it – the DNA results must have come through earlier than expected. 'I'm not resisting arrest,' I protested. 'But I am telling you that there is a man with a gun in those bushes just twenty metres away. He's already tried to shoot me once. You need to call in an armed response unit.'

The officer reached for my hands, snapped metal handcuffs around my wrists and patted me down. Immediately, he located Buffy's voice recorder. 'What's this?'

'It's a recording device. The man with the gun is called Max Vargman. He is hiding in those bushes that I keep telling you about. I recorded his confession to several murders on that device.' I struggled to keep the impatience out of my voice.

There was a crackle from the officer's radio. He muttered into it, 'Suspect in custody. Potential shooter still at large. Request immediate back-up to—'

There was an ear-piercing crack as Max fired his gun again. This time he didn't miss. The bullet smacked into my shoulder with such force that I fell back against the officer and both of us dropped to the ground. A moment later, I felt excruciating pain.

'Shot fired! Shot fired!' the officer underneath me screeched into his radio.

I writhed in agony, struggling to clear my head, to think clearly. 'Fuck!' I screamed. 'Fuck!'

My swearing screech worked, because my curse somehow acknowledged the pain and allowed me to deal with it. Blinking away involuntary tears, I clenched my jaw and threw myself upwards, using the momentum to get back to my feet.

Max was there in front of me, an oddly serene expression on his face, the gun pointed at my head. 'Shoot her,' he said in a flat voice. 'Shoot him.' He nodded. 'Get hold of the voice recorder and her body. Hold her corpse to ransom in return for any uploaded recordings that incriminate me. Horvath will come through.'

His brow furrowed. 'But I'll still be in trouble. I'll still be arrested even without the recording.'

I stared at him, confused, then I realised he was talking to himself. He was working through the problems facing him until he found the right solution.

'Hide her body. While everyone is scrambling to find her, get on a ferry to France. Get a car. Drive to Spain. The escape route from last time is still there. It's still valid.'

The officer behind me was trying to stand up. Not a good idea. I took a step backwards and all-but kicked him to the ground again. He'd only get himself killed.

'It's all that's left,' Max droned on. 'There's no other way. Bang. Bang. BANG.'

I couldn't wait any longer. I threw myself at him, my head down as I aimed for the side of his body so I could avoid the damned gun but, between my shot shoulder and my cuffed hands, I couldn't do it. Max side-stepped to avoid the collision. He swung the gun around until it was pointed directly at the centre of my chest.

Oh, Jellybean.

'I really am sorry, you know,' he said quietly.

I shifted my weight carefully and pressed down on my toes, then snapped my leg upwards and kicked Max's outstretched arm. The blade concealed in the sole of my shoe was already protruding. It had been placed there by Reginald and Beatrice, the ever-so-helpful cobblers who'd been more than happy to come to my aid once I'd described what I was looking for.

It slashed into Max's flesh, cutting him deeply. The shock made him jerk back. Before he could recover himself, I kicked again and caught him on his cheek. He howled in agony and dropped the gun in order to clutch at his bleeding wounds. I used my other foot to kick the weapon out of his reach once and for all.

Max gasped and wheezed as blood spurted through his fingers. 'Why?' Pained confusion glittered in his eyes. 'You always die. Why couldn't you die this time?'

'There's a lot more to life than death, Max,' I told him. 'Even when it comes to me.' I touched my belly.

And then I smiled.

THIRTY-ONE

Warm sunlight glinted off the church spire. I touched the heavy jewellery around my neck. Sunbeams were reflecting off the rubies on the Tears of Blood necklace that Lukas had given to me months before, and which proclaimed who I was to the world. I was not a Cassandra, or the phoenix or a kick-ass member of Supe Squad; I was the person who held Lukas's heart, in the same way that he held mine.

Reverend Knight, standing by my side, grimaced. 'I've said this before and I'll say it again. It's highly unorthodox to hold a supe wedding at this church, regardless of our proximity to the supernatural community.'

I raised an eyebrow. 'You can still back out, you know. It's your church. It's your prerogative.'

He glanced at Scarlett in her figure-hugging dress. 'I wouldn't dare – I might get eaten.' He grinned suddenly. 'Besides, I want this to be the first of many supernatural weddings here. The world is changing, Emma, and I'm changing with it.'

I patted his arm and smiled back, then glanced across at one of the old stone headstones. It was the very spot where I'd first died – at least as an adult. I couldn't stop a shiver from running down my spine, but it wasn't an unpleasant sensation; it was more an acknowledgment of who I was and how far I'd come.

I looked around the small group waiting outside the church. No, I amended silently. How far we'd *all* come.

'You have that weird look on your face again,' Liza's tone was faintly accusing.

I smiled at her. 'I can't help it.' I nodded at her. 'And I'm not the only one who looks ... weird.'

'It's all this bloody make-up,' she grunted. 'It's caked on my skin.'

'It's not the make-up,' I said gently. 'It's the glowing colour in your cheeks and the shine in your eyes.'

'Yep,' Laura said, sidling up. 'You almost look as happy as the blushing bride.'

'You know,' I sighed. 'I think my heart is going to burst with joy.'

Reverend Knight shot me a look of mock alarm. 'Don't do that. The cleaning bill will be enormous and I'm a busy person these days. I don't want to delay the wedding for twelve hours while you do your thing.'

Scarlett called across from the church entrance, 'Are we doing this, or what?'

Knight bowed, then hastily marched off and disappeared inside the church. Scarlett winked at me and followed him in as the first strains of Wagner's Bridal Chorus boomed out from the church organ.

Laura nudged me. 'We have to go.'

I drew in a breath. 'Yes.' I plucked at my white dress while Laura and Liza adjusted their bouquets and fell into step behind me. I couldn't keep Lukas waiting any longer.

~

I TILTED my head from side to side, trying to shake off the confetti. As Lukas handed me a glass of orange juice, his eyes met mine. 'It's a shame you can't have champagne at your own wedding,' he murmured.

I gazed at him. 'I don't need alcohol. I'm already intoxicated enough.'

He wrapped an arm around my waist and pulled me close. 'We could send all the guests home,' he growled into my ear. 'We've done the ceremony part. The rest is just window dressing.'

'We should probably feed them first.'

'Probably.'

I leaned in towards him. 'But we could always slip out between courses.'

His black eyes danced.

There was a click of heels and somebody behind us cleared their throat pointedly. Lukas and I turned. 'I have a bone to pick with you,' Buffy said, her hands on her hips.

'With me?' I asked.

'Yes!' she snapped.

By her side, Fred sent me an apologetic look followed by a helpless shrug. I glanced from him to Buffy. 'You're wearing matching clothes,' I said faintly. It was true. Fred was wearing a pink three-piece suit with a navy-blue tie, while Buffy was in a pretty dress of the exact same shade of pink and with a navy trim.

Fred beamed. 'You should have seen the hat that she tried to make me wear.' From his expression and the way he touched the still-visible scar on the side of his head, he'd have been delighted to wear anything that Buffy asked him to.

'Yes,' Buffy said impatiently, 'we both look gorgeous. I already know that.' She glared at me.

'Go on then,' I said, relenting under the force of her stern expression. 'What have I done?'

'Why did you make Laura and Liza bridesmaids but not ask me to be matron-of-honour?' she demanded,

I pressed my lips together.

'Well?'

I leaned across and kissed her cheek. 'Love you, Buffy.'

She huffed. 'I love you too, detective.' She wagged her finger in my face. 'But next time, don't you dare leave me out.'

Next to me, Lukas raised his eyebrows. 'Next time?'

She raised her shoulders in a shrug. 'I'm just saying.' She looked down at my belly. 'You could call the baby after me, if you like.'

Lukas choked on his drink. Fortunately, I was saved from responding by Grace limping over in our direction. 'Emma! Congratulations!'

'Thank you. How are you feeling?'

'The physio is working wonders. I'll be back to my old self in no time.' He flicked a look over his shoulder. 'I see Fred and I aren't the only police who've been invited.'

I followed his gaze to DSI Lucinda Barnes, who was deep in conversation with Phileas Carmichael. Both of them seemed to sense they were the focus of our attention and turned towards us. Phileas bowed, his cheeks staining red as if he were still embarrassed about recent events. Barnes only raised her glass in a silent toast and smiled.

'DSI Barnes and I had a meeting last week,' I told him. 'Everything is resolved and I'm in the clear.'

Lukas snorted. 'I should think so too.'

'There have to be checks and balances. Nobody is above the law.'

'And that,' Lukas told me, 'is why the supernatural community have finally learned to trust Supe Squad.'

I bit my lip. The re-building of the Supe Squad headquarters was already underway, and it wouldn't be long before we were back in our old place. I'd already had assurances from the supe leaders that any criminal acts committed by supes would fall under our jurisdiction. The fact that Max had slipped under everyone's radar for so long had been more than enough for the last barriers to fall away, and even the likes of Lady Sullivan had acknowledged the need for an independent, autonomous organisation like Supe Squad. We were already making plans to encourage more supes to join up to avoid any hint of bias towards one group or another.

From a few metres away, Devereau Webb caught my eye. 'You are positively glowing, Detective Constable Bellamy,' he said.

'You look rather glowing yourself,' I replied.

He smirked. 'Trust me, there's nothing quite like married life.'

We exchanged a look of mutual satisfaction, then his expression turned serious. 'I'm sorry that my friends couldn't come up with anything for that car tracker we found. It's too easy to buy that sort of thing on the internet these days.'

'It's okay. We don't need it. There was more than enough evidence without it. I really appreciate that you tried.'

'Of course. Us supes have to stick together.' He raised his head for a moment before returning his attention to me. 'I think there's somebody hovering outside who wants to talk to you,' he said.

I frowned. Everyone I knew was already there. I turned towards the open door but I couldn't see who he was talking about. 'Supe?' I asked.

He shook his head. 'Human.'

The furrow in my brow deepened. 'I'll be back in a moment,' I murmured to Lukas. He gave me a quick kiss, then I went out to see who it was.

Alistair Stubman looked as nervous and angry as ever. His hands were shoved deep into his pockets and his shoulders were hunched. When he saw me approaching, he scowled with even greater ferocity. Maybe that was simply his way of protecting himself.

'You can come inside,' I said. 'I sent you an invitation.'

Stubman's lip curled. 'I'm not coming to a fucking supe wedding.' And yet he was here, right outside that very wedding. Despite his angry façade, there was still hope for him.

'I only came to give you this.' He thrust a crumpled envelope in my direction.

'Is that a card, Alistair?'

'Thought I'd say congratulations,' he mumbled. 'I suppose you're alright. Even though you're a supe. Even though you're a copper.' He scowled again. 'I'm not saying we're mates or anything, though. And you'd better keep that fanged husband of yours away from me.'

'You don't have to be frightened of Lukas,' I said.

'I'm not frightened!' he glowered. 'But I'm getting my old job back at the hotel next to your place once all the building work is done and I'll be working days from now on, so I can start evening classes. I don't want to be bothered by him. Or you. Or anyone else, for that matter.'

I met his eyes. 'Are you sure that you don't want to come in?' I asked.

Stubman was already backing away. 'Fucking sure.'

Baby steps. I smiled, all the same. 'Thanks for the card.'

'You're welcome.' His mouth twisted into a half snarl, but I couldn't quite tell if it was directed at me or at himself. He spun around and stomped away, nearly colliding with a cyclist who had to swerve to avoid him at the last moment.

The cyclist came to a halt while Stubman continued on his way. 'Hi detective!' He waved at me enthusiastically. 'You look fab!'

I peered more closely and recognised the teenage goblin. He knocked on his helmet and grinned. 'I'm still wearing it!' he yelled.

'Good!'

'Thanks for making me put it on. A cat ran out in front of me a couple of weeks ago and if I'd not had the helmet on, I could have ended up with stitches or a fractured skull – or maybe something worse.'

Something far worse. 'Safety first,' I told him.

He saluted and cycled away. 'Congratulations,' he called out over his shoulder. I smiled, watching him go.

'D'Artagnan.'

I turned to Lukas, my breath catching in my throat at the sight of the sunlight glinting off his black hair and the warmth in his gaze.

'They're about to seat us for the wedding supper. We should go in.' He held out his hand.

I reached for him but as soon as my skin touched his, my vision swam. A shock of bright-blue hair. A petite figure. And blood. Lots of blood.

'What is it?' Lukas asked, alarmed.

I shook my head to clear the violent images. 'A pixie,' I said. 'Not far from here. I have to go.'

'Do you need help?'

I considered, then declined. 'No. It won't take long. You should keep our guests happy. I'll be back before the soup is served.'

Lukas gave me a crooked smile and I realised that the look

in his eyes was one of pride. 'You'd better be,' he murmured. 'I love you.'

'I love you too.' I pushed myself onto my tiptoes and kissed him. Then I scooped up my wedding dress, spun around and started to run.

ACKNOWLEDGMENTS

The Firebrand series feels as if it's gone by in the blink of an eye, even though I actually started writing it in a different time and a different world before the COVID-19 pandemic. All I can hope for is that it provided some respite and entertainment during that time and that it's continued to be a fun ride for everyone afterwards.

As always, there are many people who deserve a heartfelt thank you for their support and help in getting all the books ready. My editor, Karen Holmes, whose hard work and unstinting support deserves a special mention, Clarissa Yeo at Yocla Designs and now Joy Cover Design for her amazing work on the book covers, and Lynne Thompson-Hogg, the real life detective who got in touch early on and has been helping ever since with any and all questions and points on police procedures. Despite Lynne's sterling and detailed advice, I have still taken considerable liberties so rest assured that any mistakes are all mine.

There are many beta readers who've been invaluable - special mention must go to Laura, Mindy, Vannessa, Lisa, Marsha, Carrie, Ceri, Andrea and Belinda. And a huge thank you also to Heather G Harris for being a fabulous cheerleader.

Last but not least, thank you so much to my family and friends who all know who they are, and to Marlowe, Buster, Lara, Scout and Mavis, without whose furry companionship would make writing a seven book series a much lonelier proposition!

Helen xx

ABOUT THE AUTHOR

After teaching English literature in the UK, Japan and Malaysia, Helen Harper left behind the world of education following the worldwide success of her Blood Destiny series of books. She thanks her lucky stars every day that she's able to do so.

Helen has always been a book lover, devouring science fiction and fantasy tales when she was a child growing up in Scotland.

She currently lives in Edinburgh with far too many cats – not to mention the dragons, fairies, demons, wizards and vampires that seem to keep appearing from nowhere.

Also by Helen Harper

A Charade of Magic series

The best way to live in the Mage ruled city of Glasgow is to keep your head down and your mouth closed.

That's not usually a problem for Mairi Wallace. By day she works at a small shop selling tartan and by night she studies to become an apothecary. She knows her place and her limitations. All that changes, however, when her old childhood friend sends her a desperate message seeking her help - and the Mages themselves cross Mairi's path. Suddenly, remaining unnoticed is no longer an option.

There's more to Mairi than she realises but, if she wants to fulfil her full potential, she's going to have to fight to stay alive - and only time will tell if she can beat the Mages at their own game.

From twisted wynds and tartan shops to a dangerous daemon and the magic infused City Chambers, the future of a nation might lie with one solitary woman.

Book One – Hummingbird

Book Two – Nightingale

Book Three – Red Hawk

Made in the USA
Monee, IL
13 August 2023

40957100R00163